FLESH TRAP

MAGEN CUBED

Copyright © 2014 Magen Cubed
Cover image © Philip Rogers

All rights reserved.

www.postmortem-press.com

All characters appearing in this work are fictitious. Any resemblance to real persons, living or dead, is purely coincidental.

No part of this book may be reproduced in any form or by any electronic or mechanical means including information storage and retrieval systems, without permission in writing from the author. The only exception is by a reviewer, who may quote short excerpts in a review.

FIRST Edition

ISBN: 978-0615890067

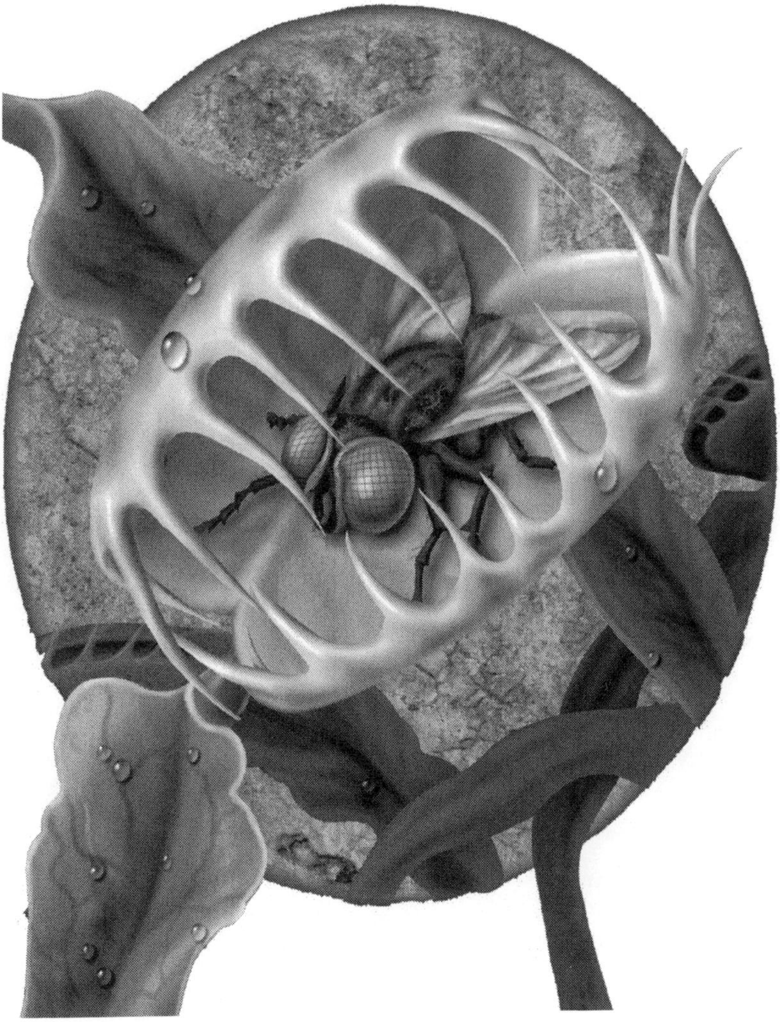

Chapter One

For twenty years, Casey Way dreamt without sleeping. He slipped into the spaces between death and waking where his father still walked the streets behind Casey's eyelids. There his father met him, in alleyways between city blocks and in the basement beneath the library, tucked into the corners of his apartment and hiding under tables when he wasn't of mind. It was his father that woke Casey now, dreaming of David Way's face as raw meat, lips peeled from straight teeth and nostrils flayed open to the bone. He sat down beside Casey on the three-twenty-five cross-town bus with the squeak of plastic upholstery. From his seat, Casey watched sunlight filter dirty-gray through the sweat-filmed glass, a halo around his father's missing face. He felt nothing, just the hole his father left there.

"Hey, kiddo," David Way spoke with a skeletal mouth.

They were alone on the bus. It made his father's bony smile seem somehow colder.

"Yeah, Dad?"

Casey was thirty-two years old and staring into the cavities of his father's eye sockets. The last time Casey had seen his father he was twelve-years-old, made of a boy's skinny geometry and freckles that had faded with time. In his mind, his father still towered over him in broad shoulders and large hands, made of steel and stone beneath his Oxford shirt and tie. Strong like Casey had thought of buildings as strong, from his good posture to his straight nose, the definition of his jaw to the blue of his eyes.

"You know it wasn't your fault, right?" The bus's empty gut lurched. Flesh hanging from his father's cheekbone dangled above his collar, a dangerous pitter-patter of blood. "I would've just ruined her, anyway."

"Yeah, Dad," Casey said. His hands felt sweaty against his

jeans, alternately hot and cold from wanting to rip the meat from his father's skull or push it back into place, preserving the semblance of his character. "I know."

Casey woke with a start of sweat and tangled sheets. The bedroom spun above his head until he shook it clear, rooted to his side of the mattress by the arm and leg Joel slept with thrown over Casey's side. Fingers skimmed the fine ridges of Joel's knuckles, and closing a hand around his wrist. Casey sighed. Practice allowed Casey to ease away quietly, out of bed and toward the doorway. His head was still full of blood and bees and Joel slept, anyway, all skinny bones and a rooster's crest of blonde hair against Casey's stolen pillow. He slipped on his red Chucks, gathered Joel's Manchester United jacket from the closet and his composition notebook from the bedside table, tucking both under his arm. Outside the door he waited until he heard Joel turn over in bed before pulling it shut.

Down the hallway and into the living room, he stared past his mother's picture on the wall at the sliding glass door to the patio. His Venus flytraps slept outside under the yellow warmth of streetlight, gathered in neat clusters in pots and stands. For a moment Casey held a breath and half expected the door to open, but Joel didn't wake and neither would they. The city seemed half-dead at this hour, empty save for shadows as Casey walked the four city blocks to Jay's 24-Hour Coffee on Walker Avenue. His cigarette drooped half-smoked from his mouth, armed with a notebook and pen until the apartment on Davis Street vanished between alleyways and the bobble of headlights at his back.

Navigating stoplights and crosswalks, Casey followed old habits to the corner booth in the smoking section where a waitress named Sherrie with milky blonde hair waited tables during the graveyard shift. His corner was under the air conditioning vents at a booth with cracked fake leather seats. Customers never wanted to sit there, where it was too cold and noisy. Casey could smoke cigarettes and drink coffee there, and no one would watch him write.

Casey took out his notebook, black cover with white pages, college ruled and taped back together where it had torn at the spine. It was the latest in a series of journals that he had kept since high school, one of the few things he learned from his hack of a therapist, Dr. Randolph. The idiot had concluded in the summer between ninth and tenth grade that Casey's nightmares were rooted in unresolved sexual issues with his mother. Casey had spent eight sessions trying to convince Dr. Randolph that his tendency to smoke cigarettes and make-out with Jimmy Carmichael behind the gym after school ruled out most sexual feelings toward women in general. Eventually he threw one of his journals across Dr. Randolph's office, killing a potted fern and ending their relationship.

He laid the notebook open on the table in a haphazard cut-and-paste of newspaper clippings, sun-bleached fliers and bus tickets, articles of life collected and remembered. The clippings sold headlines of man-hunts in sleepy neighborhoods and missing grocery store clerks and teachers, telling stories about people thought dead and never recovered. They sat sandwiched between photos of smiling faces, stolen from lamp posts and store windows where they were to like a lost dog sign and Casey knew they wouldn't be missed. That was the thing that Casey found strange about missing persons fliers. People never noticed them, even to see when they were not there anymore. Underneath them he kept a journal of his dreams in black ink and blocky paragraphs, sectioned off by dates and places, twice underlined for emphasis and smeared by elbows and knuckles. If asked about the notebooks, Casey would only say they were a matter of survival.

4/1/10, At home

Dreamt of Dad again, third time this week. He said it wasn't my fault.

Staring at what he had written, Casey took a drag of his cigarette. Inside Joel's oversized jacket he yawned, the weight of sleep still heavy in his limbs. Behind his eyes Casey could make out the shape of his father's skull beneath the dripping meat, the whiteness of his teeth, wrinkles gathering at his eyes when he laughed.

Fuck him, anyway.

"Rough night, huh?" Sherrie asked, stopping by his table with the coffee pot in hand.

It was already the end of her shift. Casey knew this but Sherrie didn't say anything. She never did. He closed his notebook. She dipped her head to the side in a jostle of her high ponytail and refilled Casey's half-empty cup. Casey knew Sherrie as a twenty-two-year-old from Vancouver who studied pediatric nursing, reading cheap pulp novels when she wasn't serving coffee in the middle of the night. She knew Casey as a librarian with a cute English boyfriend, kept a garden in his apartment and had trouble sleeping. Casey didn't have the heart to correct her. He was content in what Sherrie did or didn't know.

"Oh, you know." Casey pressed an unruly piece of black-brown hair back against his scalp and put on a good face. "Better than some, worse than others."

"I bet. How's Joel?"

"At home, asleep, like a sane person." Casey tugged intuitively at the zipper of Joel's borrowed jacket, rolling the faded metal slider between his finger and thumb. "How's school?"

"The usual: Stealing all my money and time." Sherrie shrugged good-naturedly. "But what can you do?"

He nodded. "So are you off yet?"

"Almost."

She smiled at him warmly. Casey must have looked worse than he thought.

"You know you can just throw me out of your section if you need to," he offered. "I can park myself at the counter for a while so you can clean up."

"Nah," she said, "you keep me company."

Sherrie patted Casey's wrist and moved three booths over to a table of cops. Through the partition window to the kitchen and the clarity of black coffee, familiar chords rattled out of the tinny old speaker system the tattooed fry cook was listening to. If he concentrated, Casey could hear Mariska's voice on 92.5 KVBS, the smoky rumble of her laughter slipping into the dining room between tracks of ZZ Top and Led Zeppelin. She was the late-shift DJ, seven at night to one in the morning. Monday-through-Friday, Classic Sounds with Mariska. It was easy to imagine her sitting in a hazy studio booth in her favorite cowboy boots, all long legs and jeans, wearing sunglasses at night like a poster from a cheap exploitation movie about drug culture and rock-and-roll. The way she looked since she was old enough to spend money at thrift shops on the clothes her mother hated, where she would drag Casey after school and hide bags full of old combat boots and leather jackets in his book bag so her mother wouldn't see.

For all my little lovelies out there who can't sleep tonight, Mariska said. The way she always did between commercial breaks, voice dark from too many cigarettes. You know who you are and you know why you're here, so just shut the hell up and listen to some good music.

It was a comfort between cups of coffee and Sherrie's table visits, settling in Casey's bones like nicotine and the urge to sleep. Thinking of his father's face, dripping from his skull in strips of flesh and sinew, Casey sagged against the booth and sighed. Sherrie filled salt and pepper shakers at the next table and hummed along, and listening to his sister's voice over the radio, Casey closed his eyes. Soon he would pay for his coffee and walk home again, to slip back into bed before the alarm clock could blow his cover. When Joel asked, Casey would say that he slept okay, that everything was fine, and kiss him to distract from the lies and the black droop of his eyelids. He would then get up to shower and dress for work, and see his therapist to talk about his dead father with his rotting face and bony smile.

That night he would not sleep, either, but for now, he was content to hide in the diner and try to forget.

Chapter Two

Casey borrowed the space at the end of Paul Orman's black sofa. His dark jeans and t-shirt helped him fade into the upholstery, cross-legged, shrinking away between the cushions he slouched against. Paul's office was a cave carved out of cinderblocks and mahogany on the eighth floor of a high-rise building, black leather and wood stain stretching from wall to wall. In the center of the room was a high-backed leather armchair with heavy pleats and ornate brass decorations, an end table, and the sofa. Paul on one side, Casey on the other, silence between them.

"What would you like to talk about today, Casey?"

Flanked by the tall arms of his chair, Paul was sallow with thinning gray hair and grayer eyes. The bony peaks of his skull recalled Max Schreck, Count Orlock, Nosferatu, stalking dark corridors and staircases. The notion that Paul Orman had ever instructed a classroom of future therapists made Casey uneasy. That Paul held a fond place in Joel's heart as his thesis advisor ultimately left a bad taste in his mouth.

"I don't know." He said nothing about vampires. "What should we talk about?"

Casey saw Paul on Tuesday mornings with black coffee still fresh in his mind. Joel made terrible coffee, half-caff piss-water, not at all like the black tar Casey needed in his veins every day. Joel made up for it on most mornings, when squeezing Casey's small bicep Joel kissed him goodbye at the door and warned him to play nice. For the first three sessions Casey agreed. This morning Casey had promised nothing.

"You know it's up to you, Casey." Paul smiled vacantly. "You can talk about whatever you like here. It's a safe space."

Casey shrugged. "There's not a lot to talk about. I told you that last week." And the week before that.

"Humor me, Casey."

"I'm pretty sure Joel already told you everything you needed to know. I mean, you're on his Christmas card list, right?"

"Joel only came to me and asked me to review your case. That was all."

"Then you already know I'm just here so Joel will feel better, right?" The thought of Joel sitting bright-eyed and gullible in the front row of Paul's yawning classroom, some cathedral-auditorium, all dark glossy wood fixtures and overcompensation, made Casey uncomfortable in a way he couldn't fully articulate. "And you get paid either way, so I think it's a win-win no matter what happens."

"I don't think so. Now I would like to know more about you, Casey." Paul reached for the pen and legal pad sitting on the arm of his chair. "I think hearing it from you would be more useful. So tell me a little bit about yourself."

Casey folded his hands and sighed. "Where should I start?"

Paul smiled reassuringly. It fell short. "Anywhere you like, Casey."

"Well. I'm thirty-two. I work as a library cataloger and I live with Joel."

Paul nodded. "Do you enjoy your work?"

"It's okay. It's quiet. I like working alone so it suits me, I guess."

"How long have you and Joel been together?"

"You already know all this."

"Tell me anyway."

"Four years." Casey straightened against the cushions, uncrossed his legs. "We have an apartment together. Joel's a therapist and rape crisis counselor, but you already knew that."

"Yes I did." Paul scratched something into the pad. "What about your parents?"

"Dead." Shrug. "My mother died when I was three, my father when I was twelve. My sister is my only family."

"Biological?"

"Step. Her mother married my father when I was four."

"I see. Do you have any hobbies, Casey? Anything that you enjoy doing, anything to help you relax?"

"Reading, going to the movies..." Casey made a point to omit his journal. A book's worth of missing persons fliers was nothing to brag about. "I also keep a garden, on the apartment balcony. It isn't much."

"What kind of gardening do you enjoy?"

"I keep Venus flytraps."

"Flytraps?" Paul almost laughed. "That's a somewhat peculiar choice, very exotic."

The meat in Casey's jaw ticked. "My mother kept them. It's kind of a family tradition, I guess."

Paul let his pad rest on his knee and folded his hands. "So I hear you've had some trouble sleeping, Casey."

"Sleeping? That's kind of been an issue for a while now." Casey let out a little laugh-cough. "I don't sleep at night, and if I do I have nightmares. So I take sleep meds to put me out, but the pills make me drowsy during the day. Coffee keeps me up most days but I can't drive anymore because I might doze off. But I'm not really dozing off, you know? I drift but I'm still awake. It happens at work, on the bus, in the grocery store – I just kind of drift off and see things."

Paul straightened in his armchair. He looked small between the rigid arms. Casey noticed that the buttons on Paul's gray cardigan sweater were brassy to match the ones stapled into the pleats of the chair. "What kinds of things do you see, Casey?"

"I don't really want to talk about it."

"You don't have to, but I think it would help."

"Yeah, well, I think I'll pass."

"Alright then." Paul closed the pad and placed it on the end table. "Are you at all familiar with hypnotherapy, Casey?"

Casey laughed. "See, this is the part where you tell me how safe hypnosis is, right? What a useful tool it is and how well it can treat insomnia? Then I'm supposed to get all bright-eyed and say, Gosh, tell me more. It's not like I haven't seen this pony trick before."

Paul took a moment before he smiled.

"Well, I'd say that's a fair assessment given your past. You see, Casey, I've done a little research on you since our last session and pulled up some of your records." Reaching for the side-table he unbolted a small drawer, produced a file folder and opened it across his lap. "You've had, what, eighteen therapists now? Now that seemed a little unusual, but then I noticed some references in your records to a few periods of hospitalization and psychological evaluation when you were younger. I see all of these treatment notes were added to your to file around April 1990. This would make you around twelve at the time, yes?"

"Yeah, that sounds right."

"This would then coincide with an incident around the same time, which would be the murder of your father by your stepmother. Am I correct?"

"That's amazing. Can you pull a rabbit out of your ass, too?"

Paul closed the file folder and leaned forward. From this vantage he looked every bit Casey imagined a vampire would, sneaking around a young woman's bed at night with bony fingers and teeth. Casey took a deep breath.

"Here's how this is going to work, Casey. I believe your problems are treatable, but it's going to be a long process. I'm going to require your total honesty and willingness to examine these aspects of your past to begin addressing these issues. Can you give me that much?"

"You know I've heard this all before, right?"

"I'm sure you have, but I'm very good at what I do. Joel wouldn't have sent you to me if I wasn't."

"And you already know I'm just doing this for Joel."

"Then we already have that much in common."

Casey's jaw twitched again. Paul replaced the folder for his legal pad and leaned back into his seat.

"We'll need to set up an aggressive treatment schedule, either Mondays and Wednesdays or Tuesdays and Thursdays. I can squeeze you in on Thursday and we can go from there."

"Yeah, fine. How about two o'clock, on my lunch break?"

"Sounds perfect." Another note and Paul smiled again. "Good decision."

Sinking into the sofa, Casey said nothing.

Chapter Three

Casey spent seven days at Sunnydale Hospital and Counseling Center in April of 1990.

Everything smelled like medicine and glass cleaner and Aunt Cheryl was talking again. Casey could see her pink matte lipstick mouth move in circles around the words he couldn't hear. He wanted to listen, but his ears were too stuffed up with cotton, his mouth like rubber when he tried to speak, joints like plastic doll pieces when he moved. Underneath him the fake paper cotton of his hospital-issue pajamas crinkled when he shifted, sitting on his hands in regulation paper cotton sheets. People had talked to him for three days. Nurses in white smocks and doctors in white coats and Dr. Stevens, who said he could call her Nancy and that everything would be okay. They each gave him candy-red pills in small paper cups and their mouths moved to smile when they patted him on the head. Sometimes they gave him books or used crayons and coloring pages, and sat next to him to watch him like he was going to do something amazing the moment they looked away. All of them wanted to talk.

Casey couldn't really hear them, just parts of words. Consonant and vowel sounds, big O's and hard T's. He didn't really want to speak, anyway. He just wanted to know where Mariska was. She had cried the last time he saw her, sitting outside with the cop cars and the ambulance and the neighbors that had gathered around like vultures. Her hand had been over her mouth and her makeup was running down her face, blue eye shadow and mascara smearing together when she sank down to sit on the curb in her too-big combat boots. There was blood on the Easter yellow dress and cardigan sweater her mother made her wear, the one she bought for Mariska for Christmas, because yellow was a pretty color for a pretty girl. Nobody was talking about that.

There were children in rooms down the hall, in the same cottony paper pajamas. Sometimes Casey could hear them crying through the walls at night. Nobody wanted to talk about that, either.

"These doctors are going to help you, alright?" Aunt Cheryl was saying again. "They're here to make you better so you can come home. But not your home, Casey; my home, with Jeff and Heather, do you remember them? You and Mariska can stay with me. We'll take care of you. We'll get you through this. But just listen to the doctors, and take the medicine they give you, and it'll be okay, Casey. I promise."

There was a television in his room, if he could call it a room. It was a prison cell with soft white curtains and a nurse that came in every four hours to give Casey fluids and fake a smile. The television sat up in the corner across from his stiff bed. It was always switched on but there was never anything to see, screen snowed over in static. Out of the corner of his eye, Casey watched it, the gray between the black and white. Sometimes at night he could see faces in it, his father and his mother, hands on the glass, reaching through to him. From the chair beside the bed, Aunt Cheryl leaned forward and gripped his shoulder. Her eyes were red from tears she wasn't crying.

"Do you understand me?" she asked. "Can you hear me?"

Casey heard enough of it to nod.

"Do you know about your father?"

He shook his head. She nodded and spoke very slowly.

"Something very bad happened to your father, Casey. There was an accident, okay? Your step-mother, she was a part of it, and that's why she isn't coming back. That's why you have to come live with me and Uncle Jeff and your cousin Heather."

Snow danced across the television. Aunt Cheryl shook Casey gently.

"Casey. Look at me, okay? You need to look at me, sweetie, this is important right now."

"My father."

The words clawed out of the back of his throat, sticking to his tongue like a paste. In the corner Casey could see a person in the static, a skull with hair but no face. Aunt Cheryl looked pained.

"Yes, he's been hurt. He's not coming back."

"Good," he said. It felt like talking with glue in his mouth. Her fingers gripped him even tighter. "I'm glad he's dead."

"No, Casey. You don't mean that. You're hurt, you're sick, you need your rest. Your father loved you, he did. I know he did. He was a good man, he was just flawed. He was broken. He hurt Mariska and I'm sorry, Casey, I'm so sorry."

Aunt Cheryl kept talking. She cried and held him and kissed his forehead. She told him everything would be okay. Casey didn't really care. He spent seven days at the Sunnydale Hospital and Counseling Center, locked in a white room with his broken television, because everybody thought he was broken and needed medicine. He was twelve then. Aunt Cheryl came back on the morning of the eighth day with a suitcase of clothes and Mariska in jeans, white t-shirt and a leather jacket. He had never seen Mariska in those clothes before, just the combat boots still sagging at her ankles.

On the car ride to Aunt Cheryl and Uncle Jeff's, Casey slept in Mariska's lap in the back seat. She ran her hands through his hair and promised he would be okay. Because she loved him and they had each other, and his father was dead and he would never hurt them again. He closed his eyes and believed her, and never thought about the faceless person in the television again.

Chapter Four

The Rosedale Glade Mental Facility was the third in the string of hospitals that Mariska had visited on greeting card holidays and birthdays since she was fifteen. It hadn't changed in seven years. She didn't know whether the nameless feeling she got in her stomach every time she came back was disappointment or something else. After seven years, she didn't even know what she expected anymore. Blue flowers still bloomed from broad shrubs outside every wing of the complex and beside the sidewalks connecting them, and the same lanky, gray, uniformed guard waved Mariska's car through the gate. An orderly in a wrinkled smock escorted her down long white corridors lined with shatter-proof windows and tall locked doors to rooms she had never seen. Mariska was glad not to have seen them, in a guilty part of her mind that only acted up when she was here.

In the commons room, Mariska could feel the eyes of the hefty orderly posted at the door, staring at her back as she sat on the dingy yellow sofa. She swiped some grass from her pantleg and sighed. The room was gray, white plaster and tile made cloudy by old fixtures and inadequate natural light. Around her, patients played board games or watched television in patterned blue smocks and pants, regulation pajamas. Some talked to themselves while others fidgeted in their seats like restless children, or plucked at their clothing as to put holes in their collars or sleeves. Mariska chewed her lip, tasting lip gloss and ash. She had worn makeup for the first time in months: eyeliner, mascara, shiny pink gloss that was supposed to complement the subtle redness of her hair. It didn't cover up the smell of cigarettes that still held to her blouse, or the thick feeling in her throat. She had told Billy where she was going today. The sweetly encouraging way he said, Yeah, sure, babe, that's a good idea, made her regret it. Telling him meant she had to do it, that she couldn't back out this time.

From an opened door across the room, her mother walked in and took a seat across from her. Alyona Kovol was a ghost of a woman in her regulation pajamas, skeletal under her clothes and thinning red hair. In another time, Alyona had a full face and bright eyes, filling out floral sundresses in photographs that Mariska still kept in a shoebox under her bed. Alyona was happy then, with soft skin and a big smile. The show of teeth when she smiled this time was sad. Mariska drew forward to take her mother's hand. She wouldn't tell her mother that she had been up all morning, smoking cigarettes and chewing her bottom lip, afraid of this.

"Hi, Mom." Mariska squeezed her mother's fingers, bony as they were.

It was the same visit, same sad pageantry since she was fifteen. The Kovol Family Reunion, held annually in mental health institutions across the state. Some times in the commons room, others through plastic windows and closed-line telephones.

"You look lovely today," Alyona said. Whispers of her native Ukrainian still lingered on her tongue, her childhood in Donetsk hardening her consonants and straining her vowels. Mariska had only ever seen it in photographs and postcards, but she could imagine it when her mother spoke, the mountains and the coal mines. "It's been a while, hasn't it?"

"Yeah, it has. Did you get the birthday card I sent?" Mariska smiled when her mother nodded. "You look good, though, Mom. You look healthy."

"How are things?"

"Things are good. I'm dating this guy now. He seems like the dumb stoner-type, but he's kind of smart. I think I really like him." Mariska found herself laughing. She checked under her eyes to make sure her makeup was still in place. "His name's Billy. He owns a head-shop around the corner from the station. He has his life together, you know? I think it's going to be good for me."

"Still no grandchildren, I see."

Mariska faked a smile. Her mother knew she was sterile. She just chose to pretend it would go away one day, if Mariska settled down, married a nice man.

"Well, we're talking about it, for the future."

"That's good." Alyona folded her hands, sighed. "So I see it's coming up. Twenty years next week. I read, you know. I can take a guess that's why you're here."

"Yeah, it is." Mariska sighed. "It just got me thinking, I guess."

"About what?"

Mariska didn't answer. Alyona squared herself.

"I have nothing to say to you about this. You know that."

"I just want to know what happened that night, Mom. It's been long enough."

"You know what happened." Alyona leaned away. "You know why. What he did to you, and how he humiliated me. He betrayed us. I had no choice."

"That doesn't make it okay, Mom. What about Casey?"

Alyona jerked her head as though slapped. "I did nothing to that boy. Besides, it's not like he lifted a finger to stop what his father was doing. He belongs here as much as I do. Don't let him lie to you."

"We were just kids. What was he supposed to do?"

"He knows what he could've done. That boy is sick, Mariska, he's wrong in his head. I've seen it. He's wrong."

Mariska reached for her mother's hand. Alyona drew away. Mariska leaned back.

"But it's what you did, Mom. You think we're gonna be okay after that?"

"You always defend him. He isn't even your blood and you defend him. Sitting there like you always do, judging me. You still think I'm crazy, after everything I've gone through for you. I only began seeing David for you, you know, at first. So you could have a stable home, a right home, with a mother and a father. After what your father did to us, you needed a whole family."

Mariska sighed. "I didn't come here to fight with you."

"Then why did you come at all?"

Alyona's hands shook, stubby nails digging into her pantlegs. Mariska reached for her bag to fish out her menthols and lighter.

"Because I'm not a little kid, anymore." Mariska lit the cigarette for her mother, passed it to her. She looked at the orderly. He said nothing. "I don't hate you, Mom, I don't. And I don't think you're crazy. I just – I just need some perspective."

Alyona closed her eyes, sighed around the filter. "I don't know what I can offer you."

"I don't want you to offer me anything. I just want the truth."

"I loved David, you know. It's sick but I still do, somehow. Even after everything." Alyona opened her eyes and looked at the floor. The room made them brown instead of green. She smiled. "He was beautiful, really, with his big hands and strong back. I think he knew it, too. He could have any woman he wanted."

Mariska swallowed. "Are you really going to say that to me now?"

Alyona slowly wrung her fingers together. "I did what I had to do."

"What happened that night?"

"I did what I had to do. I protected you."

"You killed him."

"I saved you from that pig."

"That's just it, Mom. You didn't."

"Well. I don't see it that way." Alyona stubbed the cigarette out in the arm of the sofa, made the room smell like burnt fabric. "I wish I could get you to see that."

"Yeah, me too." Mariska felt sick. She shouldn't have said anything to Billy.

"I do love you, Mariska. You know this."

"I know, Mom. I love you, too."

Tears threatened to smear her eyeliner, but Mariska didn't bother to wipe them away.

Chapter Five

Casey made a habit of watching Davis Street from his balcony on the fifth floor, waiting out the sunlight from the cracks between skinny brownstones and fat old shops until it disappeared. It was quiet. He needed quiet. The street below breathed with the shuffle of feet, young professionals walking home, old ladies carrying grocery bags. He smoked cigarettes alone and waited for Joel's old blue hatchback to creep down the street into the parking garage like it did every weeknight, kept company by his garden of flytraps.

They surrounded him on the patio in knots of hungry little mouths, pink on the inside like flesh, seated in a skeletal nursery of wrought iron tables and plant stands salvaged from estate sales and curbsides. Dinner, boxed Thai food from the tiny ramshackle Indochinese restaurant around the corner, cooled on the kitchen counter inside until Joel came home. In his garden, Casey breathed smoke and closed his eyes.

The sun was gone by the time the soft glide of the patio door told Casey he was no longer alone. Joel wrapped his arms around Casey's shoulders from behind and sighed against his hair, pressing himself into the curve of Casey's spine. Casey closed a hand around the cross of Joel's wrists and leaned back into the contact.

"Hey."

"Long day?" Casey asked around his cigarette, limp and nearly-burnt.

Joel closed his eyes and breathed from the nape of Casey's neck. "It usually is."

Joel Britton's office was a closet in the Turning Point Counseling Center with chipped wood paneling and smoke damage on the ceiling. It afforded him enough space for a desk, two chairs, and a filing cabinet. He spent his Monday-through-Friday each week amid the clutter of opened case files and Pepsi cans in front of his computer, the telephone wedged into the crook of his shoulder when he had time between appointments. When he had a spare moment he checked his messages on his smartphone, mostly news or updates on soccer matches. Joel invited his patients into his office for counseling most days; others he jogged the four blocks to the court-house to go with them to trial. On particularly busy days he responded to calls from officers in Sex Crimes to aid with taking statements or filing reports, either at the hospital or down at the station. On the speed-dial of at least five cops, three lawyers and two doctors, Joel's days were longer than most.

This afternoon he held a young woman's hand, waiting in the hallway outside the courtroom. Her name was Stephanie and she was twenty-one, a theater major from Scarsdale. She had to swear on a Bible and recall being raped in the parking lot of a laundromat, because her dryer had broken and a man with a knife was waiting in a station wagon. Joel didn't want to talk about that.

"You smell like an ashtray," he said instead. "I told you to quit."

Casey plucked the filter from his mouth, stubbed it out on the rail. He ignored the indignant sound Joel made when he flicked it to the street below. "I told you to stay off my patio."

"I was going to cook, you know. You didn't need to get food."

"You're tired." Casey patted Joel's wrist. "Go inside, okay? I'll be right there."

Inside meant for Joel to skin out of his beige suit jacket and vest, toeing out of his white hi-tops at the bedroom door. With a sigh, he raked a hand through his hair and crawled across the mattress in a liquid sprawl. As promised, Casey followed with two forks, two boxes of Chicken Pad Thai and two bottles of Mexican beer, sitting cross-legged beside Joel to eat in the silence of their room. Casey found that he enjoyed this kind of quiet most of all.

"How are things going with Paul?" Joel asked around a mouth of noodles.

"Well." Casey chased a piece of chicken around his to-go container with his fork. "I showed up today. That's kind of like an improvement, right?"

"Casey."

Joel looked at him like a mother looked at a child covered in dirt. Casey made a face.

"It was fine. What?"

"Did you at least say anything this time?"

"I guess. He asked me about my life. I talked about it. It's fine."

"Paul is really good, Casey. I've seen him turn some tough cases around." Joel's expression softened around a sigh. "I think you need to be more open-minded about this. He could really help you. This might be a good change for you."

"No offense, but Paul is kind of a creeper."

Joel snorted. "You think all your therapists were creepers."

"Well, fine." Casey made another face and took a drink of beer. "But I'm about ninety-percent that he's a vampire. Even you have to admit that."

"Contrary to whatever you have going on in your head, therapists aren't all just sitting around plotting ways to ruin your life."

"I've done this song and dance since I was twelve, Joel. You know that. Hypnosis, group therapy, I've been through it all, okay? All I know is no one can tell me what's wrong with me."

"There's nothing wrong with you, Casey, it's just." Joel sighed. "I want to make sure you're on the right track. So does Paul. That's all, alright? I just want you better."

"Paul's an idiot." Casey leaned forward and pressed a kiss to Joel's temple. "But you're alright."

"No, I'm lovely. Now tell me you'll be good and you won't act like an idiot at your next session."

"I won't act like an idiot," Casey agreed and took up Joel's empty takeout box. "Now go get in the shower. You smell like a sweaty office chair."

Joel tasted like spicy noodles when he pecked at Casey's mouth. "Only if you clean up."

Casey gathered up the remains of dinner as Joel showered, threw away boxes and bottles, rinsed and dried the silverware. That was the way they did things. Joel worked longer hours and cooked, kept the lights on and the utilities paid. Casey worked less and did the dishes and the laundry, and picked up the groceries and the prescriptions. Kept house and tended to the plants and took out the trash, and fixed the leaking pipes and made sure the car ran on the mornings when Joel forgot to change the oil or change the filters. They went to bed at the same time, woke up at the same time, because Casey didn't like to sleep alone, if he ever slept at all. He didn't say a word about these things to Paul. It was none of his business.

He locked the patio door with a last glance at his mother's picture, and then went to the medicine cabinet in the bathroom and the pillbox inside. Tuesday PM, bold yellow letters on clear plastic. There were only three rules to the pillbox: No drugs, no driving, and no drinking. It was like being fifteen again. Each pill was for a problem another pill caused, or maybe just a problem it didn't treat, lined up neat rows to be taken with breakfast and before bed. The blue pill was for insomnia, red for anxiety; green, orange and brown pills for vitamin deficiency, liver function and depression. Some pills helped more than others.

Casey swallowed them with a cupped palm of water and looked in the mirror. He had his mother's round blue eyes, his father's straight nose and strong jaw. The rest of him was two sizes too small, cut in sharp angles, like the jut of his diaphragm and the shallow indentions between ribs and knuckles. More like his mother's portrait in that respect, the softness of her features and the slightness of her frame. It didn't stop Casey from slamming his fist against his reflection and the traces of his father trapped inside, quietly grateful it didn't shatter and Joel hadn't heard it. His knuckle bled in nicks and scrapes underneath the bandage he used to cover the evidence, but not enough to regret it.

When Joel emerged from the shower to towel his hair dry, Casey faked a smile and said nothing about the bathroom mirror or the hairline crack in its center. He exchanged his jeans and t-shirt for pajama bottoms, waiting for Joel to crawl into bed, curl up close. He switched off the bedside lamp and, knowing he wouldn't sleep, closed his eyes.

Chapter Six

Casey always woke up twenty minutes before the alarm clock went off if he had slept the night before. This morning he slept between the dreams in black stretches of quiet, waking only to listen for Joel's breathing before closing his eyes again. It was the same nightmare every time, skipping forward then back to the beginning, staggered and jumping, like reels of broken film. He dreamt of David Way without a face, bleeding thick and molasses-slow across white tile beneath Casey's bare feet. The floor was cold, wet as fresh snow between his toes and falling from the ceiling like television static. His step-mother screamed somewhere in the dark, a hateful, animal sound, off-panel, off-camera. From the floor, his father smiled.

"What that bitch cut out of me," he said, "it left a hole in you. You know that now, don't you?"

"Yeah, Dad." Watching the blood puddle at his feet, Casey felt helpless. Flecks of manufactured snow caught in his lashes, stuck in his hair. "I know she did."

Casey could still see the blood and the snow-tile when he awoke, melting behind his eyelids. He found his composition notebook on the bedside table, smoked a cigarette and wrote down what he dreamt while it was still fresh. Rubbed the sleep from his eyes, took his pills, and nudged Joel awake before the alarm had the chance. The coffee burped and brewed in the kitchen as Joel got up to dress and found the broken mirror.

"I guess I'll have to go to the hardware store after work. It's the strangest thing, though," he said from behind the half-closed bathroom door, applying deodorant under his arms. "I didn't even notice it was broken last night."

"I know." At the closet Casey buttoned up his shirt,

tucked it into his slacks and smoked another cigarette. He only felt comfortable enough to lie with Joel in the next room. The blood on his knuckle had dried, the bandage discarded. "Weird."

When his cell phone rang from the dresser across the room, Casey didn't have to check the caller ID.

"Hello, Sister."

"Hello, Little Brother." Across town Mariska was sitting in front of her vanity mirror in a t-shirt and underwear, smoking a cigarette. Casey could hear the rasp of her voice from smoke and too much talking. "You're up awfully early."

"Or you're up awfully late." Casey buttoned and straightened his collar. "Been to bed yet?"

"Nope." Mariska snuffled, rubbed her nose. "I was out with Billy after I got off work this morning. Kind of wired for sound, I guess."

"If you called just to tell me how drunk you are, I'm hanging up."

"Yeah, right. Are you free tonight? I need to talk to you about something."

"Tonight? I don't know." Casey glanced over his shoulder to the bathroom. "Why?"

"I just need to see you. It's that time of the year, you know?" The dip of her voice gave him pause. "Twenty years."

"Yeah," he sighed. "I know."

"I got to take a shower and go to bed in a minute, but let's meet tomorrow then, okay? How about that diner by your apartment before I go to work? The cheap place with the good burgers."

"Yeah, it's Joel's group session night at the community center. I can get there by five-thirty. That okay?"

"Five-thirty's good. Love you, Little Brother."

"See you, Sister." Casey snapped his phone shut.

"Who was that?" Joel stood at the bathroom door, dressed below the waist.

"Mariska." Casey dropped his phone into his pocket as though hiding evidence. "She wants to meet me after work tomorrow at the diner."

Joel tipped his head, leaned against the doorframe.

"The anniversary's coming up, with my Dad and all." Casey tried to smile reassuringly. "You know how we both get this time of year."

The paces were familiar. Mariska got out her family photos from underneath the bed and drank a little too much, and hid from her boyfriend, and always wanted Casey close. Casey wanted to start fires, bloody noses and rip the flesh from his dead father's face. Instead he found himself having nightmares, lying to Joel and doing whatever Mariska asked of him because if Mariska asked he didn't say no. That was the way it worked between them, ever since they were kids, big sister and baby brother.

"You know I can come with you." Joel sounded hopeful. "If you want me to."

"You have group tomorrow, it's fine." Casey turned to the closet to find his shoes. "She just wants to hash it out like she does every year. We'll probably just end up at a bar, she'll drink too much and I'll have to get her home. Don't worry about it."

"Do you want to hash it out again?"

"Not really." Casey shrugged. "But it doesn't really matter much, does it?"

"Of course it matters, Casey. What about what you want?"

Casey never answered. Joel finally sighed.

"Put that thing out or smoke on the patio, okay?" Joel returned to the bathroom, pushed the door shut behind him. "I hate coming home to smoky sheets."

Stubbing out his cigarette, Casey said nothing else. He toed on his shoes, grabbed some coffee and his messenger bag. Stuffed his house keys, a bagged lunch and his notebook inside, and on the refrigerator he left a sticky-note.

J

I'm sorry. Don't be mad.

C

There was nothing left to talk about. The paces were familiar there, too.

The sun was up in splinters between trees and buildings, the sky still purple like a bruise when Casey crossed the two intersections to the Grab-N-Go. Behind the counter, Harold with the crooked nametag sat in a plastic folding chair, his skater-boy haircut over-gelled and tongue probing at a lip ring. Casey knew his name was Harold because Harold was always at the counter with the stash of porno rags that he kept under his chair. Harold knew Casey because the Grab-N-Go was within walking distance of his apartment and Casey was a creature of habit. Marlboro Reds most days, maybe 100s if the store was out.

He nodded at Casey from behind a Japanese fetish magazine. On the cover a woman in a hospital gown and leg braces was bent over an examination table. She was stuffed full of steel surgical instruments shaped like dildos and tongues, thick as his wrist and polished to a mirror shine. Casey asked for a pack of Reds, paid for them, and huffed out thanks without looking at the magazine again. The woman's eyes seemed to follow him no matter what he did, glassy and distant from too much sex. Harold with the crooked nametag never seemed to notice.

The nine-to-five lurched by, dragging itself down the halls and between the shelves. Lanyard nametag, plastic reading glasses, and a makeshift office, converted from a storeroom two catalogers ago to fit Casey's desk, chair and computer. Casey sat at his computer like he did every day, assigning Library of Congress subject headings and call numbers to the New Acquisitions folder dropped off on his desk by Debbie from upstairs. Referencing and cross-referencing, coding and sorting, updating the catalog. His office was cold and gray with dingy old fixtures and nobody bothered him. He was content that way.

That was Casey's life at the city library. Eight years spent in the basement reorganizing every inch of the library's catalog, having wandered in with four years of experience at his campus library and a useless degree under his belt. College was an exercise in futility and long weekends spent drinking, having forgettable sex and looking for fights with any guy who was willing. The only viable skill he ever picked up was how to code acquisitions and update library catalogs on the quick, learning it over the summer of his freshman year when the rest of the part-timers left on vacation. Drinking and fighting didn't pay the bills, so something had to give. In his own way, quiet and alone, Casey was happy.

At lunch, Casey ate in the break-room, microwavable noodles and coffee from the quarter machine, and tried to think of ways to tell Joel not to worry. Joel worried anyway. That was what Joel did, with his gentleness and good intentions. Joel worried and wheedled and Casey gave in, because he loved Joel and he knew Joel wanted what was best for him. Joel always knew best. That was the way things worked between them. Before Casey finished his microwaved chow mein, Kim from the front desk stopped by and asked if he could do her a favor. She smiled through a bitten lip, telling some sad story about having to pick up her kid's prescription on her lunch break.

Casey gave in to that, too. He didn't have anything else

better to do, already halfway through his list of acquisitions and four hours left in his shift. After lunch he jogged upstairs to Audio-Visual to stand in the middle of Pop A-Z with a cart of CDs. He made his way from S through W, shelving new cataloged discs and movies into the spaces Kim had made for them, listening to the shuffling of feet in the next aisle, the occasional cough or sniffle.

Between towers of two broad shelves, Casey glanced up, noticed a man in a tan suit and blue tie. The man was middle-aged, paunchy at the waist with hair graying at his temple and the edges of his well-trimmed mustache. He stared at Casey like the glassy-eyed medical fetish model on Harold's magazine, gaze dead behind wire framed glasses, tracking Casey as he moved behind the cart to step away. Inside his chest there was a hole, cut out in the shape of a fat square box. His heart thumped dully between ribs that were pulled open, expanding like the jaws of his flytraps, split wide and hungry.

"I never hurt Claire," the man said. Casey caught a breath between his teeth and held it. "I loved her. You believe me, right?"

Casey came to in a snap, brought about by steady footsteps, heavy in the soles. When he turned Walter stood at the mouth of the walkway between shelves, hands in the pockets of his dull slacks. Walter always looked just as he did in the laminated ID hanging around his neck, mouth sloping at the corners, bags under his eyes like an old basset hound. The life of an Assistant Library Director must have been more depressing than it looked from outside Walter's office on the way to the break-room. Sitting at his desk and going over paperwork and making phone calls through the tiny porthole in his door.

"You alright, Casey?" Walter asked.

His sweater of choice today was weighty and dark, blue with gray reindeer bounding across a snowy field. If it had been any other day, Casey would have laughed.

"Yeah." Casey swallowed on the knot that gathered in his throat and smiled. It was just easier that way. "Yeah, you know how it goes. Just a spell."

Walter's heavy brow sagged. "You know, after you're done here maybe we should talk in my office."

"Why?"

"I'd rather not say on the floor, Casey. You're not in trouble, we just need to talk."

"Well, then we can talk out here."

Walter sighed. "There's been some talk upstairs, about your problem."

"What problem?"

"Come on, Casey. You're a good employee; don't take this the wrong way. You always finish ahead of schedule and you don't complain. Hell, you already ran the part-time catalogers out of the building. Now I've looked the other way about your condition, but people are starting to notice your blackouts."

"I'm on meds, Walter. I'm going to therapy again."

"I know, Casey. And I know you've kept your nose clean."

Casey pushed the cart back. "So I got it under control, okay?"

Walter sighed again. "This isn't coming from me. You know I wouldn't do this."

"Then where is it coming from?"

"The guys upstairs are starting to wonder why you're working full-time with a handicap and I haven't made any mention of it."

"Handicap?" Casey's face felt hot. "I'm not handicapped, Walter. I'm just going through a rough patch right now, alright? I'm seeking treatment, I'm on medication. What did I do wrong?"

Walter was quiet.

"Take some time off, Casey," he finally said. "I know you have some personal time saved up. You can finish up your work for the week, and then just take a vacation or something, alright?"

Casey swallowed. "Do I have a choice?"

"I'll call you in two weeks. Alright?"

After a moment, Casey nodded. "Sure."

Walter nodded in turn, and watched as Casey put up his cart's worth of discs. Back in his office, Casey dug his notebook out of his messenger bag. Found a blank space beneath two new missing persons fliers he had taken from the back wall of Grab-N-Go the week before.

4/3/10, Library

Saw another dead guy at work today. He had a hole in his chest, just like the last time.

Chapter Seven

Sunlight from the windows in the waiting room sliced under the door of Joel's cold little office, as he sat between appointments amid chipping wood paneling and stained carpet. He was cross-legged in his desk chair. It creaked when he leaned back into it, reading the staff emails he had been carbon-copied into over Pepsi and a bag of pita crackers. Lunch hour had already passed, spent on the phone with a patient named Karla Simmons. She hid in her bathroom and let him talk her into going to police to press charges against her uncle for ten years of abuse. His three o'clock, Cassandra Kendrick, would be in soon, to discuss her rage toward the boy from her Business Economics class that forced his fingers inside of her after a frat party.

There would likely be no time to eat his much-anticipated Daily Special of tuna on whole wheat from the deli around the corner. Chewing on a mouthful of crackers, Joel tried not to dwell on it. At quarter-to-three, his back-pocket buzzed.

> FROM CASEY, 2:45PM, 4/3/10
> the universe is out to get me

Joel wrinkled his nose, scrolled through to his touch-screen keypad. He prided himself on his response times.

> FROM JOEL, 2:46PM, 4/3/10
> You always say that. What is it this time?
> FROM CASEY, 2:48PM, 4/3/10
> i'm being put on personal leave until i straighten my life out

Before Joel could text his response, his phone vibrated.

> *FROM CASEY, 2:49PM, 4/3/10*
> *i'll be good from now on, ok?*
> *FROM JOEL, 2:50PM, 4/3/10*
> *Do you promise?*
> *FROM CASEY, 2:54PM, 4/3/10*
> *yes. so don't be mad*

He was never mad, but Casey didn't need to know that yet. After a moment, Joel sighed.

> *FROM JOEL, 2:59PM, 4/3/10*
> *Okay.*

Chapter Eight

"So how does this work?" Casey asked, wedged into the corner of Paul's sofa. "You count back from one hundred and I just spill my guts, right?"

From his armchair, Paul folded his hands and smiled. "Not exactly. We have some ground to cover first."

Casey shrugged. "Where do we start?"

"Let's start somewhere simple, Casey." Paul drew the pen and pad from the side table. "How are you feeling today?"

"Honestly?" Casey squared his shoulders. "I'm a little stressed out."

"How so?"

Paul's pen hovered above the paper expectantly. Casey watched it for a moment.

"I'm blacking out at work. Which, you know, I've always done to some degree, I guess. But my boss caught me doing it – *again* – and put me on personal leave until I get my head together."

"I see." Paul nodded. "So it's safe to say that your problems started as a result of your father's death, correct?"

"Safe to say."

"The anniversary of which is coming up, yes?"

"Yeah."

"Can you talk about the experience?"

"My father's death?" Casey's jaw ticked. "There's nothing to really talk about. I don't remember it."

"You blocked it out?"

"No it's....the memories are there, you know? I can remember remembering it, but if I try to think back on it now, it's gone. It's like somebody just cut it out."

Paul nodded and scratched notes across his pad. Casey swallowed.

"Do you know what happened?"

"I only know what my Aunt Cheryl told me. She's my father's sister; she took me and Mariska so we wouldn't be split up. The cops called her when they found my father at the house." Casey lifted his shoulder to shrug. "What I understand is that my stepmother waited for my father to come home from work. She found a box of photos of Mariska that he kept in the top of the closet."

"Photos of your sister?"

"My father raped her for eight years. He kept pictures of the abuse, I guess as a memento."

Paul wrote something down. "Go on."

"Alyona confronted my father about the abuse and they argued. According to Cheryl, Alyona took a butcher knife and attacked him. She stabbed him thirty-seven times and cut off most of his face. I was told that when my father was autopsied he weighed about five or six pounds less than usual because of all the meat that she cut away. I don't know if that's true."

"But you seem remarkably comfortable talking about your father's death."

The sharp urge to smile made Casey uneasy. "I don't really miss him."

"And things at home?"

"What?"

"How are things at home?" Paul asked. "Between you and Joel?"

"What does that have to do with anything?"

"I think it's important to discuss your home life, Casey," Paul half-chided, "in order to get the clearest picture possible of all your issues. Wouldn't you agree?"

"Yeah, I guess."

"So?"

"We're fine. I mean, we have problems, but we work through them. We take care of each other."

"Are you happy?"

"Of course."

"And sexually?"

Casey jerked his chin up. "Excuse me?"

"I'm asking, how are you both sexually?"

"No, I heard you. I meant, how is that any of your business?"

"Casey, please. It's important."

"We're solid. Okay? It's always been good like that between us."

Paul was writing notes again. "Are you monogamous?"

"Wow, are you serious?"

"Please."

Casey sighed. "Yes, we're monogamous. And do it missionary-style under the sheets with the lights out like everybody else does. No leather, or sex-swings, or key parties, or anything exciting like that."

"Do you use protection?"

"No."

"Is that deliberate?"

"In that I'm deliberately trying to get Joel pregnant – which is impossible – or that I'm deliberately forgoing condoms because we've been together for four years? And you only use condoms when you're sleeping with other people, which neither of us are?"

"It's just a question." Paul wrote something else down. "How often do you have sex?"

"I don't know. A couple of times a week, I guess? Enough."

"Do you find Joel's sexual performance satisfactory?"

"Yeah, okay, no. We're done with this line of

questioning."

"Okay then." Paul smiled reassuringly. "I would like to try an exercise, Casey, if you don't mind. It's a form of guided hypnosis that I feel could be of some use to you. It'll allow me to observe you in a semi-conscious state, where, with any luck, you'll be more open to examining the root of your problems."

"Fine." Casey crossed his arms tighter around himself. "If you say so."

"Good." Paul smiled. "Now lie down and relax, and close your eyes."

With another sigh, Casey stretched out, closed his eyes as told. From across the coffee table he could hear Paul move between the arms of his foreboding black chair, the rustle of fabric and the clicking of his pen. Tap-tap-scratch.

"Slow your breathing, Casey," Paul said soothingly. "Allow every muscle to relax, from your head to your feet. Feel your eyes and your face relax, your neck and your shoulders. Can you feel it? Down your arms, to your hands and through your legs, right into your toes. I'm going to count back from ten to one, Casey. With each number you will become more and more relaxed. Slower and slower, deeper and deeper, until you're completely relaxed. Is that okay, Casey?"

Casey took a deep breath. "Fine."

"Good."

Paul's smile was audible. Casey exhaled and began to slip from the couch. The watery unbalance of his equilibrium told him that he was falling, sliding in liquid descent between the cushions and the upholstery of the sofa.

"Ten, nine, eight. Slower and slower…"

Casey felt limp like a ragdoll, falling through the floor. Through the cracks of the floorboards and the spaces between levels, all concrete and pink cotton candy insulation. His eyelids twitched. He took another breath.

"Seven, six, five. Deeper and deeper…"

He dropped freely through the floors of Paul's high-rise office, through the steel and wood. Gravity pressed down on Casey's chest, wind fluttering at his back. He fell through plaster and carpet, light fixtures and glass, through to the ground floor and everything underneath it.

"Four, three, two, one…"

Casey gasped when his back strike solid ground.

"When you open your eyes, you'll be home. It's the house where you grew up, Casey. Can you see it?"

Casey opened his eyes and saw the sky above him. It was a faded blue sheet pinned in place by the tops of skinny green trees, surrounded in bushels of needles that gleamed like bone-flint in Casey's mind. He blinked twice in the light of a bulbous yellow sun and felt sore all over.

"Yeah, I can."

Casey pushed himself upright, sitting in the green stretch of lawn and among the snapping mouths of his mother's flytraps. They knotted around him in thick clusters of toothy smiles, catching in his sleeves and pants as he stood. Across the yard he saw himself as a child. Three years old, he was chubby in the face under shaggy hair and freckles, tugging at his mother's skirt as she tended to her garden of mouths. They grinned cartoonishly for their breakfast, and perhaps for her as well, long and beautiful in her white sundress and sandals. Her hair dark like Casey's and tumbling past her shoulders, her eyes bluer and brighter. In the distance their home was white and fat with heavy shutters protecting curtained windows, enclosed by dense brush and tall trees. Casey watched his mother carry him across the patio, short fat fingers catching in her blouse and hair. She smiled with her whole face, from her eyelids to her chin. She looked happy.

"Where are you, Casey?" Paul asked from somewhere far away.

"I'm in my backyard." Beneath him his mother's traps snapped at him, hissing in his wake as he cautiously crossed the yard. "My mom's here with me."

"Your stepmother?"

"No, my real mom."

"What do you see, Casey?"

"I can see my house."

"Can you see the backdoor?"

Up the patio and over the steps, Casey stopped in front of the door. It was taller than he was by three heads and white like the rest of the house.

"Yes."

"Walk through the backdoor, Casey."

Swallowing, Casey grabbed the knob, turned and pushed. Inside there was only a hallway, long and white, sterile like a hospital room. The cold air blew stale against Casey's cheek and smelled like chemicals, making him acutely aware of the hairs at the back of his neck. Logic told him he was on Paul's sofa, but at the end of the hallway there was a black metal door, crisscrossed in an intricate mesh of chains and padlocks. The door was broader and taller than a man and emitting static from behind it, the snow between television stations or between Casey's toes when he dreamt of his father.

"What do you see, Casey?"

"A locked door."

"Walk through it."

"I can't. I can't get in, there's too many locks."

"Walk through it, Casey. Everything you need to know is

behind that door."

From the other side of the door there was a moan, a clanging and mechanical sound like pornography on bad speakers. Casey shook his head and against his better judgment walked forward. Moans moved down the passage in a degenerating signal, voices faded between stations to pull Casey closer. A splash and the feeling of wetness drew his attention to his feet. Water closed over his ankles, thick and syrupy, black on first glance then red. The moans spiked into a scream and Casey realized it was blood.

"Oh god." It filled the hall in a swamp that sloshed against the walls, quickly climbing Casey's legs to his knees to choke his movements. "There's nothing but blood here."

"You have to keep walking, Casey," Paul insisted coldly from the space behind Casey's head. "You have to get to the door."

Thud.

Casey looked up, jumped at the sound of steel and flesh. From behind the door something beat against it. The frantic animal sounds of fists and shoulders, bone and skin, pounding through the shackles to reach Casey. His heart thumped as he moved through blood, hands out to clutch uselessly at the chains. He screamed and tasted iron, shaking at the padlocks, scratching and tearing and--

"One, two, three, four, five—"

--biting and ripping and bleeding from his nails where they chipped away and--

"Six, seven, eight, nine, ten."

Casey opened his eyes. He sat up on Paul's sofa, the cavern-office lurching above his head, and retched. It was only when Casey looked up that he noticed Paul had held out a waste basket to catch his vomit. Wiping a knuckle across his mouth, Casey spat the taste of bile and nearly growled.

"Well." Paul sighed. "That was an informative exercise."

"Don't even." Casey shook his head, pushed the waste basket away. "You didn't say anything about the fucking K-Hole you dropped me into."

"I told you, Casey." Paul set the basket behind the arm of the sofa. "It's a difficult process. You need to be open if we're going to get to the root of your problem."

"Fuck you." Casey wobbled to his feet, made his way to the door. "Stay out of my head."

"You know I didn't plant any of that there." There was sing-song in Paul's voice that gave Casey pause. "Everything you experienced, that was already there, Casey, in your mind. I just gave you the opportunity to assess it first-hand."

At the doorway Casey took a breath. The whole of him rattled and he hoped Paul hadn't noticed. "I don't care."

"Yes, but I think Joel does." Paul smiled. "So will I be seeing you on Tuesday?"

Casey grabbed the knob, gripped it until his knuckles turned white. "Fine."

Paul's smile didn't falter.

Chapter Nine

Joel took lunch on the bench outside of Ramona's Deli. It was where he picked up his Daily Special of tuna on whole wheat and bagged pita crackers, and ate every day that he could spare the time between patients, phone calls and ritual message-checking. The bench afforded him the vantage to eye the southwest corner of his building from between two street lights, in case the receptionist Christy called him with a walk-in or an emergency. Under fresh sunlight Joel drank Pepsi from the Styrofoam cup between his legs and chewed contentedly. He didn't notice Paul approaching him under the shade of his stripped sun umbrella and the brassy fastens of his dark tweed vest, but for the click-clack of his shoes on the pavement.

Joel looked up, from black polished shoes to the tip of Paul's straight nose. He licked his lips and tried not to smile. "Casey's right. You do look like a vampire."

Paul shrugged and folded his umbrella, tucked it beneath his arm. "Casey would think so," he offered politely. Dusting off the seat he took up the space next to Joel on the bench. "Your office said you'd be over here."

"I need sunshine." Joel wiped his mouth with a napkin and dusted breadcrumbs from his pants. "It helps me clear my head."

"Long day?"

Joel shrugged. "They're all long days."

"I see you never take lunch too far from the office." Paul nodded, gestured to the sliver of the Turning Point Counseling Center peeking out between streetlights. "Still trying to change the world, I take it?"

"Not the whole world, Paul. Just the parts I don't like," Joel answered brightly. "I know that still may come as a shock to you."

"You were always one of my very best, Joel. You deserve better than a broom closet," Paul chided gently, crossed his legs. "There's no shame in having your own practice, you know. We're not all sell-outs. I think you'd do really well for yourself."

"I like my broom closet just fine. Don't worry about me."

"To each his own." After a moment of silence, Paul folded his hands. "So how's Casey been doing?"

Joel bristled and tried not to let it show. "You just saw him today. You should know."

Distracting himself with a speck of dirt on his pant leg, Paul sighed. "You know it isn't working, don't you?"

"We can't talk about this, Paul."

"I'm not telling you anything you don't already know."

"I know Casey can be a tough shell to crack," Joel said. He bagged his makeshift picnic and set it aside. "But you have to be patient with him. I think he's finally turned a corner here."

"Casey's hostile, Joel. He's withdrawn, antagonistic, self-loathing—"

"Hey. You've seen worse. I know you have."

"I've seen people that wanted to be helped." Paul sighed again. "I feel his refusal to cooperate speaks to a deeper issue here, and I don't think you're entirely aware of it."

Joel frowned. "Which is?"

"Casey doesn't want to deal with his problems. I agreed to see him as a favor to you, but he's only doing this to please you. This is an unhealthy situation to put him into, for both of you."

"Paul, he's a good guy. You just have to be patient with him. I've already been talking to him about your sessions, and I think I can get him over this hump if you give me a little time."

"I don't think Casey needs time, Joel," Paul said flatly. "I don't think Casey wants to be helped at all. And I know you care about him, I do, but I think you should take a step back and reevaluate your relationship."

"What're you implying?" Joel's stomach tightened.

"You can't spend all your time trying to fix someone who doesn't think they're broken. I don't think he's worth wasting your time on." Paul sighed, and looked remarkably earnest. "I'm only saying that as a friend and colleague."

"Well." Joel faked a smile. "Thank you for your professional advice, Paul, but I'm going to have to disregard it for the time being. And I would ask you to kindly butt out of my personal relationships and please focus on your case instead. No offense."

"None taken." Paul stood, unfurling his umbrella. "Enjoy the rest of your lunch."

"Thank you," Joel smiled, sweetly this time. "Goodbye, Paul."

"Goodbye, Joel."

As the clack of Paul's shoes receded behind the clothing store neighboring Ramona's Deli, Joel gathered up his bag and cup, each half-full, and threw them into the nearby trashcan.

Chapter Ten

Casey refused to sleep on the three-twenty-five cross-town, still thinking of blood and green grass as his fingers drummed warm spots into the handrail. He got off two blocks from the Grab-N-Go, walked the rest of the way and bought a pack of Reds. Behind the counter Harold nodded, glancing up from a fold-out of a quadruple amputee in pigtails and a metal bikini. She was spread out on the calloused nubs left of her elbows and knees, tongue out like a panting dog. Casey paid for the smokes and tried not to stare at her salivating tongue, told Harold to keep the twelve cents in change so he could leave without focusing on the strings of spit connecting the model's mouth to the floor.

"Hey," Harold said, and dropped the twelve cents into the Save the Children donation box beside the register. "Thanks."

"Yeah." Casey nodded. "See you around."

Tugging at the strap of his messenger bag, Casey walked the congested maze of evening traffic to Jay's Diner and took up his favorite booth. Sherrie wasn't on yet and Mariska hadn't yet arrived. With a false smile he ordered black coffee from a new girl named Melissa with black hair and red lipstick, promised that he would wait for Sherrie to come on if she just brought him one cup. He was a creature of habit, after all.

Once Melissa left his table Casey pulled out his notebook and pen, thumbed through pages of missing persons fliers. It was a matter of déjà vu, familiarity making his fingertips itch. Sometimes, if Casey looked long enough, he could match his written accounts of dead people with the photos in the fliers. He could put a name to the faces that he sometimes saw when blinking in and out of sleep, in line at the deli counter or waiting for traffic signals to turn. He never told anyone about that. There was nothing worth telling.

Mariska soon arrived with the familiar stomping of her booted feet through the front door, keys jangling in her jacket pocket. She smiled behind black sunglasses and bent to kiss Casey's cheek.

"Hey, Little Brother." She flopped all six-plus-feet-in-heels of her into the booth across from Casey, discarding the shades and jacket. "Buy me a Coke and a cheeseburger, man. I'm starved."

"What, you drag me out and I'm paying?" Casey straightened up to wave at Sherrie as she tied her apron at the counter across the diner. She waved back. "Let me guess, you smoked your allowance?"

"I wish," Mariska scoffed. "Not in this economy."

When Sherrie made it to the table, they both ordered cheeseburgers, well-done with mayo and bacon. Casey put his notebook away. Mariska looked tired. He already knew why. Leaning back into his seat, he still felt compelled to ask.

"You doing okay?"

She shrugged. "Okay is kind of relative these days, you know?"

"Did you see your mom yet?"

"Yeah. Kind of wished I didn't, though. That sounds bad, right?"

"Well, no. Not really," he said. "You tried. You've been trying. That counts for something."

"I guess. And, you know, sorry for not bringing it up on the phone yesterday. I thought it would be better if we talk about it in private." Taking the straw from her glass she rolled it between her fingers. "I know Joel's not exactly my biggest fan."

"Joel loves you." Casey shrugged. "He just thinks you're a bad influence...sometimes."

Mariska laughed. "Yeah, that kind of goes without saying."

Neither of them spoke, long enough to trade sighs.

"It's coming up on twenty years, man," she said. "I can't even get my head around it."

"Yeah, I know."

"So you've been having the dreams, right? I mean, you always have the weird dreams, but." Mariska chewed her bottom lip. "It's happening again, isn't it? The thing with your dad?"

"I keep seeing him. Not the way you remember him, but the way he was when he died." Casey shook his head, leaned forward. "You know the really screwed up thing, though? I don't remember anything else. It's all gone. I could recognize Dad from a photograph if you showed it to me, but that whole time – it's like somebody just cut it out."

"Hey, sorry I'm late."

Out of Casey's peripheral Joel appeared by the table. His tie was crooked, gelled hair somewhat mussed. He smiled and slid into the booth beside Casey, dropping his briefcase on the floor between them.

"Traffic was a mess," Joel explained and pecked Casey's lips gently. He smiled in Mariska's direction. "Hey."

"Hey," she forced through a smile.

"I thought you had group tonight?" Casey asked neutrally.

"I told Jennifer I had a thing and asked if she could handle the session on her own tonight." Joel squeezed Casey's knee affectionately. "So she shooed me off and I came here. Did you guys order yet?"

"Yeah, a couple burgers." Mariska slid a look to Casey. "You want something?"

Casey looked at Mariska, then back at Joel. Joel never looked away.

"No, I'm good, I had a late lunch." Joel settled into his seat. Casey nodded. "So what were you going to say?"

Mariska squared her shoulders the way she did when she was lying. Casey saw it, even if Joel didn't.

"Nah, you know, it's okay, I don't think Joel wants to hear about it." She returned to her cup to play with her straw. "I bet he's had a long day."

"Mar—"

"No, it's fine. Don't change the subject on my account," Joel insisted as the waitress returned to the table, two plates in hand, disappearing to retrieve the coffee pot before Casey could ask.

"Well." Mariska took a bite of her burger, chewed quickly, and swallowed. "I was thinking. It's been twenty years since we've been to the old house, right?"

Casey nodded, took up a knife to cut his sandwich in half. "Yeah?"

"So I was thinking maybe you and me could go back, you know? Maybe get some closure."

Casey could feel Joel bristle beside him at the suggestion.

"Well, do you think that's really a good idea?" Joel asked. "I mean, the people living there probably wouldn't like a handful of strangers lurking around outside the bushes."

"That's the thing. I already looked the house up and it's been abandoned for years. The realtors haven't been able to move it with its history. Nobody wants a murder-house, right? I figure we could drive over there and take a look around. You know, peep through the windows, or maybe see if we can get in through the backdoor or something. I mean, nobody's around to care, right? I think it'd be really good for us."

It was Casey's turn to bristle. He took a sip of his coffee

and tried not to notice Joel's burning look.

"I'm really not sure about this." Joel's voice was restrained, his appealing smile feigned. "If you want to go visit your old house, Mariska, sure, but Casey's been doing really well. I don't think committing burglary with you would help him at this point."

"I'm not doing that well, Joel," Casey said gently. "I mean, c'mon."

"Casey—"

"Which is why," Mariska sing-songed, "I think we should go. Just get it out of our systems once and for all, you know?"

"If you need to go, Mariska, you can. I just don't see how you have to involve Casey in this."

"Hey, it's not like I'm doing this out of spite or whatever. I'm doing it to try to help him. We're in this together."

"Casey and I are in this together, too. And I think you should respect his decision to seek help instead of dragging this up every year."

"What're you talking about? I'm not dragging anything up."

"You always do this, and Casey's supposed to drop what he's doing because you say so."

"Hey." Casey slid a hand under the table, caught Joel's wrist gently. "I'll think about it, okay? It doesn't sound like such a bad idea, and if it might help Mariska feel better about it, I can go. It's no big deal."

Mariska buried a nervous look in her half-eaten burger. Joel took a breath and nodded. His smile was placating and Casey didn't buy it. They said nothing about that.

"Fine."

Casey and Mariska finished eating in silence. Joel held onto Casey's wrist underneath the table, threading their fingers together where Mariska couldn't see. They said nothing about that, either.

Chapter Eleven

"You have to do this. You have to make this promise, okay? If you don't I'll hate you forever. I'm allowed."

Mariska held out the knife she had hidden in the waist her skirt, expecting Casey to take it. His step-sister's pale blue petticoat made her legs look like bones until they disappeared into the combat boots she kept in her school bag, exchanging high heels for boots once she was out of her mother's line of sight. She was thirteen then, a full head taller than all the other girls at her school and built like a boy. The dresses her mother covered her up in slipped from her bony shoulders and absent hipbones, the gathers of fabric that Mariska tugged at like a choke collar, uncomfortable in her own skin.

Casey was eleven. He still looked more like his mother then, with her rounder nostrils and softer mouth. It wouldn't be until puberty that his father's strong jaw came in, the shape of his shoulders, the straightness of his nose. At eleven, Casey could still lie about his parentage. That he was adopted or left with a relative after his mother died, and the man who shared his last name was just a cross to bear. Someday soon Casey would look like his father, but today was not that day.

Casey and Mariska stood together under the bridge on Davenport Street, halfway between home and school. Older kids hung out there on the weekends, having parties, drinking beer. The air was damp and it was cold enough that Casey could just barely see his breath. There was a trashcan for setting fires and stolen sofas for things Mariska wouldn't tell Casey about. Mariska was the one who knew about this place, leading him down the embankment and along the dried creek-bed to the cave under Davenport Street. Casey didn't ask why.

Mariska was already smoking cigarettes and fighting with her mother by then, when things were starting to get bad. She had already started running away, climbing out of her bedroom window at night and walking to her friend Stevie's house. She was already drinking stolen beer. Her mother was complaining about it all the time, shouting at Mariska over the phone. His father never said anything. Casey stopped asking about that, too. He didn't know if that was what this was, if they were running away, but when she asked him to go he knew he had to. They stuck together like that.

Standing together in the half-dark, cars rumbled over their heads like steamrollers and made the overpass shake. Casey shivered under his jacket and Mariska held out the blade. It was half her size in her little hand, almost the length of Casey's forearm. He wanted to ask where she got it, but he didn't bother. It came from the older kids where she got her cigarettes and beer, and took her to caves like this.

"I don't know." For the first time since they got here, he felt nervous. "I don't think I want to do this anymore."

"But Case, you have to." The cigarette between her lips made it hard to tell if she was breathing smoke or steam. "I don't have anybody else. You know that."

"But why does it have to be blood?"

"You have to do it in blood. Because we're a family. Because we're the only ones who aren't crazy. That's why."

Mariska didn't say it, but Casey knew what it was. It was an oath, a blood pact. People did stuff like that in movies or books. They didn't do it in tunnels with cars threatening to crash on their heads. Casey swallowed and pulled his coat tighter.

"I don't know."

Mariska looked hurt. "Then you don't love me."

"Mar, don't say that."

"And if you don't love me then nobody loves me."

"I don't think they love me, either."

They always spoke about their parents in clinical terms. He and She, Them and They. Not Mom or Dad or Alyona or David. Casey's father was never talked about, not even in private or when he was at work. It was just a matter of survival, two steps above Morse code, smoke signals or passing messages under doors. Soup cans on strings and sign language. That would be the day.

"Then we need to do this, okay? Because you're my brother and I'll make you my blood. I'm doing this for you, okay? It's not just for me."

Casey didn't answer.

"Okay?"

"Yeah, okay."

"Yeah?"

"Yeah."

Mariska rolled up a blue sleeve, dragged the blade across the inside of her arm. The blood that followed was almost black in the dark, dripping on the top of a dusty boot. She closed a hand over it and passed him the knife. Casey could feel his arms shaking in his jacket but tried to ignore it, bit his lip and pushed his sleeve back. He cut himself and felt a little sick at the sight of it, the easy way his flesh opened up and looked red underneath. Without dropping the knife he covered the wound with his wrist and Mariska stepped close. She smelled of ashes and flowers like the perfume older girls wore.

"You're my brother, Casey." She reached out and took his hand away from the cut, holding it closed with a red palm. "We share blood now. Remember that."

He took her arm and nodded dumbly, unsure of what else

to do, just trusting her lead. He always trusted her. He had to. She had been his sister since he was four and she was six, and her mother came to live with his father. Because she had no father of her own, and his mother had gone to Heaven when he was little, so they had to share a family, and what did all of it matter, anyway? They didn't want their parents. They didn't need them. Just this.

"We'll always have each other, no matter what anybody says."

"I know." He shivered even though he wasn't cold anymore. "Always."

They never spoke of the underpass, the blood or the knife. When Alyona shouted about the blood on Mariska's sleeve, Mariska didn't answer. She just looked at Casey from across the dining room table. Casey looked back. It would be their secret. Someday soon David would be dead and Casey would look just like him, and everybody would know what his father had done, what none of them ever spoke of. But for today Casey and Mariska were brother and sister, and that would be enough.

Chapter Twelve

Casey trimmed the heads of dead flytraps and frowned around his cigarette. This was just getting embarrassing now. Twelve, maybe thirteen tiny faces had shrunk together in a huddle of withered black mouths, spines like prison bars folded shut. They were fine the night before, he could have sworn. It had been warm enough to leave them out. Now they made him think of his mother, her framed portrait hanging up in the hallway. His mother could grow anything, he was told. She had a backyard of little faces to prove it. Mariska had a shoebox of pictures to prove it.

He snipped at dead faces under the patio fixture's dim yellow light, circled by humming insects, and sighed. It was the story of Casey's life. One shoe dropped, the other took out the neighbor's window, and he was always left with the mess on his hands. It was dark outside by the time he heard the door open and Joel slip out, making his way across the patio on bare feet to wrap his arms around Casey's neck. He closed his eyes to the brush of Joel's lips against his ear, held a breath.

"You still mad?" Casey asked.

"No, I'm not mad." Joel sighed, slid his arms down to Casey's waist. "Hey."

"Hey, what?"

"Just come to bed now, okay?"

Abandoning the shears on the planter stand, Casey did what he was told. Followed as Joel retreated to the bedroom, locked the patio door behind them before he did so. Turned off the light, looked at his mother's picture, and looked away. Down the hallway to the threshold of their room Joel was already undressing himself, opening his vest and button-up, skin white and clean under lamplight. Casey stubbed his cigarette out in the ashtray on the nightstand and slipped out of his t-shirt, tossed it at the corner hamper. He reached for Joel at the foot of the bed, taking him by the chin to kiss him, first softly then firm. It was easier than saying sorry or trying to explain. He didn't want to talk about anything at all.

"I didn't mean to be snotty to your sister," Joel said sincerely.

"I think she's used to it at this point."

"Rude." Joel punched Casey's shoulder lightly. Casey smirked. "I mean it."

"I know." Casey cupped Joel's face and kissed him until he was quiet. "I really don't want to talk about that right now, okay?"

"Casey."

"Hey." Caught Joel's bottom lip between his teeth, held him by the base of his throat with fond fingers. "Don't be sorry. Not right now."

They undressed between kisses, touching without looking. Sex came easily after four years together, the steps familiar, gestures measured in cause and effect, action and reaction. Across the mattress and under the sheets, Joel pressed his cheek to the pillow, breathing the smell of shampoo and Casey's hair. He opened easily to Casey's curled fingers and the kisses Casey dotted across Joel's shoulders, letting out a pleased sigh when Casey withdrew his fingers in exchange for his dick. Casey pressed again, hip-to-hip and chest-to-back, keeping Joel close. Slow rhythm, steady in the span of short breaths, all tensile strength and whispers. Easy together until each of them came, one after the other, shiver, grunt, sigh. They uncoupled, Casey's left side of the bed and Joel's right, and closed their eyes.

"You're thinking about going, aren't you?" Joel eventually said, breathing into the fleshy part where Casey's shoulder joined neck.

Casey opened his eyes. "I'm thinking about it."

Joel pushed himself onto his elbows. "I don't think it's a good idea for you to go back to that house."

"I know." Casey sat up, rubbed at his forehead with the heel of his hand. "Believe me, I do. But Mariska wants me to go, and I think she really needs to do this."

"Casey, I know you, alright? She drags you out every year to go over this and you end up right back where you started. It doesn't help."

"It doesn't matter."

"But do you want to go?"

"This isn't about me."

"Of course it's about you," Joel insisted. "It has to be about you some of the time."

Casey didn't answer. Joel sighed.

"I'm not trying to start a fight, Casey. I just don't want to see you get hurt."

Casey shook his head. "After what our parents did to us, we're responsible for each other. You know that. And if she needs me, I'll go."

"If Mariska needs to do this she can go with Billy. She's not alone. It doesn't all have to be on you."

"Yeah, but, that's the way it's always been for us."

"You're her baby brother, Casey. She needs to understand your reasons and let you get better." Joel pressed his temple to Casey's shoulder blade, listened to the clockwork of his breathing. "You need to think about yourself for once. That's all I want."

Casey shrugged. "It's not your fault, you know, all this crap. You wanted me in therapy again, on the pills. I know I've been shitty about this, but I'll stop fighting, okay? I'll go back and I'll be better about it this time, I promise."

"No. If you don't want to see Paul, then don't go back," Joel said. "I'm serious. I know I pushed you to go but if you don't want to, then don't. We'll try something else. We'll figure this out."

"Joel, don't. If you want me to see Paul, I'll do it. I owe you that much."

"I don't care about that anymore." Joel squeezed Casey's skinny bicep, held there by Casey's hand on his wrist. "Just promise me you won't go with Mariska, okay?"

Casey eventually nodded and closed his eyes again. He was tired of lying, tired of notes and messages. Tired of the pills and doctors and writing in his survival journals. His sister was going to have to let him keep his promises this time.

"Yeah," he said, and meant it. "Okay."

Chapter Thirteen

Casey sat in the green sheet of yard behind his father's house, cross-legged, grass climbing the spaces between his fingers. His mother sat beside him in her long white dressing gown, knees drawn to her chest and capped by folded arms. Sunlight brought out the muted gold amid the thickness of her dark hair, lighting the dust of freckles on her cheeks that Casey had inherited and lost after puberty. Across the stretch of the lawn and patio David Way stood at the backdoor, a meaty hand on the knob to open it. Waiting at the threshold and watching them. Sitting with his mother, Casey felt no fear.

"I wish you were here, Mom." He tipped his head back to look at the sky, licked the taste of grass from his mouth. "It all got so bad after you went away."

"It was always bad, Casey," his mother answered softly. "I just did the best I could to cover that up for you."

From the backdoor his father's face began to melt, flesh slipping from the bone to reveal the wet musculature underneath. His eyes disintegrated in their sockets, the cartilage of his nose softening, lips sinking back above teeth and gum until his recognizable traits began to drip onto the tops of his shoes. Casey sucked in a breath and held it.

"Mom."

"Casey."

Casey opened his eyes. He straightened with a blink, looking into Debbie from Acquisitions' wide wire-frame bifocals.

"Casey." She nudged his shoulder gently. "Hey, you dozed off in your office again, Hon. You missed lunch."

"Oh." Casey discarded his reading glasses, rubbed at his eyes with his knuckles. He yawned, spine complaining from the angle he had slept in. "Yeah, sorry, thanks."

Debbie placed a print-out on his desk. "Walter said to give you these. It's the last batch of recodes until you get back, okay?"

He nodded, flipped through the titles on the sheet. "Sure, I'll get right on that."

Debbie smiled behind her glasses. "Have a good vacation."

"Yeah." Casey faked a smile and came up short. "Thanks."

Chapter Fourteen

Mariska waited for Casey and smoked cigarettes. She leaned against the itchy brick-face outside the library's wide glass doors, protecting the cherry with hunched shoulders and breathing out smoke. In her car parked across the street was a case of German beer and a crowbar. She had called her station manager Cayla and made arrangements for her slot, agreeing to cover for Danny from mornings if he ever needed a favor in return for sitting in on her show. There was no going back on this now.

Going out tonight, she said to Billy's voicemail. Me and the family unit. Don't wait up for me, okay? I'll be back before you wake up. Love you.

Billy was a sweet guy with a big smile and even bigger hands. He liked to fix old cars and radios from flea markets and second-hand shops, using his talent with machine-parts to pass the time instead of going to college or trade school. Billy owned The Smoking Dragon head-shop around the corner from the 92.5 KVBS studio building, cutting a striking profile behind the counter with his wide shoulders and quarterback's thighs. He was by nature what most women she knew would call a Good Guy: Optimistic, trustworthy, kind of naive but in an endearing way. Mariska hadn't spent a lot of time with guys like that. She just knew she wanted to keep this one around, maybe for a while, maybe forever.

Billy didn't know about the Way-Koval family history. He was safe from the years of filth that Mariska and Casey kept swept under rugs, or the occasional late-night phone calls they never mentioned in the morning. Joel didn't even know about all of it, either, Mariska figured, knocking the ash from her cigarette and a scrape of her boots on the sidewalk. Joel was nice. He came from a nice Welsh family, and grew up in a nice house where the police never came by and people at school and church never talked about. Their secrets were best kept within the family, locked in Alyona Koval's room at Rosedale Glade or in the casket with David Way next to his first wife Christine, in the cemetery Casey never visited.

Sometime after five o'clock Casey emerged from the library, slinging his messenger bag over his shoulder. He looked stupid in a rumpled blue button-down with rolled sleeves and an opened collar, hands stuffed into his pockets. Mariska smiled at him broadly.

"I heard you got shit-canned, Little Brother," she said, rocking on her heels. "At least that's what the word on the street was when I called to see when you came in today."

"Yeah, thanks, no." Casey made a face at his sister. He wasn't above it. "I'm taking some personal time. What do you want?"

"C'mon, you know." She made a clicking sound with her cheek, pointing a thumb to her car parked at the meter. "I got a case of beer with your name on it."

"I can't." Casey tipped his chin up. He had practiced this in his head all day. How to tell her, what she would say, how he would back out. "Ask Billy to go with you."

"Billy's closing the shop tonight. He doesn't need to be a part of this. You know he wouldn't get it, not like you do. This is a family thing."

"I promised Joel I wouldn't."

"What, like a pinky-swear?"

He sighed. "Mar, don't be shitty, alright? Not about this."

"Shit, you're serious." Mariska stuffed her hands into her jacket pockets, took a deep breath. "Look, I'm sorry. I don't want to get you in trouble or anything. I just want to bury this, you know? You and me, the way it ought to be."

"I know that." Casey shook his head. "But I promised."

"It's gotta be us. You know I wouldn't ask if it wasn't important." She closed the space between them. In her cowboy boots she was nearly a head taller than Casey. It made her harder to ignore. "We're in this together."

"I have Joel, Mar. I'm in this with him, too."

"But it's got to be us, Case. Once and for all."

He swallowed, let his shoulders slump. "Alright."

She nodded and bit her bottom lip. "Alright."

Spiced beef simmered in the pot on the stove, filling the apartment with the smell of cooking meat when Casey came home. He tossed his bag and keys on the coffee table, unbuttoned the top of his shirt. Joel was down to a blue T-shirt and pajama bottoms, having skinned out of his work clothes the moment he came home, padding out of the kitchen on socked feet to catch Casey disappear into the bedroom.

"Hey." Joel followed behind with the beginnings of a smile. "I was about to call you. Did you walk home? I would've picked you up if you needed it."

Casey toed out of his shoes and opened the closet, discarded his button-up in exchange for a flimsy long-sleeved t-shirt. It was the one that Joel hated, with the cigarette holes in the sleeves and collar.

"It's okay. Mariska gave me a lift from the library."

Joel got close, slipped his hands over the flat of Casey's belly. "I'm cooking dinner," he said into the nape of Casey's neck. "No more take-out. It's going to make you fat."

He smelled like soap and deodorant, fresh from the shower Joel had taken when he got home. His clothes were clean where they touched Casey's skin and Joel slid a hand beneath his shirt. Casey wanted to lean into the contact, not having to think about Mariska or the house, or his father's blood. It would have been deceitful with Mariska parked on the street waiting for him.

"I'll eat when I get back." Casey moved out of reach. "Don't wait up, okay?"

Joel looked confused. "Where are you going?"

"Just out with Mariska for a bit," Casey lied. "It's fine."

"You said you wouldn't go with her."

"I won't be long. I'll just pop by the house, let her wander around, and then I'll come straight home. I promise."

"Like you promised me you wouldn't go?"

"Joel, c'mon." Casey changed into a pair of jeans, closed the closet door and slipped his shoes back on. "I'll only be gone a couple of hours. She really needs this."

Casey made his way into the living room to collect his bag and keys. Joel followed hotly.

"And you need to think of yourself once in a while and stop running off to Mariska the minute she asks."

"I'm doing this *for* her – not *to* you – alright?"

"You don't see it, do you? You'll fight me about going to Paul, but if your sister wants you to do something you don't want to, you can't get out the door fast enough, Casey. You always choose her over me, every single time."

"What do you want me to tell her?" Casey turned, squared his shoulders. "Hey, I know it's been twenty years since your mom gutted my dad. Just head back to our childhood home where my father fucked up your whole life. Sorry I can't make it, my boyfriend's pissed off?"

"You're not responsible for your father, Casey, and you're not responsible for Mariska, either." Joel swallowed, took a breath to collect himself, tried not to look as hurt as he felt. "I don't want to fight about this. Please."

"I'm not fighting."

"Then just stay home, Casey. I'm asking you this. Please."

Casey sighed. "I can't."

Joel blinked, jaw clicked shut. "If you walk out that door, don't expect me to be here when you come home."

"We'll talk about it when I get back." Casey sighed again, unlocking and pulling the front door open. "I'll see you later, okay?"

"No," Joel answered, "you won't."

After a moment, Casey walked out and closed the door behind him.

Chapter Fifteen

Casey sat on his hands on his father's front porch and waited.

He was seven years old, all skin and bones and shaggy hair he hated having cut. He still had his mother's freckles then, back before they disappeared. They were the only thing she left behind when she went to Heaven, besides her pictures on the mantel and her Venus flytraps in the backyard. Casey didn't know much about her except for the things she left behind. His father didn't say much. His father could be like that sometimes.

His bare feet were dirty from walking around all day without shoes. He didn't like shoes either. The dirt made his toes feel gritty when he scrunched them in the grass and kept his head down, trying not to look at the sun between the trees. Alyona let him sit out there, watching him from the living room window. She tap-tap-tapped a long red fingernail against her wedding ring. The gold ring, the second ring on her finger, because rings were for husbands, like the rings of a tree were for years. At least that's what Mariska said. His step-sister hadn't lied to him yet.

Alyona waited like he waited. Her step-son wasn't talking today, wasn't looking at anybody, and wasn't going to eat the bowl of cereal he had left on the kitchen table. Casey just wanted to wait. So they both waited.

Casey hadn't said a word to her since they found Rusty that morning, when Alyona went to check the mail. Rusty was the floppy cocker spaniel Casey had gotten on his fifth birthday. He had slipped out through a hole in the back fence, hadn't seen Mrs. Greeneley from next door backing out of her driveway to go to work. They found him in the street by the mailbox, eyes closed, blood on his speckled gray fur. Mariska cried but didn't let anybody see it, digging at her eyes with a sniffle. She picked yellow flowers from the garden for the funeral and sat down with Rusty in the backyard where Alyona had moved him, petting him as though asleep. In a few years Casey wouldn't remember much about Rusty, but he would remember this day.

Mariska said they were going to give him a good funeral, a proper funeral. Rusty deserved that much. Casey said nothing. He made a perch on the front porch steps and didn't move until his step-mother went inside and called his father's office. He heard them arguing through the window. They were always arguing about something.

You need to come home early today. It's important. Yes, I know it's just a dog. No, I can't talk to him about it. He needs his father. No, you listen.

Casey didn't care. He just needed to wait.

Long before five o'clock, his father's silver sedan came down the street in a glint of glass and steel. David pulled into the driveway and stepped out with his jacket and suitcase, tie loosened at the collar. His father was all shoulder and strength under the white button-down and trousers, like Casey imagined mountain ranges as strong or concrete as wise. He sat down beside Casey and sighed.

"Hey there, kiddo," he said. "Are you holding up okay?"

Casey nodded, swayed on his hands.

"Your mom told me what happened to Rusty. I'm sorry, Casey."

"She's not my mom," Casey murmured. He didn't have to say it anymore, but he did. It made him feel better to remind people of that. His mother was a picture on the mantle. His mother was the plants in the backyard.

David sighed again. "I know, kiddo. And that's okay."

"I needed you to come home. Mariska said Rusty needs a funeral."

His father nodded. "She's right about that."

"Alyona said it would have to wait until you got home." Alyona didn't dig holes. She didn't have funerals.

"That's because men usually do these things. It's part of our job. We do a lot of the hard stuff, so other people don't have to."

Casey chewed his bottom lip, kicked out his feet. "But I couldn't wait anymore."

"I know. She told me." David put an arm around his son, held him by a bony shoulder. "So how about you and me go take care of Rusty now, okay?"

His father took the key from the ring in his pocket and unlocked the door to the shed behind the house. He gathered two shovels, one large and one small. Rusty was wrapped in a blanket that Mariska had picked out, retreating to the patio with her borrowed flowers to wait. David led Casey to a small space beside his mother's garden and dug a grave. Casey put Rusty in it himself, lowered him gently into the grave and shoveled dirt on top of it while his father watched. Mariska stripped the petals from her flowers and sprinkled them in the dirt. She said a bunch of things that Casey wouldn't remember, about love and about family, and about dogs, about where dogs go when they die. She said they went to Heaven. Casey wanted to believe her.

It was the first funeral Casey remembered going to. Rusty went to Heaven, just like his mother went to Heaven. Then David put a hand on Casey's shoulder, squeezed just a little. There would be more funerals, but Casey didn't know about that yet.

"You did right by him, you know," his father said. "He was a good dog. He knew you loved him."

Dirt on his knees and under his nails, Casey nodded. "I'm glad you came home, Dad."

His father smiled. "Yeah, Casey. Me, too."

Chapter Sixteen

Casey was born David Casey Way on August 30, 1978, to David and Christine Cohen-Way. He was supposed to be the third in a line of David Ways that had worked at the Berming & Sons Bank since it opened in 1949. Two pounds underweight at birth and covered in freckles, Christine had felt that he wasn't a David Way III, insisting her only son be given his own name. His father had agreed and so he was simply Casey instead, after Christine's great uncle Casey Barton of Charleston, South Carolina. He never went by David. That name was saved for the little brother he would never have.

Christine stayed home with her baby while David carved out a comfortable living as a housing loan officer as his father had been before him, affording them the quaint white house on 6621 Mooreland Street. Casey grew up there, behind manicured shrubs and pristine white shutters, two cars in the long driveway and a white picket fence. Christine kept a garden of flytraps in the backyard, transplanted from her father's home in Greeneville, to David's passive dismay. He wrinkled his nose at them whenever he looked out the backdoor, flytraps a more morbid choice than the roses or perennials found in their neighbors' yards. Flytraps made Christine happy, just as leaving her marketing position in the city had made her happy when Casey was born, and so David said nothing of the traps. There were a lot of things they didn't talk about, but Casey would never know about that.

The traps fanned out across the small garden off the back patio. Hundreds of tiny snapping mouths that seemed to follow in Christine's tread across the porch every morning, in her dressing gown, Casey in her arms. That was all Casey knew of his mother, memories formed in the layers of her dark hair and between the prison-bar teeth of her traps. Those were the only good memories that Casey could glean from the house on Mooreland Street. When her car was struck by a pickup one September morning after Casey's third birthday, Christine took them to her grave. After his fourth birthday, David was already courting a Berming & Sons administrative assistant named Alyona Kovol and her six-year-old Mariska. Before his fifth, their families were married together.

Mariska drove in silence down the highway. In the passenger seat, Casey had said nothing about Joel. He had resigned himself to the sick feeling in his gut as he watched the stripes on the road run under Mariska's headlights in rolls of tape. The old house at 6621 was an exit ramp, two rights and seven lights from the highway, in a planned community with the name Rocky Springs written on the decorative fencing that circled the ends of all the streets. The neighborhood hadn't changed much in twenty years, a sprawl of sleepy cul-de-sacs and sport-utility vehicles parked behind tall hedges and leafy trees. Driving down wide streets through pools of yellow lamplight, the old house crept up on them in the lurching of Mariska's squealing breaks and the wet sigh that slipped out of Casey.

"Hey." Mariska pulled up to the curb across the street. "So here we go."

The house at 6621 had been long abandoned, sitting empty since going back on the market in 1998 to little interest and few prospective buyers. The house itself exhaled in shudders of glass and finishing nails, tired from disuse and obscured by the knee-high grass and knotted bunches of flytraps that had overrun the yard. White siding cracked, window shutters hanging from hinges and paint peeled away by long summers and storms. It was nothing as Casey had dreamt it, beautiful and Technicolor in his mind's eye. He found himself only vaguely unsettled.

"You wanna do this?" Mariska undid her safety belt, opened her door.

"Not really," Casey answered, following her lead. "But I'm here."

At the trunk, Mariska unlocked the hatch and popped it open to retrieve two flashlights and a crowbar. "Get the beer."

"Wait," Casey said when he saw the crowbar. "What the hell are you doing?"

Mariska shut the hatch and flicked on her flashlight. "We're going inside." She tossed him the other flashlight and tucked the crowbar under her arm. "It's been twenty years, man. I want to know what it looks like."

"You said we were going to take a look around, not break in," Casey hissed. "I told Joel we'd check it out then come right back. If he finds out about this he's going to kick my ass."

Mariska marched determinedly up the driveway through the twisting weeds and traps, toward the warped and buckled back fence. Casey had no choice but to follow, going back only to grab the beer from the backseat.

"Don't tell me you haven't thought about it, Case." She squeezed between two fallen slats to slip into the backyard. "All that shit that happened here when we were kids, we're grownups now. Don't you want to stand up to it?"

"I don't need to prove I'm a grownup. I pay my taxes and vote, okay? I don't need this."

"Our parents fucked us up, Casey." Mariska stopped and looked at him sincerely through the fence. "We owe this to ourselves. So are you coming or not?"

After a moment, Casey shook his head, bunched his

shoulders to fit through the fence. "Fuck it. Whatever, let's just go."

They made their way through the overgrowth. It caught at their pants and crunched beneath their feet in skeletal branches and crooked flowered traps, ducking their heads to walk beneath the trees, webbed by silk of worms nesting between the branches. The trail of broken concrete slabs brought them to the backdoor and Mariska used the crowbar to break the window, reaching inside to turn the deadbolt. Casey shook his head but said nothing as she pulled it open, held a breath before she gestured inside. The kitchen was hot, the air tasting stale as Casey breathed in. Dust danced past them in visible specks, paint peeling from the cabinets and mold growing in the cracks between the counter and the walls. Past the musty opened refrigerator Mariska found the doorway to the living room, leaving Casey behind, crowbar firm in her grip.

Unease lumped in Casey's throat. He discarded the beer case on the nearest island counter, took a deep breath. Ran a hand through his hair and turned his flashlight to Mariska, peering around the corner, lighting up the rooms.

"We good now?" he asked.

From across the room, Mariska grinned.

She swung her crowbar like a baseball bat in the living room for the hundred times she was scolded for playing catch in the house. Stomped in the bathtub across the hall from her old bedroom until the porcelain groaned, knocked out the rust encrusted fixtures and broken yellow wall tiles, splintering the decorative flowered tiles at the baseboards. Her mother had picked the tile out herself, standing in the home improvement store the spring that she insisted David remodel the bathroom. Yellow like the party dress she got for Christmas in 1989 and her bedroom curtains and sheets. She smashed them under her boots and ground them into dust, and smiled. In the kitchen with a roar she kicked over the old refrigerator and laughed until her hair stuck to her face with sweat and tears, and didn't care if anyone heard.

Casey watched from the safety of the living room floor, knees tucked under his chin. He nursed a warm beer and counted the spaces between the curtain blades where moonlight striped the dirty carpet. His fingers and toes were warmed by the slow burn of alcohol, making his brain feel soft. After two year's sobriety under doctor supervision and the strength of his prescriptions, it didn't take much of anything to get him drunk. Casey couldn't drink more than three times a year for fear of damaging his liver, slipping into a coma or stopping his heart in a cocktail of alcohol and sleeping pills. He couldn't drive or he could fall asleep behind the wheel, his father sitting beside him, dribbling onto the upholstery. The world was dangerous when Casey was around, something he had to fret about and manage with pills and therapy sessions. Sitting on the floor he didn't feel afraid, just loose.

In the old fireplace across the room, Casey heard the faint scratching of fingers crinkling old newspaper. He righted himself, abandoned his beer to his left, blinked to focus his eyes. Padded to the hearth, finding it filled with half-burnt logs and magazines, condom wrappers and beer cans. Kids had squatted here, had parties. In the middle was a box, short and square, fat with a battered lock and handle. Casey blinked again and saw the dents and scratches of violence, the edges of colored stickers tacky on the lid from being scraped away by a fork. Something scratched inside of it, the gentle scrape-scrape-scrape of claws or fingernails. He reached out to the box, skimmed two fingers across the handle, and was jarred by a sudden heavy thump.

"Casey. Hey, Case."

Casey turned to see Mariska at the doorway. Smiling, sweeping a sweaty section of hair from her face. She popped open a can of beer, dropped her crowbar, plopped down into the corner.

"Feeling better yet?" he asked. "Or should I go so you can finish killing the kitchen appliances?"

"You should try it sometime." Mariska laughed and took a drink of beer. "It'll save you a butt-load on therapy."

Casey looked at the lockbox, the colored edges of torn stickers and the dents from carelessness and disuse. It shivered as though cold and left Casey even colder, tracing the dirty hinges as the scratching died. Behind him Mariska swallowed loudly. He stared at the box a moment more and then gave up, followed her cue and turned away.

"What is it?" She tipped her chin up, moonlight lighting a line of sweat down her neck.

"Nothing." He sat against a nearby wall. "Just déjà vu, I guess."

"You know what happened that night? After I left?" she asked. He said nothing. "I was going to go to some older kid's party with my friend Stevie. I told Mom I was going to the movies, 'cause it was a school night, you know? You wanted to come but I called you a dork and made you stay home." She shrugged, looked down at the dirt ground into the carpet. "I should've let you come. I shouldn't have left you here."

Casey dropped his head back with a sigh, connected the stains on the ceiling in an invisible line. "You can't blame yourself."

"What do you remember?" Mariska sounded more hesitant than she meant to.

"I don't remember much. I was watching TV when Dad

got home from work. He and Alyona were yelling in the kitchen. I thought it was another argument, but then she was just screaming, over and over. Then Dad started screaming, and there was this loud, wet sound." Like carving pumpkins on Halloween, or tearing the legs off a turkey, he didn't say.

"Aunt Cheryl said that when the police came you were in the kitchen with your dad, just sitting in the blood. She always said that they told her Mom was there with you, just screaming."

He shook his head. "I don't remember."

"I should've never left you here with those fuckers." She dragged a knuckle across her eyes, digging the tears out before they had a chance to fall. "I'm so sorry."

"Hey. Mar, hey." Casey leaned in, nudged her knee with his foot. "Don't. I'm not sorry."

"I know I shouldn't have taken off all the time. I just hated him, you know? I hated him so much; I couldn't stand to be there when he was home. The way he looked at me, the way he touched me, always telling me how beautiful I was. He said he loved me even more than Mom, because she didn't take care of him the way he needed. She didn't make him feel good. Can you believe that shit? Like I was doing him a fucking favor."

Casey felt five-years-old again, padding down the hallway in green dinosaur pajamas in the middle of the night. Mariska's door was always closed. In the morning there were bruises on her thighs whenever her nightgown pulled up, thick like his father's fingers. He brought his knees up to his chin, hugged them to himself.

"I could've said something," he said to the ceiling and the constellation of tobacco and smoke stains. "I was down the hall for eight years. I could've done something about it."

"Who would've listened to you? Mom?" She scoffed into

her beer. "She was married to him, slept down the same hall, too. She was too busy being June Cleaver to see anything. We didn't really have anything before my mom met your dad. He could do whatever he wanted to me as long as we all played happy fucking family at the church picnic and PTA meetings."

"Do you hate her?"

After a moment, Mariska shrugged. "No. I mean, not anymore. There's no point in it. We all made our beds."

It was Casey's turn to shrug. "You know what the worst part of it is?" She shook her head. "I loved Dad so much. He was Father of the Year since day one. Baseball games, Disney World, fishing trips. He never hurt me, he barely even yelled at me. Now I can't help but think he was just buying me off so I wouldn't tell anyone. All along I knew, though. It should've been me, instead."

"No, Casey. Don't say that. You didn't deserve it."

"It should've been me, Mar. I'm his son. If somebody was supposed to take the brunt of it, it should've been me." Casey hadn't felt his arms shake until his fingers dug into his shins, leaving bruises that he would find in the shower later. "I could've taken it."

"Casey, don't. It wasn't yours to take. It didn't belong to anybody. This shit just happened."

"He ruined your life."

"Yeah." She sniffled, smiled. "And my mom ruined yours. I think we're even."

The laugh that rattled out of his chest was cold and ugly.

"Happy anniversary, Little Brother."

"Happy anniversary, Sister," Casey answered when he finally stopped shaking.

Chapter Seventeen

Casey shuffled down the hallway on socked feet, rubbed the sleep from his eyes with a knobby knuckle. He was warm in the cotton shirt and pajama pants and five years old again, all elbows and knees under his mop of hair. The hall was dark but for the sliver of light coming under from Mariska's bedroom door, lighting a segment of carpet all the way to his toes. Casey was drawn to it, comforted by the light of his sister's bedside lamp whenever he couldn't sleep at night, as he was her fuzzy yellow blankets and blue pillows. They always seemed softer than his at night, even if his father swore that they weren't. He reached for the handle, turned and pushed it open to hear something other than the creak of hinges.

Inside Mariska's room was bright. She was lying down with fists made of her hands, and had no sheets or pajama bottoms. His father lay beside her, a hand inside of her underwear. She couldn't look at him. He had no face, only wet meat that slipped from the bone, dripping onto Mariska's shirt until she whimpered. Casey just stood there.

"Hey. Go back to bed, kiddo," his father said. "And close the door behind you."

Casey woke at three in the afternoon to a sour taste in his mouth and throbbing in his skull. Joel's side of the bed was empty, the sheets cold. He blinked through the fog of sleep and alcohol and found himself alone. The taste of beer and cigarettes that had dried like paste to the back of his tongue jogged Casey's memory. The house, the night before, where Mariska had spun like a top or a dangerous wind-up toy, running, laughing, crying. Telling him that she was sorry and this didn't belong to him. Casey rose and shook the cobwebs from his head. He was still wearing the same clothes and the curtains were pulled shut, standing with watery knees and unsure feet. He was definitely hungover. In the bathroom, Casey washed his face and brushed his teeth, rinsed away the evidence of the night before. The mirror still had a crack. He remembered he hadn't told Joel that he had put it there, and felt guilty.

Casey toed out of last night's shoes and changed out of his clothes, finding a pair of clean jeans and a T-shirt. In the living room he called out across the apartment in a dry cough, scratched at the mess made of his hair. Joel was gone, his jacket and shoes usually kept at the front door missing. It was Saturday and Joel didn't have office hours on the weekend. There was no sticky-note on the fridge or bathroom mirror, as Joel was prone to putting up if he had to leave unexpectedly. Then he remembered the fight and the look on Joel's face, and felt so stupid for forgetting. Joel would be angry to know that he had. Casey set up the coffeepot in the kitchen and waited for it to brew, digging his cell phone out of the back pocket of his old pants. He threw himself into the sofa with a groan, flipped his phone open. There were no messages. He frowned, thumbed through his short contacts list for Joel's name.

FROM CASEY, 3:33PM, 4/5/10
where are you?

Casey waited three minutes. Joel never took more than two to answer a text. He would live on his phone if he could; checking email, CNN, BBC America.

FROM CASEY, 3:36PM, 4/5/10
we need to talk

He closed his phone. Intuition told him he had gotten plastered with Mariska and she had dropped him off at his house. Joel had been mad at him and they argued before he left. Anything beyond those concrete facts made Casey's head hurt. He flopped back across the couch with a grunt and waited for the coffee. He fell asleep before it finished brewing.

Ringing eventually woke Casey in a start, grabbing for his phone from where it had slipped off the couch onto the floor.

"Joel?"

"Nope, it's me," Mariska yawned into the mouthpiece.

"Oh." Casey tried not to sound let down. "Hey." He looked around. The sun was already going down outside the windows, making the room pink. "Did you just get up?"

"Yeah. I didn't even sleep 'til eight o'clock," she answered. "My head was just buzzing, you know?"

"Yeah, I guess." Casey hauled himself up, rubbed his eye with the back of his hand. "What time is it?"

"Six, I think."

"Figures." Casey coughed. He was disappointed to find his head still throbbed. "Hey, did Joel call you by any chance? Bitch you out or something?"

"Um, no, don't think so. Why? Was he supposed to?"

"Joel's pissed at me. He won't answer any of my messages."

"What'd you do?"

"Nothing." He bristled. "When I said he made me promise not to go with you last night, I really promised him I wouldn't. Like, you know, a cross-my-heart kind of thing."

"Shit." Mariska groaned on the other end. "Look, I'm really sorry, okay? I figured you were just balking. If I knew you'd get your ass chewed I wouldn't have even pushed it."

"Forget it." Casey sighed. "I'll fix it. I just need to – oh."

The front door scraped open on the other side of the living room. Casey sat up to see Joel appear on the other side, step in, close it behind him. He didn't take off his shoes or jacket, just palmed his keys.

"Hang on, I'll call you back."

Casey clicked his phone shut and shoved it into his pocket. He climbed over the back of the couch, even if Joel hated it when he did, quickly met Joel at the door. Joel looked like he hadn't slept, still wearing the same t-shirt and pajama bottoms, hair still stiff with gel from work the day before. Casey flattened his own hair back into place and failed to be subtle about it.

"Hey, where'd you go?"

"My mother's." Joel brushed past Casey, made his way to the bedroom. "When you didn't come home."

"Wait, what?" Casey followed close behind. "Are you serious?"

"I told you last night." Joel opened the closet, took out a suitcase. "I'll be at my mother's. She's going out of town to visit my grandmother and she's letting me borrow a key to stay while she's gone."

"Can't we at least talk about this first?"

Joel packed quickly. "We already talked. You go and I'm leaving. You went, Casey, so, what do we have to talk about?"

"I didn't think you were serious." Casey stood at the doorway, watched Joel disappear into the bathroom to retrieve his toothbrush, toothpaste, deodorant. "I mean, Jesus, I thought we were going to finish arguing when I got back. I just went with Mariska because she asked me to, okay? I don't see what the problem is."

"The problem?" Joel slammed his things into his suitcase and tugged it shut. "The problem is I begged you not to go. I told you I'd walk out if you left and you still did it, Casey."

"She's my sister, Joel. What did you want me to do?"

"I wanted you to listen to me, Casey. I just wanted you to listen. For once I didn't want you to fight me on something and make me out to be the villain while you and Mariska run off together. But you chose her over me, just like you always do."

"I didn't choose her; I went with her because she needed me to. We've always only had each other, you know that."

"And you have me, Casey." Joel stepped close, invading Casey's space. "You've always had me. And you still go with her, or hide out at the diner, or write in your stupid notebooks. I'm in the bed next to you, and you still won't tell me anything."

Casey licked his lips, took a deep breath. "I'm fucked up, Joel, I know this. You just don't need to know all the shit in my head, okay? You shouldn't have to put up with that, but Mariska gets it."

"I'm next to you, right next to you, Casey. For four years." Joel shook his head. "And you never tell me."

Casey reached for Joel's hands, held them firmly. "Look, I know I'm stupid, Joel. I'm stupid and I can't trust people. But I only go to my sister because I don't have to feel like I'm a burden to her. We need each other, okay?"

Joel swallowed audibly. "Is that all she is to you, Casey?"

Casey let go of Joel's hands. "Don't say that to me."

Joel sighed. "Casey—"

"You want to be mad at me, Joel, fine, but I'm not sorry."

"Fine." Joel took up his suitcase, headed for the living room. "When you're ready to be honest about this, let me know."

Casey didn't bother to make his last stand. He heard the front door slam from across the apartment, making the windows above the dresser rattle in their casements. Balled his fist and grabbed the first thing he found that belonged to Joel, the alarm clock on the bedside table, and hurled it into the nearest wall. He enjoyed the sound it made when it shattered into chunks of metal and plastic, scattering across the floor with its guts exposed in wires. Kicking the bedside table it followed to the floor in a clatter, the lamp shattering in glass shards and the pop and fizzle of the exploding bulb. For a moment, he seethed. Alone in their apartment, with his pounding skull and empty bed, his satisfaction was short-lived.

Chapter Eighteen

"Hey, Mom."

"Oh." On the other end, Alyona sounded cold. "Hello."

Mariska crushed her cigarette out in the glass ashtray on her vanity. Folded it in half and squashed it down. "Hey, I just wanted to call to see how you were doing."

"I'm fine. You know I can't have callers past five o'clock."

She knew she shouldn't have called. Knew it would be more of this bullshit. Knew it, knew it.

"I know, Mom. I just." She squared her shoulders under the ragged baseball jersey she slept in, sighed against the mouthpiece. "I just wanted to call and talk to you, just for a bit. See, I went back to the house. Our old house, you know, with Casey."

"You did," Alyona deadpanned.

"Yeah, and I think it was good for me, for both of us. I mean, I hope so, anyway. So I just wanted to let you know I'm okay, you know? About everything that happened."

"I see."

"I'm trying to say I forgive you, Mom. I don't hate you. I never did. I may never understand why you did what you did, but I'm okay about it."

Her mother didn't say anything else. Mariska shook all over with nervous laughter.

"Yeah, so, that's it, I guess."

"I love you, Mariska."

"Yeah. I love you too, Mom."

It wasn't until after Mariska hung up that she stopped shaking.

Chapter Nineteen

There was no sleeping on Saturday night. Casey left the glass on the floor and the table overturned. Joel would have hated that. On Sunday morning Casey took his pills, left three messages on Joel's phone, and didn't sleep. He ate the leftover meal Joel had cooked, microwaving the baked pasta with meat sauce and eating it alone at the kitchen table. The apartment was silent. For once, Casey hated it. On Sunday night, he cleaned up the mess he made in the bedroom, put on his shoes and left.

At Jay's Diner, Casey drank coffee and wrote in his journal. Harold sat in the booth across from him, long and skinny with his lip-ring and mess of greased hair. His skin stuck to the leather seat where his colorful t-shirt and cargo shorts showed, making a squeaking sound when he covered his mouth to cough. Up close he had a white stud in his nose and gold irises, details Casey had taken for granted under the dingy light of the Grab-N-Go. There was a neat square carved into his chest, heart thumping wildly between his splintered ribs, peeled open like knotted fingers. The blood trickling from the corner of Harold's eyes made Casey lean away as it began to pool on the scratched tabletop. Harold licked his dry lips.

"Hey," Harold said wetly, mouth beginning to fill with blood. It oozed down his chin to collect with all the rest, running off the table and onto the floor. "I think you left something at the store, man."

Casey's vision cleared like the snap of fingers. Black to Technicolor, his skin was hot and his stomach tight with the urge to retch. He was alone at his table with his open notebook, pen and coffee cup, ink smudging his knuckles between journal entries.

4/6/10

I dreamt about Dad and Mariska yesterday. Joel won't answer my messages. I don't know what I'm going to do.

Looking at what he'd written, Casey sighed. Blinked, rubbed Harold's face from his eyes and felt sick with himself.

Somewhere across town, he was sure Joel was asleep in his mother's guest room, on some downy bedspread with a thread-count and department store label Casey couldn't afford. The thought of Joel stretched out in a bed other than his own was distressing, strange sheets wrapped around his long legs that for four years had bracketed Casey's ribs while he slept, when he did sleep. He had taken Joel's body for granted, the weight of it beside him on the mattress, the ebb of Joel's breathing and the way his stomach tautened each time Casey turned to sleep against Joel's diaphragm. It was like a shiver held in place as he sighed into Joel's navel, fingers tracing the tips of Casey's ears until he slept again.

"You having another bad spell, hon?"

Casey looked up. Sherrie was at his table with a fresh pot, looking at him like a wounded animal. Her eyes were wet-looking, hemorrhaging pity every time she came by to fill his cup. It only made Casey feel more pathetic than he already did, hiding in the corner trying not to think of Joel.

"I've come to the conclusion that I'm a horrible human being," Casey answered. He closed his notebook, slid it to the end of the table, even if the ink on his hands gave him away.

"You're not horrible, Casey. You're just a human being." Three booths over, an old man waved his tea glass at Sherrie, the spoon clacking loudly against the plastic cup. "Sorry. I'll be right back."

"It's okay." Casey got out his wallet. "I won't keep you."

"Hey, don't worry about the coffee." she smiled. "Just take care of yourself, okay?"

His smile was so faked it hurt. "I will."

Casey left a ten dollar bill on the table when Sherrie's back was turned. He packed his notebook and pen in his bag and made his way to the door before she could come back and be nice to him. He didn't need nice. Instead, he shoved his hands in his pockets and walked to the Grab-N-Go, navigating crosswalks until he saw the sickly orange neon sign blinking from across the street. Looking both ways, he jogged across two lanes until reaching the yellow double line, stopped.

There was a box in the middle of the street, battered and made of metal. Casey stared at it for a moment, nudging it with his foot. There were three dents on the belly of it, the torn edges of faded color stickers pocking it where they had been scrapped away. It had been left there without evident purpose, abandoned on the street. It looked like the box at the house, sitting in the fireplace with the old magazines and condom wrappers. *Déjà vu* made his palms sweat in his pockets, but Casey just stared. After a moment he shook his head, left the box in the street and jogged the rest of the way to the corner store. Inside Harold nodded at him, setting his magazine on the counter. He found himself inwardly grateful for that. Trying not to think of blood, Casey bought two packs of Reds and paid with a nod of thanks.

"Hey man," Harold started to say and pushed the cash drawer shut with his hip.

"Yeah?"

"You feeling okay? You look like shit."

"Yeah, sure," Casey lied. "Have a good night."

He put one cigarette in his mouth before he left the store, stuffing the pack into his pocket. Cupped a palm around the tip, lit it in a sigh and a stream of smoke from his nostrils. Outside, the box was still in the street where he had left it.

He stood for a moment, expecting something to crawl out of it and inch its way across the street, like a half-dead animal or a disembodied hand, lurching to the stoplight. Neither would have surprised him but neither happened. Casey let out a breath he hadn't realized he had been holding and walked home in the dark, trying not to look back.

Chapter Twenty

There was a girl on the closed-circuit television behind the counter of the Grab-N-Go, wrapped in white bandages and electrical tape beneath her tattered gown. Behind the counter, Harold didn't see her, leafing instead through the pages of his magazine and waiting for his shift to end. There were beautiful women there, lying across sterile floors and black bedsheets. They had faces smudged by heavy makeup and bruising, swollen eye sockets and cut lips, bandaged at their joints in braces or cupped by steel pegs to replace amputated legs. Harold squirmed in his plastic folding chair, trying to ignore the erection digging against his fly. He licked his lips and turned the page.

Mrs. Rainey walked in with a jingle of the door chime, a crooked slip of a woman in pink lipstick and blue eye shadow. It matched the blue of her hair and cardigan sweater as she hobbled past the counter on her walker toward dairy and beer. Harold rolled up his magazine, sticking it between the cash register and the lottery ticket display. Mrs. Rainey smiled around her dentures. Above him the television flickered and stuttered into snowflakes and pepper. Neither of them noticed as Harold rang her up, made change for her twenty dollar bill and dropped her half-gallon of skim milk into a sack. Mrs. Rainey stopped to tell Harold about her granddaughter Becky, studying to be a hairdresser and in need of a nice boyfriend. Harold tried to ignore the hard-on still digging into his jeans. He thanked her for her business three times before she took her sack and left.

The Grab-N-Go closed at nine o'clock every night. Mr. Kwon was a madman about store hours, never opening the doors before nine in the morning or allowing a customer in past nine at night. He hated the people that came in after dark, often part of the bar crowd that wandered in from the clubs and restaurants in search for beer and smokes. They were mostly young professionals, working in the corporate high-rises that made up the skyline, yuppies in suits and fast cars that liked to get loud and obnoxious after a few drinks. Mr. Kwon wanted nothing to do with them. Harold didn't care either way. He just liked getting out of work before ten o'clock, catching the last bus to his friend Tony's house to play Xbox and drink beer.

At eight-thirty, Harold looked at his wristwatch with a yawn. Closing duties meant cleaning the bathroom and taking out the garbage. He folded his magazine and with a glance at the closed circuit monitor retrieved the trashbag from under the counter. Combining it with the bag in the bathroom Harold dragged it into the storeroom in the back of the shop. The storeroom was the size of a cereal box with inventory shelves on one wall, racks of price tags and cleaning supplies on the other. There was a computer and desk for file-keeping in the middle, next to the mini-fridge and microwave where Harold cooked his boxed noodles for lunch. He searched the supply racks on the back wall for the trashbags, picking through boxes of steel wool pads and printer paper that had been tossed there amid the clutter. Mr. Kwon may have been psychotic about his store hours, but he didn't care to keep house.

Harold grabbed a floppy stack of grocery sacks and noticed a lockbox, sitting where the paper towels were usually kept. He frowned and traced the beaten pad lock. It was different from the blue cash bag and safety deposit box Mr. Kwon kept under the front counter, used for moving cash between the register and the bank. Perhaps it was his son Steve's, or a secret cash stash. He picked it up and gave a firm shake. For all he knew it was the money that was supposedly missing every time Steve counted the drawer between shift changes. Holding it to his ear Harold shook it again and heard nothing but the rattle of the handle and lock.

"Whatever."

He dropped it where he found it, found the trashbags he had been looking for, and left the storeroom. On his way to the restroom to replace the bag in the trashcan, Harold was stopped by the sound of the door chime tinkling softly, the gentle patter of feet.

"Can I help you?" he sighed, walked back to the front counter. There was no one at the door or between aisles. "Hello?"

Leaning over the counter he looked around the store for the tops of heads peeking above shelves, and received no answer. The closed circuit monitor fuzzed into nothing and Harold shrugged. He set about his closing duties, placing trashbags in all the cans and cleaning the employee bathroom. He dragged three bags of garbage from the storeroom and out the back door to the alley. The pavement was slick beneath his hi-tops as Harold hauled the trash behind him, to the sliver of light coming between the building and the dumpster at the mouth of the alley.

The girl on the closed circuit television was there, a stripe of shadow against a gray burst of streetlight. She was skinny in the hips like a boy, one of his porno models in a cheap white party dress and plunging neckline. Strips of gauze and electric tape crisscrossed to cover bruises on her arms and thighs, pressing her breasts together under her blouse. Beneath the elbow her arms were amputated and healed in thick scars, a wrapping of hospital bandages the crown on her head. It obscured one eye and part of her nose in blood-and-dirt smeared bindings, the other eye blackened with bruises.

She opened her mouth to let out a sound like television static and he took a step backward. Dropped the bags and his feet skittered across the greasy concrete, unsure of his footing when she took a step toward him, bare foot and silent. Hot panic worked through Harold's stomach to his groin. She came to him, dress transparent around her hips and breasts as to outline the pink of her nipples and slit between her thighs. It made Harold's heart thump as the girl got down to her knees, mouth open and damp like her good eye when she blinked in a lazy flutter of lashes. Harold reached down cautiously, combed through the hair sticking from her crown of bandages. She leaned into the touch like a cat and he stroked her for it, enjoying the way she rubbed her stubby elbows against the front of his pants.

"Did somebody leave you like this?" he rasped. He slipped his fingers through her sweaty hair, between the bandages to rub into her scalp. Spit ran from her mouth in a thick string as she drooled eagerly against his pantleg. For it Harold sucked a breath between his teeth, hardening against his fly. "Okay. Okay, I'll give you what you want, baby, no problem."

The girl motioned to the bandages on her face, rubbing at them with a distressed rear of her head. Harold moved to peel away the bindings, grubby with decay, opening to the girl's empty socket. The sight of it gave Harold a sharp spike of excitement, curling guiltily in his balls with a shiver. Her lids were slack around the cavity and dark with infection, the hole swollen and wet, trickling down her cheek in shades of blood and pus. She dipped her head, mouth leaking onto the tops of his sneakers. He opened his pants with one fumbling hand, tugging his dick out. She widened her mouth for him but it was primitive curiosity that brought Harold's hips forward, testing softness of the flesh, the wetness of the socket. Sliding in and out of it Harold shuddered, pleased by the pulpy sound it made. He gripped her by the hair to keep her head still and thrust quickly to his satisfaction, until as he filled the opening with semen and a hard shiver.

The girl brought herself down to sit at Harold's feet, ejaculate oozing from her infected socket. Harold caught his breath, sagging boneless against the wall behind him. Rolling back like a little worm, she laid down on the concrete, her knees apart to spread herself open in the filth, mouthing wordless promises that begged Harold closer. He licked his lips with a grunt, clutching his dick to feel it start to swell at the way every one of her openings seemed to leak, just for him. Harold took two quick looks over his shoulder and followed after the girl, sitting on his knees between her legs and licking his way inside her waiting mouth.

Harold squeezed her breasts through the tape that bound them, his other hand lifting her skirt to finger impatiently between her thighs. He ignored the stench of garbage and the slime beneath his knees, felt the skeletal ridges of her collarbone and ribs, left red marks wherever he gripped and fumbled. Between her breasts his fingernails caught a pleat like a seam down the middle of her chest, ridged by the rise of stitches or staples. Harold didn't see the girl's chest open, pushing up from beneath her ribs to bubble up in the tearing of meat and muscle. The sound of snapping bone alarmed him. Looking down, her chest cavity began to expand, first fat, then muscle and ligament bursting from neck to navel in a gaping, toothed mouth. The jaws were lined by snarling ribs, jutting out unnaturally and interlocking like folded fingers or prison bars, shielding the throat that sat where the girl's heart had been.

Harold screamed and scrambled away, feet kicking on the

grease-slick concrete for advantage above the gnashing maw. On the ground the girl laid there, still drooling, eyes dead and limbs doll-slack as her second mouth bit and snapped at Harold's sneakers. If only for a moment, and surely a trick of moonlight and Harold's panicked imagination, she seemed to smile. He put his hands up to defend against her but there was no fighting the teeth that slammed shut around his ankle. He screamed again, fingers scratching at the trap of fangs but the mouth only grew him closer, snapped up by the jaws, twisting and kicking as he slid down the throat in the girl's black center. The mouth shut behind him, teeth folding together again, swallowing every trace. He left only blood on the alley floor and the slow static of breathing. For a moment the girl laid sleeping, belly sealing itself shut again in its seam of hidden stitches, full of meat and blood, then died without a sound.

Chapter Twenty-One

For the last ten years Sarah Britton returned to Cardiff in the spring, taking three weeks off to visit with her mother and sisters Beth and Angie, their husbands and children. It was the only way she could deal with living in America, having packed up her life in Wales and followed her husband Jimmy to a manager's position at cousin Arthur's aluminum foundry, a bigger house, and a nicer car in the driveway. Even after Jimmy died of the stroke when Joel was away at university, Sarah stayed for her son and the home they had carved out for themselves so far away from Cardiff. Every year since, she's packed her bags and left Joel her spare apartment key, so he could tend to the potted plants and feed her Pomeranian Jules.

This year Joel turned up on his mother's doorstep with a suitcase, telling her that he and Casey had fought. That Casey was being ridiculous and Casey was being irrational and that Joel didn't know what to do with him anymore. Sarah offered him the spare bedroom and a kiss on his forehead, and said nothing more of it. She gave her son her key from underneath the crystal vase on the fireplace mantle. Joel gave her a lift to the airport, a hug, and a promise that he would be fine and she would have a lovely trip. Since then he had been alone, in her nice clean apartment surrounded by her nice sterile things and framed art on the walls.

On Monday morning, Joel woke to the strange chime of his mother's reproduction antique wind-up alarm clock. The queen-sized guest bed was softer than the one at home, the ornate bed-set nicer than the Target brand sheets and comforter he was used to sleeping under. His father had done well for his family when he was alive, making a living with his hands at the foundry at Bedwas, until middle-age set in and the arthritis took his grip, and cousin Arthur had a position open up for a man of his experience. His mother had her respectable trust and her inheritance from her grandfather, affording her the polished oak furniture and plush beds Joel remembered even from their home in Cardiff, when his father insisted they still drive a modest car and live in a modest house. Jimmy never wanted to live too easily, to spend too much, requiring that his only son be raised to know the meaning of an honest day's work. Once he was gone, Sarah could spend her money however she wanted, but Joel still had enough of his father in him to always sit up straight, square his debts, and to be content with what he had.

Joel's wages covered the rent and monthly bills, while Casey's paid for groceries and any other expenses, with very little to spare on luxuries like brand-name sheets. Waking up in his mother's bed felt like a small betrayal, an act of measured infidelity that made the pit of his stomach knot when Joel sat to turn off the alarm, shake out the sheets and make the bed. In the guest bathroom, he washed in a shower stall twice the size of his own with travel-sized soap, shampoo and conditioner. Everything came in small decorated bottles, like the ones from the hotel room he and Casey had stayed at when they drove to Hallmark to attend the wedding of Casey's cousin Heather.

He remembered, because there was a full bathtub in the bathroom. They hadn't made enough money put together to afford an apartment in the city with a full bathtub, only the cramped shower stall, and he hadn't taken an actual bath since high school. Just being able to sleep in and take a bath together made the trip worth it, even for a weekend spent navigating strange looks and awkward conversation with prying cousins and aunts. Why hadn't Casey called, why hadn't he visited, why hadn't he written, why hadn't they ever known about Joel. Joel could only smile and say he didn't know. Squeeze Casey's hand under the table at the reception, and go back to their room to sit in the tub with him and wash his hair in cupfuls of water. Wait for the water to cool off and their skin to prune and then listen to Casey breathe.

Joel made half-caff coffee in his briefs with his mother's strange coffee-maker, a tall black machine with buttons and settings that he didn't recognize. He tried not to think about those things, or about Casey. Instead he applied deodorant and hair product, dressing in the bathroom while the coffee brewed, fastening up his shirt and vest with a sigh staggered between buttons. Rolled up his sleeves, ran a hand through his hair, and sighed again at his tired-looking reflection.

"You know he started it," Joel assured himself. Tugged at the bottom of his vest and smoothed it with a nod. "Let him stew in it."

Over toast and eggs with coffee, he flipped open his phone. He checked his work email and personal email, his news highlights from CNN and BBCAmerica. Something beeped. There were four new text messages. Joel stared at his phone before he finally opened them, almost regretting it the moment he had.

FROM CASEY, 4/6/10, 9:45AM
i think youre being really fucking childish about this
FROM CASEY, 4/6/10, 11:02AM
i dont know what more you want me to do
FROM CASEY, 4/6/10, 1:12PM
can we talk about this?
FROM CASEY, 4/6/10, 2:03PM
just talk to me

Joel tapped his stylus on the screen for another minute.

FROM JOEL, 4/7/10, 7:31AM
I'll talk about it when you can be honest with me.

He waited three minutes for Casey to thumb stupidly across the keypad of his clunky phone and respond. When no answer came, Joel couldn't help but think of Casey alone in their apartment. Of his long profile on the patio smoking cigarettes in the dark, the bed cold and untouched without Joel there to herd Casey to it every night. He shook his head and put his phone away. Work, lunch, home, and sleep. Casey never answered.

Chapter Twenty-Two

Carroll Robinson lived at 5160 Mooreland Street. He was six feet tall and weighed two-hundred-ten pounds. Fawn colored hair, a graying mustache and glasses. No one had seen him since he last left his workplace three weeks prior, the Sherman Brothers Bank branch location at the intersection of Thatcher and Marigold. Casey knew this because of the missing persons flyer tacked onto the sign post at the intersection of Commerce and Houston, bearing a grainy colored photo of Carroll Robinson smiling in his best red Christmas sweater. He hadn't been smiling when Casey had last seen him, bleeding between shelves at the library from the box cut into his chest.

The signal changed, white man for the red palm. Pushed ahead by the jostle of elbows and purses as foot traffic moved across the intersection, Casey grabbed the flyer, folded it twice and stuffed it into his messenger bag for later. He walked the remaining two blocks to The Smoking Dragon. Casey knew Mariska was there in the afternoons before her show started, visiting her boyfriend and having lunch in the loft space above the shop where he lived and slept. Casey hadn't bothered to call to let her know he was coming. He had a feeling Mariska already knew.

The Smoking Dragon was a hole in the wall with Bob Marley and Timothy Leary posters in the windows and shiny holographic stickers on the doors. Through the beaded bamboo curtain at the front door Casey navigated the dim maze of shelves and display cases to the front counter. Billy was behind the register, blonde and broad all over like the old-fashioned, football-playing American varsity dream. He was the kind of guy that Casey remembered spending his high school and college careers brawling with if he had enough beer in him. Instinct still squared Casey's shoulders when Billy looked up from his inventory log.

Casey had made a job for himself of bloodying his knuckles in parking lots and behind bars starting at the age of sixteen, eager to fight any big, smug-looking guy that tried to hustle him after class or at a pool table. Guys like Billy liked guys like Casey because he was a head-case, a faggot, pillow-biter or queer-bait. Having been pinned against car doors while guys like Billy pounded his ribs in for a cheering crowd, Casey learned that full Heineken bottles hurt more than fists. If he put his elbow in a guy's throat, kneed him in the dick, rolled him to the ground, people stopped cheering. If the captain of the football team got his face laid open by the faggot from English class, people stopped bothering Casey entirely.

"Hey, man," Billy said, leaned over the counter. He was a full head taller and nearly bursting out of his t-shirt. "What's up?"

"Hey." Casey tried not to puff himself up too much. "Is my sister here?"

"Yeah, upstairs." Billy pointed to the staircase on the back wall, obscured by a partition decorated with candles and thrift store knick-knacks. "I think she's cooking lunch."

"Thanks."

With another nod, Casey ducked around the counter to the staircase, jogged up to the second level and the walkway to the apartment door. He knocked once before entering, shrugged off his messenger bag and jacket onto the beaten leather sofa by the door.

"Mar, it's me."

Crossing the cluttered living space to the kitchen doorway, Casey found Mariska at the ancient stove, smoking a cigarette as she chased chorizo and eggs across a skillet with her spatula. Potatoes sizzled on the next burner, tortillas and cheese warming on the nearby countertop. With a sigh, Casey dropped into one of the rickety wooden chairs of Billy's thrift store dinette set and put a hand across his forehead. He closed his eyes. They burned under the lids, a bone-deep ache that travelled behind the sockets and down the back of his neck.

"Hey, I'm just making some lunch before I head off to the studio." Mariska looked at Casey from over her shoulder. "You look like asshole."

"Thanks." Casey opened his eyes just to roll them emphatically. "I still can't believe you're dating that thing downstairs. I could swear he kicked me in the ribs in eighth grade once."

She laughed. "He probably did. And sorry if I'm not particularly torn up that my big gay brother doesn't like my taste in men."

"I don't fuck Neanderthals, thanks. You feel better? You know, about things?"

"I think I do, actually." She omitted her mother. Couldn't let that ruin a good thing. "Going back to the house, I think it helped me in a way. It just felt good to get it all out of my system, you know?"

"Yeah," Casey lied with a nod. "Good."

While Mariska's back was turned, he reached for his phone, flipped it open. Thumbed through the menu screen to expand his empty message inbox, and in his peripheral saw her backward glance. He put his phone away.

"You haven't slept, have you?" She knocked the ash off the end of her cigarette in the ashtray balanced on the edge of the counter. "Don't tell me you've been up since Saturday. I will kick your ass."

"That's really not the point, is it?" He didn't want to tell her that he had been up, kept awake by coffee since his exhausted nap waiting for Joel to come home. The pills didn't work and the black-out in the diner didn't count. Sleeping with his eyes open never counted, especially when he only slept long enough to see people with holes in them. "Joel's at his mother's."

"Shit." Mariska set the spatula down, pushed the skillet off the burner. She shook her head. "I shouldn't have pushed you into going."

"Don't do that. You wanted me to go with you, I went. That's it."

She turned, leaned against the counter, still smoking. "You talk to him yet?"

"We've messaged each other." Casey shrugged. "He thinks I'm incapable of trust and honesty."

"And?"

Casey drummed his fingers across the scratches grooving the lacquered tabletop. They felt like teeth marks or knife wounds. "And I may've told him I wasn't sorry for breaking my promise, and generally treating him like shit."

Mariska sighed. "I'll go talk to him."

"No, don't. The last thing I need is for you poking around in this. I fucked it up, I can fix it."

"If you could fix it, why did you come here?"

"I don't know. I just felt like bitching at someone. It's still allowed." Casey dug the urge to sleep out of his eyes with a knuckle. "I really don't know what to do about this anymore. I'm starting to think that going to the house was a bad idea, and now I don't even have anything to show for it."

"Why not?"

"I don't feel different. I don't feel better. I'm still seeing things, but, different, I guess."

"Different how?"

Casey got up, retrieved his messenger bag from the sofa, and emptied its contents out onto the table. He unfolded Carroll Robinson's flyer. "I saw this guy in the library the other day, when I had one of my spells. He had a hole in his chest like it'd been cut there, telling me about some girl. Then last night I was having a conversation with the clerk from the convenience store where I buy my cigarettes. He had a hole in his chest, too."

"You're hallucinating?" Mariska took the poster, read it over. "I mean, I knew about the nightmares, but. These people you keep seeing, what does it mean?"

"Hell if I know. I think going to the house made it worse somehow." Casey shook his head. "Now Joel's gone and I can't even go back to work. I don't know what I'm supposed to do."

"Have you talked to your therapist about this? Shown him all this stuff?"

Casey didn't say anything. Mariska leaned forward.

"You are still seeing your therapist, right?"

"Yeah, I am," he said shortly. "Joel wanted me to go, so I'm going. I still can't exactly pop in tomorrow and tell him I'm seeing dead people, can I?"

"Well, I don't know." She folded the flyer up again, handed it back. "You're talking about people with holes in the middle. I'm just trying to help."

"I know." Casey sighed. "Look, this stays between us, okay? Just until I figure out what to do with it." He stuffed the flyer into his notebook, tucked it back into his bag. "I just have to try to get through to Joel, and then I can deal with the rest of this."

"You know it'd be easier to fix shit if it you didn't do it on your own," Mariska chided softly. She turned to shut off the stove, threw the potatoes in with her eggs and chorizo. "I can talk to him if you need me to. I mean, if he's mad that you went with me, chances are he's mostly mad at me for taking you. Take the heat off of you for a bit."

Casey slipped his messenger bag over his head, tugged it into place over his shoulder. "Don't come crying to me if Joel scratches your eyes out."

"I got six inches on him in heels," Mariska smirked. "I think I can handle your boyfriend."

"Whatever. Eat. Go to work," Casey said, heading for the living room. "I'll see you later."

"Go to bed, Little Brother," she called behind him.

"Doubt it," he called back, opening the door and closing it behind him.

Down the stairs and out the front door of the shop, Casey stuffed his hands into his pockets and kept his eyes to the tops of his red chucks. Carroll Robinson's face followed him home from the smiling photos on lamp posts and traffic stops, watching his every move like the models on Harold's dirty magazines. Casey ignored it and swallowed the knot in his throat. Had he been of mind he would have noticed the lockbox at the bus stop on 3rd and Henderson, waiting for him on the bench beneath the black metal sun shelter. Casey didn't look. A young boy came up to the box, long and bony under a mop of dark hair. He stooped to pick it up and walked away.

Chapter Twenty-Three

"I went back to my old house the other night."

Casey had worked himself into the corner of Paul's couch, to sink into the cushions and vanish. The office felt smaller than it had before as Paul stared him down. He felt like retching, but the waste bin from his last session was nowhere in sight. He couldn't tell anymore if it was from exhaustion or a side effect of being in Paul's office.

Paul lifted a brow. Casey crossed his arms.

"What? You wanted me to be honest."

Paul settled into his armchair with the creak of leather pleats. "How did that go over, Casey?"

"I don't know yet." Casey shook his head. "I don't think it helped. I don't think this is helping, either."

"That's because you've been resistant to treatment." Paul kind of smiled. Even that was smug.

Casey sighed. "I didn't even want to go. I only went because my sister asked me to go with her. She thought going there would give us closure."

"Did it?"

"Maybe for her. I'm still having nightmares, still blacking out. I'm starting to think I'm just wasting my time."

"Do you think facing your problems is a waste of time?"

"My life hasn't exactly taken a turn for the better since I started seeing you, if that's what you mean." Casey kind of laughed. "Before I thought I was at least coping with it. All the shit just feels compounded now."

"You were on and off medication and blacking out in public, Casey. I don't think you were doing as well as you thought."

"I had Joel. I had it under control."

Paul perked. "You had Joel, which means you don't have

him anymore?"

"We argued about going back to the house. Joel didn't want me to go." Casey lifted his chin, defiant. "I did, and he left."

"Where did he go?"

"His mother's place. What does it matter?"

"What did you argue about?" Paul looked far too concerned for his own good.

"My apparent pathological inability to trust and love others. Whatever. I really don't want to talk about this."

"Do you think he's right?"

"Right about what?"

"Do you think you're incapable of trusting people?" Paul canted his head. "Do you not trust Joel?"

Casey bristled. "I trust Joel. We take care of each other. We always have."

"I see." Paul reached for the pen and paper on the side table, jotting down a series of notes. "Tell me about the house, Casey. What happened?"

"Nothing happened. We went in through the kitchen and Mariska tore through the place until she felt better. I hung back in the living room and waited for her to finish. We talked for a while, then we drank too much and she drove me home."

"You got in through the kitchen?"

"Yeah."

"Isn't that where your father was murdered?"

"Yeah, I guess so."

"How did that make you feel, Casey?"

"It didn't make me feel anything." The ease of the words caught him off-guard. "I didn't even think about it."

Paul jotted down another note. Casey swallowed.

"Have you been sleeping, Casey?"

"Yes." Sporadic naps only counted when Casey said so. "Not well, obviously."

"You still dream about your father?"

"Yes."

"I see."

"And just what is that, exactly?"

"Well." Paul set his pen and paper aside. "Honestly I'm a little troubled, Casey."

"Are you?"

"You're telling me that you revisited the source of your childhood trauma because your sister asked you to, and you felt nothing."

Casey's jaw ticked. "And?"

"You won't like what I have to tell you, Casey," Paul all but tutted.

"I usually don't, Paul."

"It sounds as though you're so far in denial about your issues with your father that you've totally separated yourself from him," Paul said smoothly, folding his hands on his knee. "You've based your sense of self-worth on the distance you've placed between yourself and your father, and yet you fail to see how afraid you are that you're like him. On the other hand, you're emotionally dependent on your sister out of the guilt you feel for her abuse. You'll jeopardize your own happiness to please her and in some way atone for her rape, and drive away anyone else that happens to be in the way of that. Up to and including Joel, apparently, whom you use as a crutch because he enables your asocial behavior under the guise of caring about your emotional well-being."

Paul waited ten seconds before he smiled. "Does any of this sound familiar at all?"

Casey swallowed the returning urge to retch. "Fuck you."

"I told you that you wouldn't like it, Casey."

"I never used Joel, alright?" The muscles in Casey's arms began to shudder, the initial tiny tremors that circled after nightmares or black-outs. "I may've hurt him, but I never used him, so you don't get to fucking say that."

"I know you love Joel, but even you have to see that your relationship is unhealthy." Paul sighed, leaned back in his armchair. "He pressured you into seeing me in an attempt to fix you. You agreed in order to appease him and keep him close to you, even though you feel therapy is ultimately a waste of your time. In the state you're in, do you really think that you can give Joel with what he needs?"

"Look, before him, I was in a bad place, okay? We both were. I was drinking and fighting all the time, and he was stuck with some trust-fund baby, but then we had each other. He fixed me, and I was good for him, so shut the fuck up."

"Please. Joel was fine before he met you," Paul deadpanned. "If you recall, I've known him longer than you have. He had aspirations, talent. Then you came along looking sad and pathetic and ruined everything."

"He wanted me." Casey squared himself.

"He was slumming."

"And do you always get this involved in your patients' relationships?"

Paul's smile broke into a small flutter of laughter. "I don't know what you mean, Casey."

"You just seem really invested in Joel."

The smile widened. "He was my student."

"Yeah? Was that all?"

"I don't know what you're talking about."

Casey leaned forward. "So is that it? I beat you to the punch? Joel went with me, now you hate my guts?"

"You're changing the subject."

"I don't like being bull-shitted."

"Neither do I, Casey."

"I guess we have that much in common, don't we?"

Paul's smile faltered, dissolved into an inaudible sigh. "Will you be coming back on Thursday?"

Casey leaned away. "Will you see me?"

"Of course I will, Casey. We still have much to discuss."

Chapter Twenty-Four

Casey hadn't lost a fight since he was eighteen, when the high school quarterback Joe Redbird broke his nose behind the gym one Friday afternoon. That was until he met the bull with the dirty right cross at Barkley's Pub on East Dallas Street. The bull didn't have a name that Casey could remember, just some bad movie poster name like Brody or Caleb or Troy or Tray. He only knew the bull had six inches and fifty pounds on him, and he could hit like a ton of bricks. Bottom lip busted wide open and nose dripping down his chin, Casey spat red onto the pavement and sagged against the back door behind Barkley's. The bull wiped the blood from his knuckles and spat between his teeth.

"You done?" He had chipped front teeth and a mole under his eye that Casey hadn't noticed before with his head still fuzzy with tequila, fingers loose before balling them up in a fist.

Casey snorted, tasted the copper in his sinuses. "Yeah, fine." He hugged his ribs where they ached. "Whatever."

The bull spat again and picked up his jacket from the ground, slipped it on and shook his head. "Don't start shit you can't finish," he said over his shoulder as he disappeared to the left of the alleyway's mouth.

Casey swiped at his bloodied nose with his wrist. He held himself tighter to push at the door and slink back down the hallway, past the kitchen door to the men's room. In the mirror he took in the damage, busted lip and nose and a scrape on his cheek, ran water in the sink to clean himself up. In retrospect, it wasn't worth it. The bull was just a jackass in a bar, running his mouth with his white trash friend. It shouldn't have bothered Casey, but when the guy bumped him and laughed and sloshed his beer around stupidly, he couldn't back down. He should have backed down. He should have gotten the guy in the nuts and slid his elbow in the guy's collarbone and that should have been it. The bull got the drop on Casey and he didn't keep his guard up, didn't cover himself.

He should have won. Instead, Casey cleaned himself up, swallowed the taste of his blood and left the restroom. He pushed his way through the crowd around the bar, past the tables and cocktail waitresses to the front door. On the street, he dug the smokes from his jacket pocket, lit up, and heard his name.

"Casey?"

The bells at the door jingled when he turned, saw a man in the doorway. Slender, his blonde hair gelled in place. Dressed too nice for Barkley's mostly college crowd in a white button-up, cream vest and slacks to match, all smooth and crisp and clean. Casey recognized him from the Thursday night Rape and Incest Survivors group meeting at the community center. The name scribbled on his nametag said Joel and he held hands with a circle of people in the too-cold gymnasium and told them everything would be okay, week in and week out. The sight of him made Casey's throat stop up, his gut stupid and tight.

"I'm sorry. It is Casey, right?" Joel smiled pleasantly and closed the door, walked out onto the street. "From the meetings?"

Casey wiped at his nose. "Yeah. Yeah, Joel, right?" Like he even had to ask.

"I saw you come through just now. I didn't know you came here." When Joel got up close his smiled faltered. "Hey, are you okay?"

"Oh. Yeah, just a stupid fight," Casey lied. "It's nothing."

"What? Why? What happened?"

"It was just some guy. Whatever, I'm fine."

"Let me see." Without permission Joel tipped Casey's head back, looked over his bloody nose, lip and cheek. "You should go to the doctor. Your nose looks pretty bad."

"It's not as bad as it looks." Casey snorted, wiped more blood away. "I'm just heading home to put some ice on it."

Joel wasn't convinced. His hands felt warm where they touched Casey's face, thumbed at his jaw, edged into his hair. Casey changed the subject.

"What're you doing here?"

"I'm with my boyfriend," Joel answered. "Look, really, you don't have to go to the emergency room if you don't want to, but there's a decent free clinic just around the block. I'll walk you there."

"Oh." Boyfriend. "And, no, it's fine. Thanks, but I'm okay."

"Joel?"

Another guy stood at the door now. He was tall, nice suit, good-looking, healthy tan and a nice watch and everything. This was becoming a thing and Casey slid away from Joel like he had been caught stealing.

"Yeah, excuse me, hi," the guy said, stiff with his runner's legs and big shoulders. "Joel, are you coming? We're going to be late for our table."

"Lee, this is Casey. He's one of the people at the group." Joel made it sound like they were friends.

"That's nice. Hello, Casey." Lee didn't even look at Casey. "So are we going? I need to pay our tab."

"You go on without me," Joel said. He looked back to Casey, who looked between the both of them. "Let me go get my coat, okay?"

"What? No, Joel, we're going." Lee stepped out to block Joel's path. "Who is this guy supposed to be?"

"He's hurt and I'm taking him to the clinic around the

corner. I'll catch up with you later, alright?"

Joel went back inside and Lee followed. On the sidewalk Casey felt like taking off or trying to hail a cab, anything to make an escape. Joel came back out with his coat and Lee exploded after him, all righteous indignation and sputtering as Joel took Casey by the arm and moved him along. Casey just did as he was directed and walked with Joel, with no idea of what else to do.

"Are you serious? You cannot be serious," Lee said, hot on their heels. "You barely even know this guy."

"Just go to dinner, Lee, you'll be fine without me."

They walked half a block before Lee gave up, kicked at a trashcan and retreated. Joel didn't say anything. He just squeezed Casey's arm.

"So." Casey gave up on the cigarette, flicked it off half-smoked. "Was that your boyfriend?"

"Yes. Well. Ex-boyfriend," Joel said simply. "He'll be fine. He drives a Camaro. Chances are he'll find somebody to give him a blowjob by the end of the night and he'll forget all about me."

"Oh." Casey looked back. Lee jerked open the door at Barkley's and stormed inside. "I guess I should say I'm sorry for your loss."

"Don't worry. I was going to break up with him tonight, anyway."

"For obvious reasons?"

"Yeah. Obvious reasons."

"Well. Thanks, then," Casey said. "I guess."

For it, Joel laughed softly. "No, I should probably be thanking you."

Casey was eighteen the last time he lost a fight. He was twenty-eight when he met Joel Britton. After that night at Barkley's, he never fought again.

Chapter Twenty-Five

"Hey."

Joel looked from his cross-legged perch on the bench outside of Ramona's Deli, to see Mariska had found his hiding place between his two-thirty and four-fifteen appointments. She put a black outline between him and the afternoon sun, silhouetting her brown peasant dress and cowboy boots. Blinking, Joel swallowed, straightened his slump against the bench seat into something more presentable.

"Hey," he said pleasantly, compensating for the thickness in his throat. "You're up early."

"You got a minute?" Mariska's eyes were unreadable behind her sunglasses until she slipped them off. "I think we need to talk."

"Sure." Joel relocated to the end of the bench, moving his lunch with him to make room. "Please."

Mariska sat with a jingle of keys and jewelry, tucked the skirt under her knees. Joel sighed.

"Look, I know you're mad," she said. "You have every right to be, but you have to give Casey another shot. He can't do this without you."

"I guess Casey sent you, then." He tried not to sound hopeful.

"He tried to talk me out of it." Mariska looked too earnest to be lying. Joel knew she was terrible at it, anyway. "I felt like I owed him. It's my fault, anyway."

"Mariska." It was easier to look at the shop windows across the street than at her with that sorry look on her face. "This isn't about you, alright? Don't worry about it."

Joel didn't feel like telling her that he hadn't been sleeping well in his mother's guest bed. Nothing about the time or place made it okay to complain to Mariska about that. Even if she had been the only friendly face he had seen since dropping his mother off at the airport.

"I knew it pissed you off when I asked Casey to come with me, but I figured he was just balking." She shook her head. "He would've never gone if it weren't for me. I just wanted you to know I'm sorry for pushing this."

He looked at his sandwich, tossed it into its wrapper and sack. "I know. I'm not mad at you. Well, I am mad at you, but I think I'm over it. I'm just tired of him fighting me, and hiding, and keeping his secrets."

"Joel, Casey loves you, okay? I know he's stupid and stubborn, but he loves you so much. And he's hurting right now. This isn't his fault."

"Of course it's his fault. It's both our faults. But what else can I do? If I run back to him and nothing changes..." He sighed again. "I can't do it. I need him to trust me and I don't know if he can."

"Casey trusts you, Joel. You have no idea how much."

"I really don't. That's kind of the problem, isn't it?"

"A lot of things happened in that house when we were growing up. I got away from it, went to college, went through a lot of stuff. Did a lot of things with a lot of people that didn't really care about me, and I think it almost killed me once or twice. It took me a long time but I learned how to live with what happened, and how to not let it run my life. But Casey? He was just a baby. He never really learned how to move on. That's why it's hard for him, so he hides it from you. He's not trying to hurt you, Joel. He just doesn't want to be a burden to you."

"But he's not a burden. He's everything to me."

"Yeah, I know that." Mariska shrugged. "But he doesn't."

"Yes, well, he should by now," Joel said. "I don't want him

fixed, or medicated, or neutered, or whatever else he thinks I'm trying to do to him. I just want him home, and healthy, and with me. That's it. He just doesn't seem to get that."

"Well. Maybe you should go tell him that."

"And if nothing changes? What do I do then?"

"Tell him I'll kick his ass."

"And if that doesn't work?"

"Then you can kick his ass."

Joel tried to laugh and came up short. Mariska reached between them to squeeze his wrist.

"Just talk to him," she said. "Okay?"

He smiled, if only just, and nodded his head, "Okay."

Chapter Twenty-Six

You remember when we first met, right?

I was still going to my old therapist then, Dr. Jones, the one who thought my problems were all rooted in sexual relationships. Which was bullshit, but whatever. He thought it was would be a good idea to look into support groups for rape survivors, because it would help me with my guilt about my sister. I kept trying to tell him it wouldn't work, because me and Mariska were fine that way. But I wasn't sleeping anymore, and anything was better than nothing, so I said okay. You were still working on your thesis, remember? You were volunteering through the community outreach center then, having these meetings in the basketball court after the youth mentor group left. It was always too cold and the chairs were three-hundred years old, and the coffee tasted like shit, but you just kept coming in every week. You were always smiling back then. You looked so much younger. I mean, I know you were younger, but, I just. You were – I don't know, you were happy then. You were good.

Every Thursday night I sat there, in a broken metal fold-up chair and listened to these people talk. It was always the same stories, about pervert uncles or fucked-up cousins or step-dads. I felt like a voyeur for being there, you know? Asking myself why the hell I ever listened to my therapist. But you just listened. I watched you listen, never judging, never asking too much, telling everybody "Nobody gets through life without scars." You never asked me to say anything, week after week. You never called me out, just let me sit there. I just remember you there, too good to be in that grubby little gym, telling people like me that we're all going to be okay, and I just.

It took me a month to get myself together enough to talk

to you, after a meeting. People were standing around talking and grazing from the complimentary cookie tray, maybe laughing a little. I remember because I came up to you, reached past you for the coffee pot sitting on the makeshift card-table counter. I said something stupid, like "Whoever made that piss-water needed to have their ass kicked." You laughed and said something like "I'll keep that in mind for next week." I felt like an asshole but you didn't seem to think so. We talked for a while, about next to nothing, and you still didn't think I was an asshole. I knew it then, right then, that I wanted you in my life.

I don't know what I'm doing anymore.

I just need you back, okay?

I just.

I miss you.

That was the message Casey wanted to leave. Staring at his cell phone in the back corner booth of Jay's Diner, he drank coffee and smoked cigarettes. Notebook open, he tap-tap-tapped his pen on the blank page. Sherrie kept his cup full, smiled at him with a bounce of her ponytail. He tried to smile back and came up short, and said "Thanks" instead.

For five minutes Casey looked at his phone, Joel's number in the contact list, and finally snapped it shut.

Chapter Twenty-Seven

At ten-forty-five Casey opened his eyes to follow the bobble of the overhead fan. The sound of breathing from Joel's side of the bed made him aware of another presence in the room. When he looked over his shoulder his father was lying beside him. His face had fallen to further decay since Casey had last seen him, the muscles disintegrating into loose threads of tissue, jaw sliding free. The wheezing sound of his breathing forced fluids out of his nasal cavity, dribbling onto Joel's pillow and the cold sheet Casey had skinned off at some point in the night. Watching the trail of mucus made Casey's stomach turn.

"You can't fix this," his father said. "We were built to destroy things. That's in our blood, kiddo."

Casey's mouth felt dry, brain cottoned by sleep. Before he could answer, his father reached for his throat to choke him, squeezing and crushing, snapping the vertebra under his fingers. It was the final crunch of tissue that woke Casey, grabbing for his throat to pry his father's hands from it. Coughing, the room lurched until Casey righted himself and saw that he was alone. The urge to retch settled. He stood and made his way to the bathroom to wash his face and rinse his mouth. In the mirror, his face was hollow from sleeplessness, dark around the eyes and under his cheeks, distorted by the crack he had put in his reflection.

"You can do this," he told himself. "Get your shit together."

He held a breath and opened the medicine cabinet, found his pillbox, Wednesday AM. He swallowed the handful of pills with a gulp of water and waited for the last wave of nausea to pass. On the patio on bare feet, Casey smoked the second-to-last cigarette from the pack, watching the lazy dance of flies above the dew-filled mouths of his traps. He counted seven of the one-hundred-ten heads in his garden closed. The dying twitch of fly-legs through veined green skin was soothing to Casey, like the subterranean sound of his mother's breathing if he thought hard enough about it, watching the spasms slow in an inevitable tick-tick-stop. He breathed smoke and took fleeting satisfaction in the tiny death throes. In the back of his mind, he was sure Joel wouldn't have approved.

By one o'clock Casey showered, changed, drank three cups of coffee and documented his nightmare while it was still fresh. He pasted Carroll Robinson's picture beside it and closed his journal, left it on the nightstand where it could do more good. Casey checked his phone twice, frowning at his empty message inbox each time. Before one-thirty, he was walking down Davis Street, hands in his jacket pockets, bag in tow to the library. Today, Casey decided, he would talk to Walter. He stopped first at the Grab-N-Go for a pack of Reds, surprised by the guy in a red plaid shirt who stood in Harold's place behind the counter. His nametag said Steve and he smelled of a woodsy aftershave Casey could taste at the front door.

"Pack of Reds," he said with a nod. "Hey, where's Harold at?"

"That shithead ditched the other night. Haven't seen him since," Steve answered blithely, ringing up the pack and sliding it to Casey. "He just went out the backdoor before closing. If my dad hadn't been driving by and saw the store still open we would've been looted. That'll be six-forty-seven, man."

"Oh." Casey handed Steve seven dollars and felt his stomach knot. "Keep the change."

Without looking back Casey left. He shoved aside paranoid thoughts of Carroll Robinson and his collection of missing persons fliers, certain in his knowledge that he didn't dream of Harold's death in the corner booth at Jay's

Diner. People went missing on the drive home or left work without reason. Things just happened like that. Hands made into fists at his sides, Casey walked the last seven blocks to the library. He shrugged through the automatic doors into the clean white lobby and made sure to smile politely at Kim behind the front desk. Don't stop to chat, don't let them corner you, he told himself. He couldn't handle the faked pleasantness. It was the kind of invasion of space he couldn't afford.

Casey jogged down the wide staircase past the glass doors to Audio-Visual, descended to the basement level where the main catalog was kept. Through the narrow maze of broad shelves in a path laid by grayed ceiling fixtures, beyond the reference archive and rows of computer stations and down the hallway marked Employees Only. He wandered the hard turns past the break room to the administrative offices until he came to Walter's. Casey stretched himself to peer through the porthole in the door and found Walter at his desk, leafing through a stack of papers. He was wearing an unfortunate green sweater with brown plaid patches. Casey knocked twice and didn't bother waiting to be let in.

Walter frowned before Casey had a chance to drop into the old wicker-back chair across from him.

"I told you I'd call you, Casey."

"I know, I know, Walter." Casey swiped at his mouth with the back of his mouth and sighed. "You know I don't beg, alright? I've worked here eight years and I've never asked for anything. So you know that if I come to you, it's only because everything's gone sideways. Right?"

"I know, Casey." Walter folded his arms and leaned back. "I didn't do this to punish you. You know that."

"I do." Casey leaned forward to fill the gap between them. "But I need to work right now. The last thing I need is to be sitting around doing nothing."

Walter just frowned harder.

"Please, Walter."

"I can't let you back for at least a week." Walter lowered his head to regard Casey levelly, the droop of his eyelids making him look more like an old dog than he did before. "Look, the people upstairs are asking questions about your hours, alright? If I bring you back now it's only going to get worse. Just take the rest of the week off and try to get your head on straight. I'll call you."

Casey shook his head. "I can't just wait around my apartment with this shit in my head, Walter. Joel's gone and I'm on my own here. I need this, okay? Cut my hours, give me half-days, I don't care. Just let me work."

"Casey, I'm not going to try to pretend I understand what's going on in your personal life. I do know that you're on medication and you're seeking help, and that's the best thing you can do for yourself right now." At least Walter looked earnest, that he actually meant what he said. "Whatever this is, you can move past it."

"I don't know if that's possible right now." Casey's shoulders slumped. "What I'm dealing with...I don't know where it ends and I begin."

Walter took a deep breath. "I did something once. I did something so terrible that I didn't think I could ever forgive myself for it, or that anybody else would either. I struggled with that for years, hiding from my family, from the guilt. But I finally got right with myself and I accepted it, moved on. I may not be going to Heaven, but I don't have to hate the face that stares back at me every morning."

Casey felt flattened under the weight of Walter's big, well-intentioned eyes.

"Go home, Casey," Walter said. "I'll call you next week."

"Yeah." Casey swallowed and nodded, and knew nothing would change. "Sure."

Walking out of Walter's office he closed the door and didn't look back. He headed down the opposite end of the hall to the service elevators that connected the basement to the lobby. He couldn't bear to walk the floor again, the thought of Kim and Debbie smiling at him making him sick. Casey waited for the shaky grind of gears to open the battered-looking elevator doors. The flicker of the overhead light caught his eye, a jump that traveled down the corridor from bulb to bulb. At the end of the hall the last fixture flashed twice and popped in a hiss. Beneath it the lockbox waited in the middle of the hallway, abandoned in the library's gut.

Casey stared at it. Familiarity crept down his arms to his fingers, making them itch when he curled them against his palm in a fist. He swallowed again, this time on the taste of bile. He remembered the box now, from the fireplace at the house, when he sat drunk in the living room while Mariska smashed through their childhood with her crowbar. It had been outside the Grab-N-Go the last time he'd seen Harold, alive behind the counter and dead in his dream. He reasoned that it had now had been left outside of Walter's office by someone that could anticipate his actions. Whether in taunt or hostility he didn't know, brain churning over a list of suspect names and faces. Walter wouldn't have known, or Kim or Debbie. Joel couldn't muster the villainy to even try, as wholesome and earnest as he was. Mariska had nothing to gain by tricking him, and Paul. Paul was always of suspect.

The bell chimed and the elevator doors grated open. Casey motioned forward on uncertain feet, stepping inside. With a shake of his head, he walked back out, taking quick steps to the middle of the hallway. Stooped to pick up the box, tucked it under his arm, and hurried home with the lockbox.

Chapter Twenty-Eight

The lockbox sat on the kitchen table. Casey paced around the room from counter to counter, studying the box from a safe distance. He had locked the doors and shut the curtains, closing himself in with it as he moved around the box, inspecting every dent, every nick or scratch. Worked through possibilities, the how's and why's behind it. No one had known he was going to the house but Joel and Mariska, neither of whom had anything to accomplish from placing the box there. It wasn't Paul trying to confuse him, even if he was likely psychotic underneath that tightly buttoned sweater, and he knew it wasn't his father. David Way was dead, no matter how easily he crept into Casey's bed or into the corner of the living room, flattened between the bookshelf and the corner table when Casey wasn't paying attention.

Someone could have taken it from the house and followed him with it, but for what he didn't know. Casey knew he wasn't worth following; he didn't have money or useful connections. He wouldn't even have left the apartment every day if he hadn't had a job to go to, or Joel going on about fresh air and sunshine. That left the box itself. The box, which had somehow crawled out of the fireplace, dragged itself down the highway and to the Grab-N-Go where it began to follow Casey. It didn't make sense, and only served to make him feel worse than he already did.

Casey tried to ignore the box. When he got home he put it in the bedroom with his coat and bag, leaving it on the bed and shutting the door behind him to watch afternoon television. For two hours, he flipped through all two-hundred-fifty channels, left a cautious eye on the hallway to the bedroom and thought of the box. With a sigh, he abandoned the remote and walked outside to tend to his garden, feeling the heat of unseen eyes under his clothes and on his skin. By six o'clock he gave that up, too, and retrieved the box, setting it on the kitchen table and watching it closely.

"Alright, you little bitch," Casey said, if only to hear himself say it. "What's inside you?"

The box did nothing. Taking a breath, Casey felt his pockets for his phone. He wanted to dial Joel but knew it wouldn't get him anywhere. Joel wouldn't believe that he was being stalked by a box. He had no proof of any wrongdoing other than the box itself, and it betrayed no secrets. Instead, he dialed Mariska and reached her voice mail.

Mar, it's me, he said. I know this sound weird, but did you see an old lockbox when we went to the house the other night? This is kind of important so call me when you get this. He hung up before the line cut off. She had a better tolerance for crazy, anyway.

Casey ran a hand through his hair and felt his gut make a knot of itself. He knew the box. He didn't recognize it at first. Maybe he didn't want to, uncertain of what he was looking at in the fireplace and later at the convenience store. Staring at it on his table, Casey knew he had seen it before, the box of photos sitting in the top of his father's closet, between a hatbox and a stack of yearbooks. It was the box where his father kept his trophies, the Polaroids he had taken of Mariska whenever he visited her bedroom at night. Alyona had found it one day while cleaning the closets for old clothes and knick-knacks.

That was what Aunt Cheryl had told Casey when he sat on his hands in hospital-grade pajamas and asked how his stepmother found out. She only knew what she had learned second-hand from police and doctors, and they didn't know much to begin with. The box had fallen off the top shelf and landed on its cheap padlock while she was pulling out the yearbooks, cracking it open and spilling the photos onto the floor. No one outside of the family would have known about the box. The police had taken it away as evidence, bagged and sealed with the butcher knife Alyona had used to carve up Casey's father. It was gone and nobody should have been able to find it.

Casey licked his dry lips and reached out to trace the edges of the padlock, sealing the box shut as though it had never been broken. He regretted his decision not to call Joel. Joel would have had something good to say, something warm and soft and reassuring. He would have made this alright. Now there was no calling him, because Casey knew Joel had no answers that he couldn't find for himself inside the box.

Retrieving a butter-knife from the silverware drawer, he pried at the lock, twisted the blade in the shoddy catch to lever it open. The lock gave out in a jerk and scrape, and holding a breath he pulled back the lid. The smell of rotting meat struck Casey first, like the stink of an animal carcass left in the sun. Inside the metal box was a lining of sweating flesh, thin and heavily veined by blue arteries. Fingernails and tiny canines like a baby's milk-teeth flanked all sides of the box in staggered rows, circling the throat at its center. A wide gullet of corded musculature, flapping open and shut in a wet slap of flesh and smelling like dead animal and intestinal juices. Slap, gurgle, sigh.

Gagging, Casey slammed the box shut and scrambled back across the kitchen, tripping, falling. The room lurched and narrowed his field of vision into a motion-sick tunnel. His pulse beat against in his temple until his sight cleared, grabbing the edge of the counter to drag himself upright. He disregarded the decorative pot of spatulas and spoons that he had sent across the floor, grabbing instead for a kitchen knife from Joel's cutlery set and brandishing it at the box. The box didn't move. The sounds of its digesting gullet thinned into a tight sucking noise. Another sigh and the box sounded pleased with itself.

Eventually, the room stopped spinning. Casey took a deep breath. He waited for his ears to stop buzzing and took careful steps to the table, mindful of the broken clay and re-latching the padlock. Without a second thought, he took the box and walked it to the patio door, forcing it open with his elbow and hurling the lockbox over the edge of the rail onto the street five floors below. It hit the ground with an awful bang that rattled in Casey's sternum and between his ribs like a punch to his solar plexus, knocking the air out of him. The pain of impact moved over him, settling in his skull and eye sockets, inside his cheeks and reaching for the roots of his teeth. Dropping the knife he tumbled over, unable to catch himself, his arm muscles seizing and knees gone to rubber. The room spun again, from upright to invert, and his back struck the ground in a thud of bone and meat. For a moment Casey stared at the ceiling in a knot of useless parts, and didn't have a clue as to why.

Maybe if he had only listened to Joel, for once in his miserable life, none of this would have happened.

When the seizure passed, the ceiling disappeared.

Chapter Twenty-Nine

Sunshine stretched through the tree-line in thin ribbons, catching in Christine Cohen-Way's eyelashes like pieces of silver. Casey lay across her lap, asleep in the folds of her white dressing gown as she rubbed slow circles across his back. The grass of his father's backyard enveloped them in a shining green sea, dotted by trees and the mouths of Christine's flytraps. Their toothed faces beamed in the sunshine and made tiny clicking noises from inside their invisible throats, stretching themselves above the meadow to be close to Christine.

Casey was jealous of them if only for the moment, the lesser siblings they were, trying to steal her attention. It made fleeting sense in his half-sleep, in some primal part of his brain that made his fingers dig into the creases of her nightgown. Casey turned his cheek and breathed through the fabric of his mother's dress. She smelled like wild flower perfume and laundry soap, and he knew that she belonged to him. She had always belonged to him. Mariska's borrowed, defective mother was a poor substitute.

"You have to go home now, Angel," Christine said, stroked fond fingers across his scalp. "You know you can't stay here."

Casey opened his eyes and tasted dirt. He was on his stomach with his face to the floor and grit in his teeth. The pain of the night's seizure was gone, reduced to a gentle throb behind his eyes. It was morning in his apartment, judging by the sunlight pouring through the open patio door and the tinny car horns on the street below. Memories of the night before came back in fragments: The box of flesh and the broken clay pot, thinking of Joel and throwing the lockbox to the street. Thinking of Joel and passing out. He felt a momentary relief in that, cheek still warmed by the thought of his mother, comforted in the knowledge that it surely hadn't been a hallucination.

From his side something vibrated. Groaning he sat up and grabbed for his phone, rubbing at his face still sore from sleeping on carpet. He coughed twice and opened his inbox. Wiped the blood that had dried there from his nose, dripping from his nostril where he had struck the floor.

FROM MARISKA, 4/10/10, 1:32AM
I didn't see any lockbox. Why?
Blinking at his sister's text, Casey sighed.
FROM CASEY, 4/10/10, 12:45PM
thanks a bunch.

Looking at the time on his cell, Casey cursed. It was Thursday and he had an appointment to keep at Paul's office. Fuck fuck fuck. He put his phone away and stumbled toward the bathroom where he washed his face and brushed his teeth. He took his pills and changed clothes, and tried not to think of the inside of the box when he closed the patio door, leaning over the rail to see that it was still there. It wasn't. The scuff it had left behind on the pavement was the only evidence that the box had ever existed, ever been thrown, ever landed there. He tried not to think of that either and swept up the broken clay on the kitchen floor while he waited for the coffee to brew. After two cups of black tar, Casey found his messenger bag and keys in the bedroom where he had left them, toed on his shoes and left for the bus-stop.

He checked his messages twice before the one-thirty cross-town lurched to a halt. The thought of Joel sleeping in strange sheets still made his chest tight. Thumbing *I miss you* into the text box, Casey frowned. He pressed Cancel instead of Send, and sighed. Sherrie was already on the bus when Casey stepped onto the crowded shuttle. He meant to wave, smile, be polite. She sat by the window in her uniform white polo shirt and jeans, black apron tied around her waist. There was a square cut into her chest and blood dripping from her ears and the corner of her mouth. It dried dark and crusty in her ponytail and across her shirt, smears and hand prints that crawled to her throat. She smiled at Casey, pleasantly vacant from her seat two rows from him, swaying at the handrail. He ignored the fine tremors that ran down his arms.

"Hey, you," Sherrie said and patted the empty seat beside her. "Sit down. You look like you had a rough night."

"You're not real," Casey told her. He gripped the rail above his head. "You're not dead, I know you're not."

"Not yet, Sweetie, but I will be. You're going to make sure of that."

"I didn't hurt you," he said. "This isn't real. I'm hallucinating."

The waitress made a sad sound and stood up, shaky on her feet in the bus's forward sway. She reached for the rail to steady herself, invading Casey's space. He could smell the blood on her clothes and in her hair, hear the rabbit-fast sucking of her heart between splintered ribs. The urge to retch burned at his throat but he swallowed it away.

"I'm sorry, but it is," she said. "And real soon, Casey, you're going to have to make a choice."

"What choice?"

"You can put a bullet in your head and stop it yourself, or you can let me die. You can let all of us die."

Under his clothes Casey shook all over, sweat creeping down his spine. "Why?"

"Why what?"

"Why tell me any of this?"

"Because it's always been you."

"What's been me?"

"Oh, sweetie, you know what I mean. The monster at the end of the book." Sherrie shrugged limply. "Your daddy's favorite little weapon."

The bus crawled to a stop in front of Paul's office building. Casey sucked in a breath and Sherrie was gone. The iron-smell of blood still hung in Casey's clothes, and he waited until he got to restroom in Paul's waiting room before he finally vomited.

Chapter Thirty

"I'm seeing things."

Casey sat wide-legged in the center of Paul's sofa. His palms were flat on the cushions with his fingers spread, taking up as much space as possible. It was something he remembered from his high school and college careers spent starting fights in bars and school parking lots. Making himself bigger, puffing himself up, ready for the fight. The lingering taste of vomit and blood made him nauseous. Paul watched from his silent perch in the armchair, notepad waiting on his knee, tap-tap-tapping the pen to his chin.

"I see," Paul finally said.

"I have been for a while now. And I think I'm being followed."

Paul nodded, but looked unconvinced. He tapped his pen twice more on his chin. Casey huffed out a breath.

"You think I'm lying."

"No, I don't think you're lying. I do think you're feeling persecuted by me, however, and likely using this to distract yourself from larger issues."

"I saw a dead person the bus today, on the way here. Except she isn't dead yet. At least I don't think she is, anyway. I think that counts as a larger issue."

"What happened?"

Paul put pen to paper in anticipation. Casey shrugged.

"She was just sitting there, smiling at me. There was a hole cut into her chest. She came up to me and said I was going to be the reason she would die."

Paul scribbled something down. "One of your hallucinations?"

"I guess. I mean, I don't know. I don't think so. It seemed like she knew things about me, about what's been going on. She said she knew about my dad." He swallowed the taste of bile. "I also saw two men last week, and both of them have gone missing."

"I see."

"Did I mention I was being followed?"

"You did, yes."

"Well?" Casey threw his hands up. "Any thoughts on that, maybe? A professional fucking opinion on the matter?"

Paul smiled patiently. "Who are you being followed by, Casey?"

"A lockbox. I first saw it at the house when I went back with Mariska. Then it showed up at the corner store by my apartment, and at the library."

"I see. And why do you think you're seeing this box?"

"Because it's there. It's real. I took it home with me last night. It used to be my dad's."

"And?"

"And I popped the lock open on it and it was full of crazy shit," Casey all but snarled. "Imagine Hell and put it in a box, and that's what I had on my kitchen table last night. It was just sitting there, sucking and swallowing, like a throat, or some kind of trap."

"Ah," was all Paul said.

"Ah, what?"

"You're not going to like what I'm going to say, Casey."

"That's not very surprising."

"I think you're feeling guilty, Casey." Paul leaned back, folded his hands in his lap with a tired-sounding sigh. "I think you've finally allowed your asocial tendencies isolate you from your loved ones, and your guilt is manifesting itself. You feel threatened, followed by visions that appear to be out to persecute you." Shrug. "It's easier to be a victim than to face how your behavior has harmed your relationships."

"This has nothing to do with Joel." Casey's jaw ticked. "And the box is real. I threw it off my fifth-floor patio last night and I had a seizure, like it attacked me for trying to get rid of it. It's not like I just guilt-tripped myself into epileptic fit or anything. I woke up on the floor where I passed out, with a nosebleed. How else would you explain that?"

"Don't you think it might be useful to at least consider that your grip on reality may not be as firm as you think it is?"

"No, I don't. And leave Joel out of this."

"I'm not bringing him up, Casey. It's you. You don't like guilt, so you create elaborate narratives to try to escape from it."

"You think I want to be this way? That this shit is easy to live with?" Casey pointed to the window. "I just pitched a box made of skin and teeth off my balcony last night and you make it sound like I'm doing all this for kicks."

"I think it's easier to be a victim than to face what you've done."

"I'm not hiding from anything. And I'm not a victim."

"I think this box of yours would disagree with you. And so would Joel."

Casey's phone vibrated. He reached for it and Paul tutted him. His heart thumped stupidly at the sight, one new message.

FROM JOEL, 4/10/10, 2:27PM
We need to talk. Can we meet?

"I have a no cell phone policy, Casey. It isn't conducive to open discourse."

"Whatever." Casey stood, stuffed his phone back into his pocket. "I have to go."

"Let me guess--Joel?" Something bitter peeked out from behind Paul's smile. "I thought you said this wasn't about him."

"Fuck you," Casey said from the doorway. "And it isn't."

"See you on Tuesday."

Casey slammed the door behind him.

Chapter Thirty-One

At Jay's Diner, Casey waited in his corner booth with his messenger bag and held a half-smoked cigarette between two itching fingers. The coffee was cold, untouched since Sherrie first came by his table with a smile and a bounce of her tight ponytail. He was relieved when he saw her but said nothing about the bus or the hole in her chest. Instead, he thanked her profusely for the coffee and rubbed the dreading look from his eyes with the heels of his hands. He couldn't tell her that he had dreamt of her half-dead, smiling through the blood and the wet stammer of her heart. Sherrie didn't deserve to have that kind of Hell in mind.

Maybe Paul had been right, not that Casey would say it aloud. Maybe his grasp was beginning to slip.

"Hey."

The sound of Joel's voice almost made Casey flinch. He stood up clumsily, bumping elbows and knees on the table to meet him. Joel looked less alert, less put-together than usual, neglecting to smooth out the creases in his vest or fix his tie. He licked his lips like he was having second thoughts and Casey's mouth was suddenly parched. Casey couldn't think of anything good to say, just raked a hand through his hair and gestured for Joel to sit down.

"I know I should've called you first." Joel took a seat. "I didn't know if you wanted to talk to me yet."

"It's fine." Casey laid his palms on the table. His hands felt empty when Joel was this close. "Still staying at your mom's, right?"

"Yeah." Joel looked Casey over. "You been okay?"

"No." The cough-laugh Casey found himself making sounded more pathetic than he had hoped. "Not really, but it's fine. How's your mom?"

"She's doing well. Last I heard she's been shopping with my aunts." Joel looked sheepish. It didn't suit him. "Look, Casey, I'm sorry."

"Don't be." Casey tipped his chin up, determined. Hopeful. "I'm just glad you came."

"I know." Joel sighed. "I shouldn't have stormed out the other night. I know you were just trying to be there for your sister and I didn't handle it very well."

"I don't care about that anymore."

"Well, I do. I overreacted, and picked a bad time to do it. But this has been a long time coming, and I think we both know that."

"Joel, please. Just come back. We can start over, I swear."

"Casey." Joel sat back, shrunk against the booth seat. "Don't do this."

"It's all gone to shit since you left, okay?" Casey leaned forward to fill the gap Joel left. "I fucked it all up, I know, and I'm sorry. Just come home, okay? I need you here."

"You always say that, you always say you're sorry and then I go back. But then nothing ever changes, Casey. You still keep secrets from me and run to your sister instead."

Casey reached under the table to take Joel's wrists firmly. "Look, I mean it, alright? I'll do whatever you want. Therapy, the meds, just tell me and I'll do it, I promise. I won't fight. Just come home."

"I'm not doing this for me, Casey. I need you better, but you have to want to get better." Joel pulled away. "You have to trust me."

"I do trust you. I know I hurt you, and I know you don't think I'm serious about this, but I am. And, shit, Joel. It's all been bad since you left. I don't know why, I can't even explain it. I just know I need you, I need you home again. I can't do this without you."

"I want to believe you." When Casey reached for him this time, Joel didn't withdraw. "I do. I just don't know if I can anymore, Casey."

"You make me want to be a better person. You make me want to try."

Joel looked at the table, the cold coffee and the ashtray. "Then you'll tell me what's in the notebook? About your dreams?"

Casey let go of Joel's wrists. "I can't."

"Why not?"

"I don't think you'd still want me if you knew."

"That's for me to decide."

"I'm not trying to hurt you, Joel, I'm not." Casey looked away, away from Joel to the other side of the diner. To the counter and the register, Sherrie and four other waitresses gathered in a knot. It was supposed to make it hurt less. "But there are things about me that I can't seem to make right, no matter how hard I try. There's something inside of me, inside my head that makes me the way I am. Maybe I got it from my father, I don't know. It doesn't mean you should have to deal with it."

"That's not your decision to make, Casey." Joel leaned forward, tried to nail down Casey's eyes. "If you expect me to come home, you have to be honest with me."

Casey licked his lips, reached for his bag, pulled out the notebook. "The things in this notebook, they're bad, okay? And I don't think I can handle what you'll think of me if you knew the whole truth."

Joel held a hand out to touch the book's duct-taped spine, the battered cardboard covers. "Nothing can be that bad."

Casey said nothing, held his gaze away. Joel frowned.

"Whatever's wrong, we can work on it. But you have to tell me what it is first. That's all I ask."

Across the restaurant the lockbox sat on the counter, ignored by the waitresses. Reaching into the pocket of her apron, Sherrie moved away to disappear beyond the partition wall behind the counter to the kitchen. She walked past the box without a glance. Casey made motion to stand, catching Joel's worried look as he slipped from his seat.

"Casey?"

"It's here." Casey braced himself on the edge of the table. He ran through the paces: Carroll Robinson, Harold and now Sherrie. The living box and the wet hot sound it made when he opened it, the spasm and the dreams. "It followed me."

"What's here?" Joel stood, got between Casey and the box. "What's going on?"

"The box."

From the kitchen, Sherrie screamed.

Chapter Thirty-Two

Danny was built like a tennis player with sandy blonde hair and a wide, wicked smile. Sherrie met him at a house party her friend Jennifer had taken her to the summer prior. He was dressed in baggy jeans and a concert t-shirt, and she liked the look of him long before he opened his mouth. They drank beer from red plastic cups and talked about horror movies and a love of cheap old crime novels. Before the night was over they had made-out on a raggedy sofa that belonged to Jennifer's friend and exchanged phone numbers. They promised to stay in touch. Within one month, they were dating, and Sherrie learned that Danny liked to pull her hair and choke her, slap her ass during sex. She liked that part. Within six months Sherrie learned about Danny's temper, and that part she didn't.

It had been two weeks since Sherrie told Danny to pack his bags that he appeared at Jay's Diner. He stood in the narrow hallway to the dry storage room, leaning against the wall with his wolfish grin and the lockbox at his feet. Sherrie didn't see the box. Danny said nothing. She forgot about the extra sugar packets for table seventeen and squared her shoulders instead.

"I told you the last time, Danny. You can't come around like this anymore. I have to work; I don't have time for your crap." Sherrie balled a fist at her side, readied herself for the fight. "Get out before I have you thrown out."

He said nothing.

"Get out or I'm calling the cops."

She shoved at his chest to warn him. He didn't move.

"Get out, you psycho. Get the fuck out of here."

Instead of an answer, Danny punched Sherrie so hard her cheek cracked at the impact. She didn't have the chance to defend herself when he struck her again, across the other side of her face and twice more in the mouth to smear blood down her chin. When she didn't scream, he punched her in the ribs and the eye, bones giving in a wet snap. She tasted metal and heard static, like a television at low volume sitting behind her teeth, filling her head with snow. Danny's knuckles were red when he wrapped his hands around Sherrie's neck, dragged her to the dry storage room and closed the door behind them. He pressed her to the wall, choking her in a firm shake. She twisted to breathe, scratched his arms, tearing at the skin with her short flat nails and leaving angry scores behind them. He didn't bleed.

Another hard shove and Danny cracked Sherrie's head against the plaster of the wall until she saw white dots. He pinned her in place with one hand, the other reaching down to the trace a thumb along the fly of her jeans underneath her apron. Down the warm stripe between her thighs, Danny unzipped her pants and dipped his fingers inside to rub slow circles in the defining crease of her underwear. There was something ugly and wild in his face, something she had never seen before. Not like the pointless anger whenever he had had too much to drink or they fought over nothing at the kitchen table, when he was being stupid and unreasonable. If he had tried to hit her then she hit him back. If he had tried to choke her during sex, she didn't mind. That was different. There was no overlap.

Danny tried to put his hand inside her underwear. Sherrie coughed wetly, caught her breath, and screamed. That was all she would be able to say had happened when she stumbled out into the dining room, holding her mouth where it bled down her hands. One of the other waitresses screamed, two others helped Sherrie to a seat at the counter, used napkins to wipe the blood from her face. Casey went to her, put his hands on her shoulders to stop her shaking, and tried not to panic.

"What happened? Did you see it?"

She shook all over and muttered through the blood that had pooled inside her lip, something like *him* and *hurt* and *choke*. The box had disappeared from the countertop, but Casey didn't notice that. Instead he took off his jacket and put it over Sherrie. Behind him, Joel fished through his pockets for his carkeys. Their eyes met in a backward glance.

"We don't know what happened here, but don't panic," Joel gently told another waitress, Pam printed on her blood-spotted nametag. Pam rattled her head. "Just call the police to be sure somebody didn't come in through the back door, and try to get everybody outside in case he's still here. We're going to take her to the hospital, okay?"

Casey helped Sherrie out of the diner and into Joel's hatchback, sitting with her in the backseat and at the emergency room. Joel spoke to the nurses and made a report with the uniformed officer that came to take statements, handled the grownup business. Hospital accompaniment during rape investigations was part of his job. Dealing with cops, doctors, lawyers and social workers was like tap-dancing: it just took practice. Casey waited with Sherrie for the hour it took before a nurse in pink scrubs came for her, squeezing her hand and dabbing the blood from her face with the wadded handful of paper towels he had taken from the restroom. After she was admitted, Casey waited with bloodied hands and clothes, and fidgeted in his seat until Joel appeared in the next seat and put a hand on his knee.

"Hey." Joel was too good at this, too practiced at seeing women in the hospital to be anything other than earnest and composed. "I spoke to the cops. They're checking out the restaurant now and Sherrie's family is on their way."

Casey let out a held breath. "Good. That's good."

"There's nothing more we can do now, so why don't we go home?" Joel nodded. "Okay?"

Casey said nothing, gathered his discarded jacket and wiped a bloody hand on his pantleg.

The car ride back to the apartment was silent, Joel's hands tight on the wheel, his spine straight. Sleep took Casey as he sagged against the passenger door with his forehead on the window. He tried not to think of Sherrie with her chest opened and blood dripping from her smiling mouth. He tried not to think of Harold, Carroll, and the lockbox that had vanished from the diner. Neither of them spoke of the red spots staining the backseat upholstery, dried hard and black. Pulling into the parking garage, Joel found a space by the elevator. Casey opened his eyes, stretched his weighted limbs, and looked at Joel. Joel smiled weakly but after a moment even that vanished.

"Are you coming up?" Casey tried not to sound hopeful.

"I don't think that's such a good idea right now." Joel shrugged gently, softening the letdown. "It's been a really long day, you know?"

"Yeah, I guess so." Casey shook his head anyway. "I just miss you."

Joel sighed. "I know."

"I haven't even really slept since you left." Casey let out a clipped and bitter laugh. "Of course that sounds completely pathetic, right?"

"No, it doesn't." Joel turned in his seat, squeezed Casey's arm.

At this distance and in the quiet of the parking garage, it was hard for Casey to ignore the smell of aftershave still high on Joel's neck, his spit-wet mouth almost unbearable to look at. Leaning in to kiss him, Casey wanted to wipe it away. Joel gripped Casey's forearm with one hand, pulled Casey closer in a tug of hair with the other. Casey let himself be dragged, urging Joel out of the driver's seat and over the armrests to settle in his lap. He straddled Casey's knees in the uncomfortable space between the dashboard and the seat and Casey held him there, keeping Joel close for the nights they had lost.

They kissed until they forgot to breathe. Joel finally pushed at Casey's shoulder and sighed.

"Okay. Okay, okay," he said. "I need to go."

Casey held Joel closer. "Stay. Please, Joel, just stay."

"I'm sorry." Joel wriggled free, back to the driver's seat. He tugged his clothes back into place, smoothed the creases from his shirt and vest. "I just don't know what we're doing right now."

Casey's lips still tingled, his face hot as though he'd just been slapped. "You're leaving me. I think I figured out what's going on."

"Please." Joel sighed, shook his head. "Casey, don't."

"Don't what?"

"I didn't mean it like that."

"It doesn't really matter how you mean it, does it?" The car was suddenly too small, the air between them hot. Casey felt sick. "You want me gone, so I'm going." He grabbed the door handle and pulled it open, slid out of the car. Swallowing, he stopped and reached for his messenger bag, took out the notebook and threw it into the seat. "You want to know how fucked up I am, Joel? There. Knock yourself out."

"Casey—"

Joel reached out across the passenger seat but Casey walked away without looking back, past two cars to the elevator bank. He disappeared behind sliding metal doors, up five floors to their empty apartment. Left with the notebook and empty hands, Joel turned on the engine and drove away, back to his mother's apartment, plush sheets, and cold guest bed.

Chapter Thirty-Three

Had another dream about my father.

Saw a man with a hole cut into his chest. Same as the last time.

Didn't sleep last night.

Going to group meetings again. Met a guy. I probably shouldn't even be writing this down.

Joel was twenty-seven when he found himself sitting in Paul Orman's cathedral office, clicking his heels together between the chair legs and smiling like the room was wired to explode. On the other side of his desk, Paul smiled back. Between them was the fifth revision of Joel's thesis on the clinical practice of social work theory and Paul's favorite red pen. Paul folded his hands and placed them on the desk, straightened his spine like he was giving a speech.

"A slot just opened up with my support group," he said. "My other grad student Tiffany had to drop out due to scheduling concerns. I'd like you to take over for her. It's an internship position at the community center so it's solely for your own education, to get a feel for therapy in a group-setting, but I feel you would do well there."

"Oh, yes." Joel practically beamed. "Yes, absolutely."

On Monday he got the address, the staff key, and a list of topics and activities. Deep breathing exercises, guided meditation, trust-building training. On Thursday, he was sitting in the gymnasium of the Open Hearts Community Center, in a circle of old fold-up chairs and blank-looking faces. Tired faces, hurt faces, shell-shocked faces, from teenage girls to young professionals to middle-aged men. Joel sat in the middle of the seven o'clock Rape and Incest Survivors group, smiled and introduced himself. Just put your name on the nametag, he said. You can introduce yourself if you want, but if you want, you can just listen. We're all here to listen. Every Thursday he led the members through personal accounts and held hands, led prayers and dried tears. He hugged grown men and soothed young women and did this every week for eight weeks.

His mother was proud of him. Lee was proud of him. Paul said he had a knack for reaching people and sent his sixth thesis revision back with a new set of red marks.

On the ninth week, a man came in through the double-doors to the parking lot. Unshaven, wind-swept, smelling like the cigarette he had just flicked onto the sidewalk outside. There were holes in the sleeves of his tissue-thin black sweater and he was average all over, from his average height and slender build to the average-looking circles under very blue eyes. He never bothered with a nametag and found a seat across from Joel, crossed his arms and sagged back into his chair. He never introduced himself, never quite looked anybody in the eye, never did anything but sit there and listen. Listen and watch, like Joel was the only one in the room, under a spotlight of dingy fluorescence across the cold gym, looking at Joel look at everyone else. Joel never mentioned any of that to Lee. It never felt like the right time or place. It never seemed like it was any of his business.

That was how Joel met Casey Way. They didn't talk for another month, until standing by the coffee pot at the snack table Casey gave his name and something like a smile. Another two weeks and Joel saw Casey at the bar, leaving his boyfriend and walking Casey home before the night was over. A week after that Casey asked Joel to eat dinner with him and Joel said Oh, yes, absolutely. On a Friday night they shared a meal and a brief kiss, and when it rained Joel let Casey stay over to keep dry. On Saturday morning they did more than just kiss, and by the following Thursday Casey had stopped coming to the meetings entirely.

That was four years ago. Joel was twenty-seven and Casey was twenty-eight. By twenty-eight and twenty-nine they were living together in a little apartment on Davis Street, with Casey's garden of flytraps and a warm bed to share.

Four years later, Joel sat alone in his mother's apartment with Casey's notebook in his lap. The spine was tattered and held together in strips of gray tape, the pages heavy with black ink scribble and newspaper clippings cut and pasted into place. There were missing persons fliers between the chicken-scratch; men and women, soft young features mixed with weathered old faces. Smiling and laughing in holiday snapshots and graduation photos, from days when these people were happy and home and safe. He couldn't read the names or the articles, the dates above the dreams Casey had about his father and strangers with holes in them, bleeding all over the floor in line at the bank or in the stalls of men's rooms. Instead he held a breath and thumbed over through the pages, taking in this section of Casey's life that had otherwise been closed to him.

It was different from the Casey Joel had known. The Casey from the meetings, the Casey he shared a home and a bed with. The Casey from the diner, the one at the hospital with Sherrie, the one Joel kissed in the car, the one alone in their apartment. That Casey liked take-out Thai food and fixed the car when it made clunking sounds, and hummed along to Elvis Presley songs on the radio and didn't smile nearly enough, because Joel loved it when he did. This Casey spilled his black, ugly dreams across the pages of his notebook, written in blood on cold sheets and in the backward-falling snow where he saw David Way, belly-down and smiling from the slit left of his mouth. Joel felt over the crinkled pages, fingers moving through the years and the faces and the chasm of space between him and Casey. From where he sat, on his mother's floor, the chasm was just the breath between them while they slept where their bodies didn't meet while they slept. It was the space Casey didn't breach when he woke sweating at night, and Joel kissed his cheek, brushed a hand through his hair, and told him it was just a bad dream.

So Joel just took a deep breath, smoothed the papers and closed the book.

Chapter Thirty-Four

Casey hadn't bothered to undress before he crawled into bed to sleep, his t-shirt still covered in Sherrie's blood and Joel's aftershave. He hadn't checked the clock on the bedside table either. If he had he would have known it was only nine-thirty-five. He would have remembered that Joel would likely not go to bed for another hour, and he would have tortured himself with the thought of Joel sleeping alone more than the smell of his body already did. Instead he stretched across the mattress, dragged the pillow to himself and hoped for sleep without dream.

Long before morning, Casey opened his eyes in the dark. He was prone, pulled up into a fetal tuck across his mother's lap. Her body was long and lanky in person, draped by her white dressing gown and long sleep-tousled hair that framed her face in an untamed crown. Above him she smiled, carding bony fingers across his scalp the way she had in his dreams and Joel did when he had trouble sleeping. He jerked away, startled awake by the touch.

"Hey, baby," his mother said.

"You're dead." Casey sat up. He couldn't help but study the line of his mother's body, the relaxed way she sat beside next him, her weight making the mattress sink. The way her nightgown looked so soft against her skin. "This isn't happening."

"Oh, baby, don't worry." Christine made a noise in the low of her throat and touched her son's shoulder. Her palm was soft, the pads of her fingers gently callused from years of handling spades and pruning shears, digging in flower pots and pulling weeds. Plucking dead faces from her garden and stroking over the barbs of the living, the lesser children that they were. "Just come here."

Casey shivered as his mother reached for him, pulling him to her breasts to lay his head beside her heart. It thumped beneath her sternum in an animal rhythm that left his knees weak, head swimming. He allowed himself to be held there, surrounded by her smooth arms and pressed to her skin. Tears gathered in the corners of his eyes but he didn't try to wipe them away, gathering a handful of his mother's gown, letting out a hoarse, dry sob.

"So I'm not seeing things. So you're here. This is real."

"Of course not. I'm right here, Casey. I've got you this time."

"I've missed you." Casey closed his eyes, breathed in the organic shampoo smell of her hair. "I missed you so much, I didn't even know."

His mother sighed against his scalp. "I know you did, it's not your fault. But we can be together now."

"You're dead, Mom. I can't fix this."

"I know I am, but I won't always be dead, baby."

Casey opened his eyes.

"You just need to come home, Casey. Just come back to me. We can be together again, forever, just like we were meant to be."

"Mom." He moved away. Christine brushed the hair from his face, thumbed the edge of his cheekbone, the swell of his bottom lip. "I can't do that."

"Of course you can," she smiled, warm and bright in the dark of his bedroom. "Don't you want to come home with me? It can just be us, without your father or your sister, or anyone else to come between us. Isn't that what you want, baby? To be a family, to feel whole again, like before?"

"You're asking me to kill myself."

"No, Casey. I would never hurt you like that." Christine canted her head, traced the line of Casey's neck, down his collarbone. Down his chest to his solar plexus, fingers splayed out to dig between the ribs. She pressed her palm there and held it. He shut his eyes again. "I just need you to be with me, and to trust me. You can do that, can't you? You can trust me?"

Casey shook under his clothes, cold like a wet dog.

"There's so much that I missed when I was gone. Riding a bicycle, your first day at school, watching you grow up." Her eyes were wet when she laughed, a silky and comforting sound. "I just want my little boy back."

"I can't."

"Yes, you can, Casey. Just let me inside of you."

"No, Mom. I can't do this."

"Just let me in. It can be the way it was. Like I was never gone at all." He could hear her smile through her teeth. "That's what you want, isn't it?"

"Mom, no."

The hand on his chest clenched into a fist in the fabric of Casey's shirt. After a moment it let go. When he opened his eyes his mother was gone. His bed was again empty but for the lockbox in her place, nestled in the skin-warmed sheets left behind. He took the box into his lap, holding it between unsure fingers.

"Alright," he breathed out. Sat up straight, steadied himself to face it. "You have my attention."

Casey didn't sleep for the rest of the night.

Chapter Thirty-Five

It wasn't yet ten o'clock when Casey started pounding on Mariska's front door. The sound woke her, the heavy thump-thump-thump rattling the chain on the lock and the floorboards in her cereal-box foyer. At the foot of the bed she found a pair of Billy's sweat pants left from the last time he spent the night, stepped into them and tied them off at the waist to make her way to the door.

"Case," she groaned, rubbed at her eye. "Learn to use a fucking phone, man, for real."

Casey stood in the doorway in the previous day's clothes and the lockbox in the crook of his arm. He didn't wait to be asked inside before he walked to the kitchen table and set the box down.

"I know, I know." He shrugged out of the jacket he grabbed when he left the apartment. "Sorry, it couldn't wait."

Mariska closed the door and padded across the apartment behind him. At the table she stopped short. "Is that blood?"

Casey looked down, licked his lips. "Yeah, it's blood."

"For shit's sake, Casey." Grabbing a dish towel she wet it in the sink. He could barely contain his flinch when she took his hands and scrubbed the red stains from his fingers and nails. "Moron. Tell me it's not yours, at least."

"No, it's. Well, it's a friend's. She was attacked yesterday. Me and Joel took her to the hospital."

"Jesus." Mariska folded the towel and left it at the sink. "Is she okay?"

"I don't know yet. That's kind of why I'm here." Casey moved to the table for his jacket, laid it open to reach inside one of the pockets. "I need you to do me a favor."

"What is it?"

He took a breath. She crossed her arms.

"Case?"

"I need you to look at this box, and tell me what you see."

"The box?" Mariska looked at the lockbox between them, the dingy, battered thing it was. "What about it?"

"So you do see it?"

She let out a tense bubble of laughter. "Look, Casey, you're scaring me. What's going on? And where's Joel, shouldn't you be with him right now?"

Casey sighed, slumped into the nearest chair. "I don't know. At his mom's, I guess."

Mariska's chin angled up sharply. "He's not with you?"

"No. He left me, again. It's kind of becoming a pattern."

"He said he was going to go talk to you last I saw him."

"Seriously? Even after I told you to stay out of it?"

"Look, I just thought I could talk some sense into him." She sighed, pulled out a chair to sit down across from him. "So what's with the box?"

"I found it at the old house last week, then again at the corner store, and the library. Last night it turned up at the diner where my friend was attacked. I didn't know what was going on at first, and I don't know how else to explain it, but." Casey leaned forward, shook his head. "But it's following me."

"Following you? How could it be following you?"

"Is it any weirder than seeing dead people? All these things I've been seeing, I thought I was just hallucinating but something happens to people when the box is around. They disappear, or they get hurt. I think they're trying to warn me." He swallowed. "I saw my friend before she was attacked. Last night it came to me as my mom, telling me that she needed me to come home to her. I think it's tied to our old house."

"Casey, this doesn't make any sense. You're just stressed, okay?" She reached past the box to grab his wrist. "You need rest."

"Mariska, this box wants me for something. It's like it's using these people as bait, to lure me in."

"You can't beat yourself up over this. People go missing sometimes, it just happens. And whatever happened to your friend is awful, but it's not your fault."

"Mar." Casey leaned away, took a deep breath. "Look at the box."

"Case—"

"Just look at it. Please. Tell me what you see."

Mariska sighed again. Taking in the torn colored stickers and the sides compressed from years of battery, it looked like the lockbox she and Casey had as children. Covered in bright cartoon animal stickers, tucked under her bed where it safehoused her notebook journals. One morning in summer it had disappeared from her room. She was eight and Casey was six. Later she learned he had emptied her journals into the fireplace after a fight and set fire to them with a box of matches when her mother was at the grocery store. They fought about that, too. The box wouldn't turn up again until she saw David bring it into her room one night with his Polaroid camera and told her to take off her underwear.

Something cold danced down Mariska's spine. She let go of Casey's wrist.

"Oh my god."

Casey swallowed. "Mar, I'm sorry."

"That's not the box." She pushed back the chair, stood up, moved to the other side of the kitchen. "Cops took it the night your dad died. Shit like that doesn't just crawl out the door."

"I know, Mar, I know it doesn't." He rose from his seat,

reached out to her, tried to keep her calm. "I shouldn't have brought it here, but I needed you to see it. See what's been going on."

"You're fucking right you shouldn't have brought it here." Mariska kicked at the nearest chair, sent it skidding in Casey's direction and crashing to the floor. "What the fuck were you even thinking?"

"Because I need your help." The next chair she threw at him, over the table and missing him by a side-step. "I'm fucked here otherwise, in case you haven't noticed."

Her hands made fists at her sides, arms taut like tension wire. "Shouldn't have gone back to that house."

"I know." He took a deep breath, hands held up. "That's why I need you, Mar. I wouldn't have come here if I didn't."

Mariska exhaled, closed her hands around her nose and mouth. "Need me for what?" she finally asked.

Moving back to the table, Casey reached into the pocket of his jacket, produced a box-cutter. "I need you to look inside."

"Why me?" Examining the blade she took a careful step in, fight-or-flight making her agile on her feet. "Why can't you do it?"

"I don't know. I can't do anything to hurt the box, or so that's the way it looks."

"So you want me to do it, instead. Nice."

"Look, the last time I pitched this thing off my balcony it sent me into an epileptic fit. If I try to hurt it, it lashes out at me, like it's punishing me for fucking with it. I don't know what it wants with me, but I do know this doesn't have anything to do with you." Casey held out the blade. "So tell me it's not worth a shot."

Mariska took the blade, sighed and shook her head. "Fine."

Casey nodded, reached for the latch, the padlock now gone. "What's inside here, I can't explain it. But don't be scared, okay? I don't think it can hurt you."

"Just open the box." She extended the blade fully.

Unlatching the lid, Casey pulled it back, wincing at the loud sucking sound that followed. The stench of decay hit them immediately, making Mariska turn away from the gaping throat and the wet flesh that enclosed it. She covered her mouth and fought the urge to retch.

"Oh my god, what is that?"

"No idea, but it's alive. Look, you took biology in college, right? We need to see what it's made of."

"You want me to dissect this? That was thirteen years ago, and I don't even know what I'm doing."

"Mar, please," he begged. "I'm only asking you because I can't do it myself."

Mariska wanted to say No but nodded her head anyway. Mouth still covered, she dragged the blade across a section of flesh, sickened at the way it shivered and shrank back. Casey moved from the table, unable to watch and instead leaned against the nearest cupboard, steadied his breathing. She did the same and pressed the box-cutter into the skin along the side of the box, drawing a long incision that quickly filled with sticky black blood. At the wall Casey's head began to pound. He gritted his teeth and pressed his temple to the cabinet door.

"Keep going," he said gruffly. "It's fine."

Swallowing the taste of vomit, she began to work her blade into the cut, widening it from the metal wall the tissue was fixed to by thick cords of sinew. Beneath the flesh was muscle, dark with decomposition like flank steak rotting in the sun. The gullet in the center sucked and swallowed and from wall to wall the flesh sweated. Inside the box the whole thing pulsed and shook as Mariska severed it from its shell, bleeding fresh and hot onto her blade. Blood dribbled from Casey's nose. He closed his eyes and gritted his teeth, licking the taste of iron from his top lip. Grunted, pounded a fist against the cabinet door to distract himself from the pain.

Mariska looked up. "Casey?"

"Do it." Casey held himself up against the countertop with shaking arms. He didn't turn to face her.

"Look, we don't need to do this—"

"Cut it open."

Her stomach tightened, ignoring her own trembling hands to peel back the layers of dying tissue. It opened beneath the blade and the box shook and stirred, the throat slapping open and shut, spitting intestinal juices and pink flakes of meat. At the cupboard Casey fought back the scream that climbed its way from his chest. He didn't notice his knees giving under the pain, gripping the cabinet to keep from slipping to the floor.

"Alright. Alright, alright." Mariska slammed down the blade, forced the lid shut in her panic. "I'm not doing this anymore."

She took him by the shoulder, led him to a chair and pushed him into it. Retrieving the soiled dish towel she wiped the blood from his nose and mouth, tipped his head back to try to stop the stream. Casey gasped for breath through the burn on his tongue and in his throat, and waited for his skull to stop throbbing.

"Okay, so, what do we do now?" Mariska asked.

He had no answer. She didn't expect one. Instead, she cleaned her brother's face and waited for the frantic sucking inside the box to thin into silence.

Chapter Thirty-Six

"I'm so glad you could join me, Joel."

If Paul's office was a cavern then his home was a system of tunnels and caves, sitting at the top of a century-old tenement building in a neighborhood far above Joel's foreseeable pay grade. It began at the imposing black French doors at the entrance to foyer, floored with black granite and lit by a dangling chandelier. Paul opened the door with a smile and an extended hand, drawing Joel in to take his messenger bag and jacket. From there the apartment sprawled out in arms of patterned gray wallpaper and dark wooden furniture, leading Joel down the main hallway to the living room and finally the kitchen. It was a wide monochromatic space, white tile walls and checkered black-and-white tile floors, dark counters and fixtures and an island counter in the center.

There was a bottle of red wine and two glasses on the island. Joel didn't pay them any mind. He resisted the urge to retrieve his phone and check his inbox, if only for the moment. Expectation and guilt made his fingers itch. He wanted to fill Casey's phone with a dozen repentant messages, spill his guts over the wire until Casey was done being angry and he was done feeling stupid for letting Casey out of the car. In Paul's home, Joel would say nothing about it, watching the older man lean against the counter and pour a glass of wine.

"You know, I wasn't sure if you would come over," he said, still smiling. "I thought you might still be sore over the conversation we last had."

"Well, you were nice enough to invite me." Joel folded his arms to keep himself from playing with his phone. "And house-sitting is a uniquely boring experience. I guess I could use the company."

It wasn't a lie. When he heard Paul's voice message as he walked out of the office to his car, he didn't think twice about spending the evening at his former professor's home. The idea of another night in his mother's guest bed and empty apartment was depressing. At the counter, Paul offered Joel the glass. Joel accepted it without thinking, but didn't drink. Paul poured one for himself and took a sip.

"Ah, right. I heard you were staying at your mother's. Is she out of town?"

"Visiting our family in Cardiff, yes."

"How is she doing these days? I haven't seen your mother in ages, since the two of you sat in on my lectures in the fall." Across the kitchen Paul laughed gently with himself. "I should probably invite her over next time, then. Do a bit of catching up."

"She's been fine." Joel smiled politely and set the glass down. "Don't tell me you invited me down here just to ask about my mother, Paul."

"I didn't." Paul set his wine aside. "Actually I wanted to speak to you about Casey."

"Paul, he's your patient. It's a breach of his confidence to discuss his case with me. I've already told you."

"Yes, but you're no longer with him," Paul dismissed casually. "And besides, I'm only asking for your opinion as a colleague. He and I are at a bit of an impasse, it seems. I'm afraid I don't quite know where to go from here."

Joel stiffened. "He told you that?"

"Yes, last week. So you see why I asked you here."

"Oh." Joel's chest felt tight, but he tried to ignore that too. "Still, I don't think it's a good idea for me to weigh in on this. He's your patient."

"Yes, but Casey's been increasingly hostile toward me. He seems to be allowing his delusions to distract him from his treatment, using them as a form of escapement."

"Delusions?"

Joel thought of blood, the faces of strangers taped to the pages of Casey's journal. He swallowed, took a sip of wine. Steadied himself.

"He feels that he's been hunted by some kind of box. It appears to be threatening him, and sending him visions of dead people that he believes this box has hurt or killed." Paul came around the counter to Joel, hands folded thoughtfully. "I think he's allowing his guilt to manifest itself as some kind of omen, in order to maintain his feelings of persecution from others, and avoid facing the reality of his actions."

"Face the reality of what actions? What're you implying that he's done?"

"Well, not done, per se, but certainly capable of doing."

Joel shrank back. "And what is that, exactly?"

"You know, you never told me why you started seeing him in the first place." Paul reached across the counter for his glass, took a long swallow. "You were about to graduate, you had your whole career ahead of you. Then Casey showed up and you're immediately following him around, cleaning up all his messes."

"Paul."

"What was it? Was he a good lover? Did you just need something to fix for yourself?"

"You wanted to talk to me about the case, Paul," Joel reminded him stiffly. "So talk."

Paul nodded, let out another sigh. "If he continues to reject my help, I feel Casey's going to suffer a break from reality. Without immediate attention he's likely to hurt himself and others. Just tell me you'll be careful, Joel. Stay away from him, for your sake and his."

Joel bristled, his ears reddened at the accusation. "Casey may be a lot of things, Paul, but he is not violent or psychotic. Maybe I wasn't always able to help him over the years, and maybe I have enabled some of his problems, but you have no right to tell me that he's dangerous."

"I just want to protect you, Joel." Paul laid a hand on Joel's shoulder, squeezed gently. "I'd hate to see something happen to you. I couldn't forgive myself."

"I don't need to be protected from anyone, and especially not from Casey."

The hand slid down to Joel's wrist, lifted it to Paul. Joel looked down and pulled away. Disappointed, Paul just sighed.

"You're too close to him, Joel. You can't see the big picture. He's in a very bad way, and I don't know if there's anything you or I can do to stop him."

"I sent Casey to you so you could help him, because I trusted you. If I knew you were going to demonize him I never would've let you see him."

"So I'm just supposed to wait idly by, sitting on my hands while you champion his virtue?" Paul asked, his voice dipping into a scoff. "And what am I supposed to do when this white knight of yours tries to hurt you, or worse? You expect me to just wash my hands of this?"

"It's my decision to make, Paul, and mine to live with." The tone of Paul's sneer made fists of Joel's hands. "I don't want you to see Casey anymore, is that clear?"

"Casey is my patient. Until he decides to stop treatment, I will continue to see him."

"Do not come near him again," Joel warned.

Paul simply smiled. "It looks like we're at an impasse as well, then, aren't we?"

Joel swallowed. "Then there's nothing more to discuss."

He walked out of the kitchen, down the hall to the foyer, retrieving his coat and bag. Paul didn't follow. Listening to the echo of the slammed front door rattle across the apartment, Paul sipped his wine alone and pondered the fire in Joel's eyes.

Chapter Thirty-Seven

It was morning again when Casey woke in Mariska's bed, lying on foreign sheets and facing the window where sunlight slipped through in dusty ribbons. He sat up from his dreamless sleep to the smells and sounds of brewing coffee and television in the next room. Across the room on Mariska's Salvation Army chest of drawers was a pile of folded clothes, a soiled wash rag and a pair of red chucks from his closet. A letter written on notebook paper sat folded in a tent beside the clean laundry.

C

Got some stuff from your place. You need a shower bad. You can thank me later.

M

It was almost enough to make Casey smile. He could still smell iron in his nostrils from his nose bleed the morning prior. For the moment he felt safe enough. Rising on unsteady feet, Casey took the clean clothes to the bathroom behind Mariska's bamboo string curtain. He washed the evidence of Sherrie's beating from his skin and threw the soiled t-shirt in the waste bin beside the toilet. There was no point in saving it. After showering he dressed without looking in the mirror above the sink. Down the hall he followed the smell of coffee to the living room where Mariska sat on the couch in front of the television, a cigarette hanging between two fingers. The dark rings under her eyes told Casey that she hadn't yet slept.

"Hey," she called out, voice rougher than usual from coffee and cigarettes. "I was about to call a doctor. I didn't know if you were going to come around."

"How long was I out?"

Through the doorway to the kitchen, the box still sat on

the table with the blade. Blood had dried on the table-top in a black puddle. Casey swallowed.

"About a day now. You, uh, blacked out yesterday morning. I cleaned you up and moved you to the bed." On the couch Mariska snuffled and scratched her nose. "I left the box there. Didn't know what to do with it."

Casey nodded. "Thanks. And for the clothes, too."

Moving to the couch, he dropped onto it with a sigh. He found himself staring at the morning news through the haze of smoke from Mariska's cigarette. An anchor with a blue tie and a gap in his front teeth made mention of the strange attack at Jay's Diner, flashing a picture of Sherrie and a thirty-second clip of a taped interview with an officer on scene. Standing outside the diner beside a squad car, she made passive assurances that the police department was taking the report seriously. Restaurant workers in the area need not be alarmed. It appeared to be an isolated personal incident. Casey learned forward and shook his head.

"Jesus."

"Is that your friend?" Mariska asked carefully. "The waitress?"

"Yeah."

She nodded. "You need a ride to the hospital?"

"Probably. I should go see her, make sure she's okay."

"Is that the game plan? Go talk to her and see what she knows?"

He shrugged. "I don't really have a game plan at the moment."

"Well, look, you think this thing hurt your friend, right? If it did, you need to find out what it did to her and what she saw. Maybe she can help you out."

Casey's eyebrow bounced. "You know you're really taking this well, all things considered."

Mariska stubbed her cigarette out in the neighboring coffee table ash tray with a cough. "Yeah, well. Look at our family, Case. Crazy shit kind of just follows us around."

"So you believe me?"

"I don't know what I believe. But after yesterday, what can I even say, man?" Her eyes jumped to the kitchen to watch the box carefully. "What are we going to do with it, anyway?"

He didn't say anything. She took a deep breath.

"So you need a ride or not?"

Casey took the box with him. It made sense enough to keep it near where he could make sure it didn't happen upon anyone else, latched shut and tucked under his arm as he carried it to Mariska's car. He watched it in the backseat from the rearview mirror during the twenty minute drive across town to the hospital, waiting for it to make some motion to attack or escape. For the moment it seemed content. At the wheel, Mariska shook her head but said nothing of it. At the hospital she stayed in the lobby with the twin rows of red leather chairs and Spanish-language television while Casey went to the front desk to find Sherrie. He left the box in the car under a jacket with the doors locked and hoped for the best.

Up the eight floors and down three right turns of the narrow pastel blue hallway to the Intermediate Care Ward, he found Sherrie in a tiny room at the end of corridor. She was one of two patients, beds partitioned by a heavy white curtain, surrounded by a small chair, an end table and a huddle of machines fixed to her arms and chest by tubes and wires. Miniscule in her oversized bed, her face was mottled in bruises. One eye was still swollen shut and black, head crowned by blood-speckled dressing where her hair didn't cover, unwashed and oily from sweat. Her mouth was discolored when she tried to smile at Casey as he moved to stand beside her bed, lips pulled back in a weak show of teeth.

"Hey." She sat up gingerly, propped up by arms that looked too weak to support her weight. "You didn't have to visit me, Casey. You guys did enough already."

"We didn't do that much." He stuffed his hands into his back pockets and met her smile feebly. "I would've kicked my own ass if I just left you there waiting for an ambulance."

"Well, I'm glad you stopped by. I realized after I got out of surgery that I didn't even bother to thank you for helping me."

"Don't worry about that. You getting out of here any time soon?"

"The doctors said they're going to release me in the morning. They wanted to keep an eye on my concussion overnight." She pointed a finger at her bandaged temple. There was still blood and skin under her nails. "It was pretty bad when I got in."

"That's good, then." He nodded, moved to sit down in the armchair. "How're you holding up?"

She licked her lips, shrugged limply. "I'm in pain. I'm scared. I jump every time someone comes into my room, because I keep thinking he'll be there. And I just feel so stupid about the whole thing, you know?"

"Hey, you have no reason to feel stupid, Sherrie. Somebody hurt you. It's not your fault."

"Yeah, well, I know that." She laughed in a soft and hateful way. "But, what I saw, what happened to me? I can't even trust it."

Casey swallowed. "What do you mean?"

Sherrie swiped at her eye, drying tears she hadn't yet cried. "I don't know. I don't even believe it myself. I guess I was just confused, but I still told the cops when they asked for my statement. Now I wish I hadn't."

"You have to know what you saw, right? It's nothing to be ashamed of." He leaned forward, elbows on his knees to give her a long and earnest look. It felt deceitful to come to her like this, but he was honest in his concerns, just not truthful in the details. "I'll believe whatever you tell me. I promise."

She took a deep breath and shook her head. "I thought it was my ex, Danny. But it doesn't make sense, right? He always had a temper, and I knew that going in. We used to fight like crazy, especially when we were both drinking, but I kind of liked that about him, I guess? He was really intense, and yeah, sometimes he got rough with me, but he never scared me or tried to hurt me. I liked it, you know, when we were together?" A dry sniffle made her shoulders shake underneath her paper gown. "We broke up a couple of weeks ago. He came around the diner a few times, tried to get me to go back with him. I told him to get lost. I thought I took care of it."

"So do you think he just...lost control?" Casey asked gently.

Sherrie shook her head again. "I don't know. It was like Danny was there, but he wasn't. He kept trying to touch me like he used to, whenever we had sex, but – but he was hurting me, trying to kill me. It was like he was possessed, but that doesn't really happen. People aren't just possessed by the devil when they're walking down the street, you know? I just...I just don't think it was really Danny."

"Who do you think it was?"

"I don't know, but I know it wasn't him. He wouldn't do this, not to me. He might be an asshole, but he wouldn't. He couldn't." Tears trickled down Sherrie's cheek and she turned her eyes from Casey, wiped them away with the back of her hand. "Now the cops are going to go talk to him, and I should've kept my mouth shut."

"Hey, you don't worry about that right now. You didn't do anything wrong." He reached out, squeezed her hand. "Just focus on getting better, alright? That's what's important."

She nodded, dried her eyes. "Okay."

The sudden tap-tap across the room stole their attention. A blue-smocked nurse peered through the doorway, fresh bandages in hand. Casey sat back and stood up.

"I'll go." He offered Sherrie a smile, less fake than before. "Stay on the mend."

"I will. Take care of yourself."

Her smile was still painful to look at as he walked away, stuffing his hands into his pockets to forget how useless they felt these days.

Chapter Thirty-Eight

"I need you to put me under again."

Casey was perched like a trapped animal on Paul's sofa. Between two bouncing knees he held the lockbox in his lap, tapping his fingers against the sides, if only to listen to the steady jingle of the lock and handle. He had taken the bus there from the hospital, promising Mariska he wouldn't make her stay in the car with the box any longer. He promised that he would go home right after, to eat and rest. She didn't believe him but she let him go, waiting on the bench beside her brother until the bus pulled up at the stop and watching him disappear inside before she got back into her car.

From his chair, legs crossed and pen to paper, Paul set down his notepad with a long sigh.

"And why would I do that?" He tipped his chin to rest it in the palm of his hand. "What do you hope to accomplish?"

Casey sat up. "Look, you were right before. There's something in my head, something I'm not remembering, behind that locked door that I saw. I'm starting to think all this shit that's been going on has something to do with it."

"And you want to find out what it is?"

"Yeah, that's kind of the point."

Paul sighed again. "Why are you doing this, Casey?"

"I just told you. You don't believe me. Why don't we just skip the formalities, okay?"

"It's not a matter of not believing you, Casey. I just don't entirely trust your motivations. The last time you came in here you were claiming that you've been hunted by lockboxes and visited by spirits. I'm concerned you're using this to justify your paranoid delusions." Paul paused, followed Casey's anxious hands to the box rattling between them. "I take it that's the box you mentioned before."

"Yeah. And? Are you going to do it or not?"

"No, Casey, I won't. Because you're not looking for help, you're looking for validation. I won't play any part in it."

"Because you don't like me."

"It's not a matter of not liking you. My personal feelings have no bearing over my professional judgment."

"Maybe so." Casey scoffed. "Or maybe you just like Joel more than you hate me."

Paul let slip a chuckle, his smile mechanical and dry. "I have no idea what you're talking about."

"Sure. Like this whole thing hasn't been about Joel since the start. That's the whole reason you ever agreed to see me, right?"

"Joel is a colleague and a former student. I respect him. You seem to be confused."

"I bet you respect him." Casey leaned back into the sofa, placed an arm over the box. He looked Paul up and down, smiled, half-crooked and vicious. "So what is it exactly? You had a thing for your student but he didn't fall for the easy A?"

In his chair, Paul bristled. "I never touched him."

"But I'm betting you wanted to. I'm betting you were gagging for it."

"You're disgusting."

"No, I just beat you to the draw."

"I just don't want to see him spend his time on trash." Paul folded his hands in his lap, straightened his spine. "He seems to be set on the task on saving you, no matter how I try to convince him otherwise."

Casey tried not flinch. "You've talked to him?"

"Yes." Paul's smile was slow to spread but sour around the edges. "Why? Did I strike a nerve, Casey?"

"Stay away from him. Joel has nothing to do with this."

"That's funny. Joel said the same thing about you, actually."

"Look." Casey's jaw ticked, hands gripped the box. "Two people are missing and one is in the hospital. They're getting hurt, and I'm just trying to figure out what's going on."

"Do you really think you can stop it?"

"I don't know. Are you going to help me or not?"

"I'm afraid not. I won't further enable your flights of fancy. You have a serious problem, Casey. When you can come here willing to open yourself up to treatment, I will help you."

"So until then I'm screwed, right?" Casey sank back into the sofa. "I'm on my own?"

"Until then." Paul smiled. "Take care of yourself, Casey. Give my regards to Joel."

Casey didn't say anything else to Paul, taking the box with him as he stood to leave and slammed the door behind them. He took the bus to the apartment and didn't look at anyone else. If he had he only would have seen Sherrie, Harold and Carroll Robinson, skin cold with death and bleeding from the wounds in their chests. They would have smiled. The box made a sucking sound as he held it in his lap, but Casey ignored even that. In his apartment he stood barefoot in his kitchen and stared into the open refrigerator, feeling only sickness in his stomach. He didn't eat, resolved only to take the day's pills with water and wash his face in the bathroom sink. The cracks in his reflection made him think of Joel, naked and sweating into Paul's sheets, the full weight of him in Casey's lap the night they kissed in the front seat of Joel's car.

Maybe Paul had lied, but if Joel had seen him behind Casey's back it left him exposed. He had no way of knowing what Paul had said to Joel, the secrets he must have shared about Casey's visions, all that he kept close to the vest and behind closed doors. These were the things he couldn't burden Joel with, good-natured and blameless as he was in the face of the horrors that Casey brought with him. Standing before the mirror, he put his fist through the cracks, creating a spider's web across its surface until he could no longer see himself in it.

Pulling the curtains shut, Casey lay down in bed but didn't sleep. The box waited beside him, making a hungry swallowing noise that made its sides tremble. He flipped through the pages of one of his notebooks, looking through sleepless notations and the faces of the dead and missing. Carroll's face smiled at him from between nightmares and spells, fifty-five, heavy build, graying hair. He had last seen in a tan suit jacket and trousers leaving his local Sherman Brothers Bank branch location, five miles from his home at 5160 Mooreland Street. Down the road from the home David Way had bought for his wife and infant son, settled in a cul-de-sac of two-story houses with leafy trees and wide lawns.

Casey sat up.

"Mooreland Street."

At his side, the throat inside the box thumped against its cage. It shivered all over but Casey paid it no mind.

Chapter Thirty-Nine

Joel had found himself operating on only a sandwich and four cups of coffee when he parked his hatchback outside The Smoking Dragon, holding a breath and drumming his fingers across the steering wheel. He had lain in his mother's guest bed for the last two nights, thinking of what Paul had said, trying to soften his wits with wine and accusations. The thought of leading Casey to Paul in the first place left a pit in his stomach, sleeping sporadically between anxious dreams of Casey with bloodied hands and dirt on his knees. Casey, standing in a burning house, flames licking at the rafters and up his legs while the walls around him gave to fire, soaked in the backward-falling snow of television static. Joel stared at the ceiling and regretted ever opening his mouth.

Each morning he got out of bed and thought about calling Casey. He managed to get as far as checking his messages before he snapped his phone shut again. The apology he had been mulling over for two nights died on his tongue every time he saw his empty inbox. When his mother had phoned him from his aunt's house that morning, Joel made no mention of Casey. Instead, he listened patiently to secondhand news of cousin Lisa's new baby boy and her husband's promotion at the law firm. He made polite conversation while he dressed for work and cooked his eggs for breakfast, swearing to look at the pictures his mother had emailed him and to come with Casey over the summer for the family reunion. It was easier to smile through the wire and make pleasantries than to tell his mother the truth. He couldn't deal with her pity, her tutting into the phone and promising that things would work out in the end. She was better off going to lunch with her sisters and thinking things were well back home.

It took five minutes to get up the nerve to go inside The Smoking Dragon, past the doors blacked out by posters and stickers with hands jammed into his jacket pockets. He found Billy at the counter flipping through a magazine. The shop was quiet but for the sound of classic rock floating overhead and the occasional footsteps two aisles over. Looking up, Billy smiled at Joel and pushed his reading aside. Joel took a deep breath and smiled back.

"Sup, man?"

"Hey, Billy. Is Mariska around? I tried to call her at her place but she wasn't there."

"Yeah, she's upstairs. Been staying over since yesterday. What's going on?"

"I just needed to see her about something. I'll be quick."

"Sure. Oh, and hey, sorry."

"Sorry about what?" Joel's stomach tightened.

"She told me you guys were having trouble. Sorry, man." Billy smiled hopefully. "But you guys are good together. You'll work it out."

"Oh, right. Yes, of course. Thank you."

Joel gave him a grateful nod before jogging up the stairs to the loft. He took another deep breath and knocked twice on the door. Mariska opened it. Her eyes flicked from Joel's shoes to the crown of his cheeks before narrowing with a tip of her chin. Joel tried to smile, anyway.

"This isn't a good time," she said.

"Can I come in for a moment? I need to talk to you."

She stared at him and then sighed. "Fine."

Opening the door, Mariska led him across the living room to the tattered rug between the sofa and television. There were three overturned shoeboxes tossed aside amid the several dozen Polaroid snapshots they held now scattered across the floor. The photos had grayed with time, turned face-up and smudged by oily fingerprints, capturing Christmas mornings, Thanksgiving dinners, and school holiday productions in varying degrees of discoloration. She sat on her knees in a clear space, returning to a cigarette set aside in a nearby ashtray. Joel leaned against the arm of the sofa and felt stupid for coming at all.

"I didn't mean to just drop in. I tried calling you but you weren't home."

"I haven't been staying at the apartment. Got too weird for me," she said around her cigarette, taking stock in the contents of three family albums strewn around her. She thumbed their edges, reading the faces cast at her feet like tarot cards or tea leaves. He wondered if this was her way of conjuring magic, but he said nothing of it. "I'm still mad at you, for your information. Casey said you bailed on him."

"I didn't bail. I just." Realizing he didn't have a way to finish the thought coherently, he abandoned it. "How's Casey doing?"

"Epically shitty, to be honest with you." From the floor she shrugged. "I don't really know what's up, but he's in a really bad place right now, Joel. You sure picked a crap time to leave him."

"I know. That's actually what I wanted to ask you about. The last time we spoke Casey said something was going on, and then his therapist expressed some concerns with me. I stopped by to check in, really, just make sure he was okay."

"Why don't you ask him yourself?"

He swallowed. "Because I'm pretty sure I'm the last person Casey wants to talk to right now."

"Seriously?" She looked at him like he was something just scraped off the bottom of her boots and let out a loud scoff. "Then you really *are* dense."

"Look, I get it. You want to be mad at me, fine, but I

wouldn't be here if I didn't care."

Mariska leveled him a hard look. "What's his therapist told you?"

"It's probably nothing." Joel licked his lips, ran a hand through his hair. "Paul seems to think Casey's having paranoid delusions. He's worried Casey might hurt himself, or somebody else."

"And you believed him?"

"No." He shrugged helplessly. "I mean, I'm terrified, okay? That's why I'm here."

At that she stabbed her cigarette out, got up to her feet. "Something's up, okay? These things he's been seeing, the nightmares? I can't explain it, but it's like they're coming true. Casey thinks it has something to do with the old house."

"So he has been seeing things?"

"It's not what you think. I wouldn't have believed him if I hadn't seen it, too."

"Seen what?" Joel was unsure if he wanted to know, but asked anyway.

"The box."

"What box?"

"Forget it." She moved back to her pile to stand in its center. "Look, I already told you, Casey's not so good right now. Maybe if you hadn't ducked out, none of this would've happened."

"Mariska, I'm trying here, okay?" It felt like a lie to say it, even if it was at least half true. He still couldn't tell her that he was afraid to call Casey. Knowing it was irrational it didn't make him feel any less hopeless. "Whatever this is, I want to get it figured out just as much as you do."

"Then why won't you go back?" she asked. "He needs you. I told you that."

"Because maybe we can't fix it this time." He shook his

head. "Maybe this is it."

She sighed. After a moment, he did too.

"So what can I do to help?"

"Honestly, I don't know yet." Nudging at the mess with the toe of her boot, she bent forward to retrieve a photo and handed it to him. "Casey thinks it has something to do with our old house. All this shit started when we went back, so I guess that's what we're going with."

Joel held it up. The picture was of Mariska and Casey at ages eight and six. They were sitting on the living room rug with coloring books and crayons, Mariska's diary and the lockbox. He swallowed.

"This box has something to do with it, too," she added, "but it's gone. As far as I know the cops took it when Casey's dad died. So unless you can pull police evidence out of your ass, I don't know what we're going to do."

"I can't." He tilted his head, passed the photo back to her. "But I think I know somebody who might."

She watched him slide his hands into his pockets and head for the door. "Where're you going?"

"I'm going to ask a favor." He stopped at the doorway, licked his lips. "Can you just tell Casey that I came by?"

She didn't answer.

"Please?"

Looking away, she nodded. He closed the door behind him.

Chapter Forty

The text message from Casey said they needed to talk. Mariska hadn't the time to respond when she got to work, dropping her phone and keys into her bag before the staff meeting. Her knee bump-bumping under the table, rolling her thumbs to the point of distraction while the programming manager Scarlett clicked through a PowerPoint presentation on the new marketing strategy coming down from the managers. It had been difficult to make it through the show, bump-bump-bump against the desk between commercial breaks and staring at her phone, hidden from view in her lap. The photos had gotten her nowhere. She hadn't even known what she was looking for in Christmas cards and Fourth of Julys, family dinners and school plays. There was something in the house that she thought she could find hidden in the faces and smiles. The house had held David Way's secrets. Nobody had said their memories couldn't do the same.

After her program, Mariska made her round of goodbyes. Goodnights to her producer Terry and Scarlett in the office down the hall, smiling politely as not to tip anyone off as she ducked down the lobby and outside without looking anyone in the eye. Outside the station, she walked the half-block to her car in the lot across the street. It was one-twenty-four and the lot was largely empty but for the cars of the overnight crew. Casey stood hunched against her driver-side door, composition notebook under his arm and messenger bag slung over his shoulder. His eyes were black under the play of shadows coming off the street lamp behind him, the lines around them made heavier for it.

"Casey, what're you doing?" Mariska crossed the concrete between them, looking her brother over for bruises or blood.

"I was going to call you back in the morning."

"I needed to see you tonight." Casey straightened up and held out his notebook. Dog-eared pages of articles and missing persons fliers, gone over with pink highlighter under street names and dates. "I've got a lead."

"What's this?"

"These are the people I've seen. They've gone missing around our old house. There's at least ten here that I've counted, with eight more that I'm unsure about. I've got to look into it further, find their records or case files or something."

She didn't bother looking through the notebook. "So you're saying it's something to do with the house."

Casey puffed up a little. "I'm saying I think it's Dad, Mariska."

"How?"

"These fliers go back twenty years, right up to a few months after he died."

She sighed, shook her head, handed the book back. "I don't know."

"Look, the box knows me, alright? It's targeting people, some I know and some I don't. And now I think somehow it started with Dad."

"Casey, when was the last time you slept?"

"I don't know." He shook his head, stuffed the book into his bag. "It doesn't matter. I'm good."

"No, you're not." She sighed again, unlocked her door. "Get in. I'll take you home."

He stiffened, opened his mouth to argue, and then did as she asked.

The car ride was silent. With Casey holding still in the passenger seat it was easy to see how tired he was. Half-asleep, shoulders slumped, squinting through the glow of passing traffic. Hands at ten and two, Mariska bounced a glance at him and back at the road.

"I was looking through our photo albums earlier," she said, unsure if it would help or hurt him. "I don't know why. I guess I just thought there might be something there. Like a clue or something? That must sound stupid."

He sort-of laughed at that, a weird bony sound. "Stupid is relative at this point."

She watched the way his eyes changed color in the bobble of opposing headlights, from black to blue to something like old silver. "Do you really think this has something to do with your dad?"

"I don't know." He shrugged. "It makes sense though, right? This started when we went back to the house. It's like it was waiting for me to come back. Who else but Dad would do something like that?"

"Your dad wasn't that bad. Your dad was bad, Casey, but he wasn't the Devil."

"I guess that depends on your definition of the Devil."

Mariska bit her lip. "I saw Joel today."

Casey straightened, caught off-guard. "Yeah?"

"He came by when I was at Billy's. He wanted to make sure you're alright."

"What did he look like? I mean, is he doing okay?"

"Yeah. I mean, he's worried about you. We both are. He wants to know you're safe. He wants to help."

"He can't," he said, sounding remarkably like his father for just a moment. "He isn't safe now."

She said nothing else.

When they made it to Casey's apartment, it was cold. The curtains had been drawn shut and the lights were out in all rooms but the bedroom and on the patio where the flytraps slept. Casey's ability to move through the dark filled Mariska with a vague sense of dread. She groped the living room wall for a light-switch as he set down his notebook and messenger bag on the dining room table, opening the bag to slide the lockbox out. Seeing the box made her step back; seeing her do it, Casey swallowed.

"I need to keep it nearby." His hand hovered over the lock, dragging his thumb across the key hole with something close to fondness. "I can't afford to let it out of my sight."

"You need to sleep, Casey."

He shook his head. "I'm fine."

"You're going to make yourself sick like this. You have to sleep." She put a hand on the box's handle. "I'll stay here."

"You don't have to."

"I'm going to."

She smiled in that fake-sweet way her mother would smile when she wanted to get something out of Casey's father. When David was digging his heels and dragging his feet about something stupid, just to make sure he had a say. When Mariska remembered she was still her mother's daughter, even when she didn't want to be.

Casey sighed and knew it wasn't worth fighting over.

"Okay."

Chapter Forty-One

Lucas Shore was the kind of man who didn't betray his nerves. Two years as a beat-cop had cut him out of steel, the kind of a man people wrote folk songs about, all strength and civic duty. Another six in the police records office downtown tempered him, made him even stronger. But his knee being blown to hell by some stupid nineteen-year-old kid, some gap-toothed wannabe with a stolen gun, left him at a desk, instead. Sitting at Jay's 24 Hour Coffee, Lucas couldn't help but wring his hands under his jacket sleeves, knuckles making dry popping sounds that made Joel uneasy.

Joel had only ever seen Lucas as steadfast and earnest, holding his wife Theresa's hands through her rape trial. A man, Rick Moppet, had raped Theresa in a convenience store bathroom, in the summer after Joel had started at Turning Point. It was his second court accompaniment, but Joel remembered the trial because he remembered the Shores, made of stone in the witness gallery through all three days of testimony and cross-examination. Seeing Lucas now made him feel guilty as he took the seat across from him with a pleasantly forced smile.

"Hey. I got your message." Lucas stood to shake Joel's hand in a loose grip. "I don't know what I can do for you, but I'm glad to help if I can."

"Thanks so much for meeting me, I really appreciate it." Joel meant every word and took a seat. "How's Theresa been?"

"Oh, she's great. We had a baby last summer, a boy," Lucas said through a smile. "We named him Michael, after her father."

"Good, that's good." Joel smiled back, and then thought better of it. "I'd hate to have to do this, and I just want you to know I wouldn't be bothering you unless it was important. See, the thing is, well. I have a favor to ask, actually. It's about an old murder case."

"You can request police records on something like that," Lucas shrugged.

"I know." Joel smiled gently. "But I need more than just records, Lucas."

Lucas looked confused. "I don't know."

"I know it's kind of a lot to ask. There's an item that went into evidence in a murder case from about twenty years ago. I need to know what happened to it."

"Look." Lucas sighed, shifted, uneasy. "You helped get Theresa get through back then, okay? Hell, you helped both of us keep it together, and I'm not going to forget that, not ever. But this? I don't know, Joel."

"It's a lot, I know, and I don't want to get you in trouble. I just need a favor."

"What are the specifics?"

"It was a murder from April, 1990," Joel said. "A man named David Way was stabbed to death by his wife, Alyona Kovol. There would've been a lockbox at the crime scene."

Lucas ran a hand through his hair. "Twenty years? I'm not sure there's going to much left to go through. The police department moved to a new building in '97. A lot of records didn't make it in the transfer. I can't say for sure if anything from that far back is still at my office."

"I'll take anything you can find."

He let out another sigh. "What do you need them for? You know I got to ask."

Joel knew his poker-face was wearing thin, but he lied, anyway. He had tap-danced his way out of worse. "It's for a friend."

"A patient?"

"Just a friend. I owe this to him."

Lucas looked unconvinced.

"Please," Joel said. "I wouldn't ask you if I didn't need this. You know that. And just know that I hate asking this, and I won't let a word of this to pass to anyone else. You have my word on that."

Lucas shook his head, took a deep breath. "I'll do what I can."

"Thank you, Lucas." Joel reached across the table to shake Lucas's hand in a firm squeeze. "I wouldn't ask you to do anything more than that."

Chapter Forty-Two

The sun was barely up when Casey woke up to the last roaming of fingers across his back and underneath his clothes, mind working over memories of Joel's mouth and hands. Opening his eyes to his empty bed left him feeling cold as he sat up, reaching for his cigarettes on the bedside table. Mariska was still sprawled out on the couch where he had left her the night before, promising to watch the box for him. He didn't fault her for sleeping. She had needed it, more than him in most ways. The box wasn't her problem. The nightmares weren't her problem.

He sat out on the patio on a chair stolen from the kitchen table and watched the sun rise between the buildings. The flytraps didn't stir. He half-expected them to, crawling upward to him as they had for his mother in his mind's eye, eager for her attention. Smoking made him cough wetly but he ignored the inconvenience to skim his fingers over the toothed cups of a red trap, grinning at him with an empty mouth. Blowing smoke into the cups, snapping closed on his fingertips. There was something comforting in the familiarity of it, the faces that didn't change.

By ten-thirty and Casey's third cup of coffee, Mariska woke.

"What time is it?" She yawned, didn't open her eyes.

"After ten," he answered from the floor in front of the television, surrounded by twelve composition notebooks. The box sat behind him, a notebook across his lap.

"Jesus." She sat up, scrubbed her brow with her knuckles, looking around to take stock. "What're you doing?"

"Going over my notes. I'm making a list for when I hit the newspaper archive at the library. Some of these people had to make it to the paper."

"Yeah, I guess so." Mariska squared her shoulders. "Do

you think it's wise?"

Casey looked up. "Do I think what's wise?"

"To keep the box."

He closed his notebook and stood. "It wants me, Mar. It won't hurt anyone if it gets what it wants from me."

"You don't know that, Case."

Gathering his collection of books, he shrugged. "I don't have any other choice."

"Or you trust it." Her voice fell flat. He said nothing. "You do, don't you?"

Casey made a neat stack, shoved them into the bag on the coffee table. Mariska rubbed a hand across her mouth and stood.

"I don't want you to get hurt, Casey. That's all."

"Go back to Billy's, Mar," he said without looking at her. "You need to rest. I'll call you later."

She nodded her head even though she knew better of it. "Yeah. Be careful. I'll see you tonight."

She kissed his cheek, took her keys and left with the clicking of the front door lock. Casey dressed, washed his face and took his pills, mindful of the face in the mirror. He walked to the Grab-N-Go for cigarettes, books and box tucked into his messenger bag, Harold's stupidly smiling face staring back from a flyer on the window. Without looking Steve in the eye he paid for his pack and left, stealing the flyer when the clerk wasn't looking. Harold Tan had officially joined his gallery of the dead and missing.

Another ten blocks took him to the library, ducking past the front desk to the stairs and down to the main archive. He couldn't bring himself to wave back at Kim behind the desk or make eye contact with Debbie when she tried to stop him on the staircase. Yeah, hey good to see you, too, I have to run. Through a short maze of shelves he made his way to the newspaper archive, flashing his lanyard at Mark at the records desk with the best smile he could muster. No, I'm not back yet, just need to do some research. Good to see you, too. Say hello to Sydney for me. Lying was becoming a remarkably regular thing. Staring at six feet of metal shelves and eight tiers of leather binders stuffed with sixty-three years of laminated broadsheets, he tried not to think about that.

Valerie Richards was a little blonde nurse with a thin pink lipstick smile. She disappeared in the spring of 1990, on her way home from the grocery store after a double-shift at the hospital. Michael Plame and Jeffery Davies, one fat and one thin, were gone by the summer of '91; ad executive Jessica Martin and firefighter Kyle Brown by Christmas. They were followed by ten others that vanished from Mooreland Street, doctors and lawyers and church pastors. Carroll Robinson was the last before Harold disappeared and Sherrie was attacked, eighteen people in twenty years that his father's house had reduced to photos and newspaper clippings. Just faces in his survival journals, names and dates underlined and circled twice in an invisible thread that connected them across dog-eared pages and Internet searches, all the way to Casey's doorstep.

"Debbie said she saw you down here."

The sound of Walter's voice jarred Casey out of his stasis, sitting at one of the desks wedged in the corner of the archive. Twelve open notebooks at his elbows, new notes scribbled in the margins, pages torn out to mix and match with articles. He looked over his shoulder to see the assistant director behind him with a beige sweater and coffee from the machine in the break-room. Walter looked slightly more cheerless than usual.

"I should've known Debbie would roll over on me." Casey almost smiled.

"I should probably remind you that I told you to get gone and stay gone." Walter sighed, pulled up a seat from the neighboring desk to sit down. His joints popped and creaked.

"But I doubt it'd do much good."

"It's not what you think."

"I'm not sure I want to ask."

"Are you going to sit here and stare at me until I give up and go home?" It sounded more distressed than Casey had intended.

"No, I'm not. I just wanted to come down here and see what you're up to."

Casey sighed. "I know what it looks like, but I need to do this."

"I can see that." Walter nudged through the papers, finding a clear spot for his cup. "This looks like quite a project you have here. Something your therapist has you working on?"

Casey closed the book on Harold's dopey smile.

"Not going to tell me, huh?"

"I don't think I can."

Walter took his turn at sighing. "I just don't want to see you burn yourself out."

"I won't," Casey lied.

"Whatever you think you did to deserve this, it can't be as bad as you think, son."

"You wouldn't believe me if I told you."

"You could always try."

Walter looked just a bit hopeful. Casey just felt tired. He laughed, sort of, and hoped it was enough.

"Yeah, well. Maybe some time I will."

Walter smiled like a basset hound would smile if it could, and gave Casey's shoulder a squeeze. "I'll hold you to that."

Casey kept up his fake smile until Walter stood, pushed his chair away. It was getting so easy to lie now. If his mouth hadn't hurt from smiling, he wouldn't have known he was still doing it.

Chapter Forty-Three

Casey had lost track of time again. It was getting easier and easier, the hours running together and the days slipping away between visions and nightmares. Like lying it was getting too easy to do, to anybody who got close enough to hear what he had to say, away from windows at his desk in the archive with no sense of sunlight to guide him. The sounds of shuffling feet had finally perked Casey's ear, caught his attention. Beside his bag his cell phone said ten minutes to six. Closing time and Mark was probably pacing around his desk by now, staring at his wristwatch and waiting for Casey to leave. Mark was always like that at closing, staring mechanically at his watch to prove to everyone that he had places to be. Like anybody cared about *American Idol*. Standing made Casey's spine pop in three directions, ignoring the dull pain to collect his pile of books and stuff them into his bag, tucked beneath the lockbox.

Overhead the lights flickered gently. He sighed.

"I'm going now, Mark," Casey called over his shoulder. "You don't have to turn the lights out on me."

Shrugged his bag on, gathered up the leather binders to fill the empty slots on the shelves, lined up neatly and pushed flat to the back wall. Behind him the lights danced again, outlining a shape amid the row of desks. He turned, ready to say something nasty to Mark for rushing him out, and stopped in a flinch. David Way waited at a desk, eight feet tall and made out of a gray suit and white button-down. His face was healed, the flesh new and holding fast to his skull in the façade that Casey remembered from family albums and Christmas cards. It was like his own face, with a stronger jaw, smaller eyes and a thinner mouth, his father's features decidedly more defined than his own softer qualities. Cut from something better than Casey, assembled in the hard angles that made men bigger, better, more male than he could have hoped to be.

Casey dropped his bag. From his seat at the desk his father smiled the same way Casey remembered from car rides to school, waving goodbye from the driver side window with a broad hand. The same hands had hauled Casey up on his shoulders more time than he could count, holding him by the knees, his own wiry legs wrapped around his father's neck. They used to laugh together once, just like that, at the park or on the Fourth of July parade that Casey remembered going to the summer after his mother died. The summer his father met Alyona and everything changed.

"So you do remember me," David said. "I thought you might've forgotten."

Panic rolled over Casey in hot sheets, the urge to crush, scratch, tear and destroy making his fists tremble at his sides. "Don't." He moved back. "This is you, isn't it?"

"This is me what, Casey?"

"It was you at the house. You're the one hurting people."

"If that's what you want to hear."

"Don't you fucking say that to me." Casey's voice verged on a quiet terror that echoed in the forest of books and binders. He swallowed, tried to stop his shaking. "You don't get to tell me what I want."

David sighed. "Casey, we need to talk."

"What do you want?"

"You already know."

"No, I don't."

"I need to go home." David stood. Just two inches taller now and two sizes bigger, taking three steps forward that brought Casey one step back. "You need to come with me. That's the only way this is going to get any better."

Up close, his father looked human for the first time in twenty years. Wisps of premature gray colored fine strands at his sideburns and crow's feet creased at the corners of his eyes from laughing and smiling. That, too, was a lie, like all of Casey's lies. Compacted, compounded.

"You're dead, Dad. I can't help you." Casey grabbed his bag. He slung it over his shoulder, pushed past his father. "You deserved to die."

"You still don't get it, do you?"

Casey shook his head. "I don't care."

"I never had a choice, you know. I was born with this inside me, Casey. We both were." The soles of David's shoes clicked on the floor, turning to stare hot holes into Casey's back. "Don't you at least want to know why?"

Casey stopped between desks, stared at the floor, his hands still shaking. "You always had a choice, Dad."

"You know that's not true, Casey. You feel it in you, too, that sickness. That hole inside of you that you can't fill? It only gets deeper."

"I won't let it. I can't."

"So come with me. We can do this together."

"And then what happens?" Casey closed his eyes. "Does it stop?"

Silence in the library, his father's broad shoulders shrugging in a rustle of slick fabric. Moving like mountains must have moved if they could, or sighing if buildings could sigh. His father's smile was audible in the dark, steps heavy when they circled him, a shark in the water.

"It never stops, Casey. Not really. It just gets easier to hide."

"Dad, don't do this. Not now."

"Just let me in. It'll be easier for both of us."

"No." Closed his eyes tighter, couldn't breathe, couldn't

be here. Casey thought of his mother and of the flytraps and green grass. He thought of Joel and soft sheets and something warm and safe and far from here. "I love you, Dad, but I want you to stay dead."

"Casey—"

"You deserved to die." Joel's hands and Joel's mouth, clutching and smiling and sighing and laughing. "I just wish it'd been me that did it."

His father said nothing else. Casey opened his eyes and was alone again. Closing his hands over his mouth, he let out a dry sob and waited for his body to stop shaking. Overhead the lights flickered into darkness, the click-clack of soles thinning and finally dying away.

Chapter Forty-Four

Walter left the library at seven o'clock every night, after the clerks had all finished and he said his goodbyes to Chuck and Leslie upstairs. Checked, signed and passed off on the reports from Technical Services and Acquisitions, and finally filed his spell-checked amendments to Bill's budget proposal for Monday's staff meeting. Checked the drawers at the front desk and locked them. He was drinking his last cup of coffee in the employee break-room when the night janitor Jeffery pushed the mop and cart down the hall outside with the creak of plastic wheels and leather soles.

Jeffrey had a crooked lanyard ID around the collar of his blue work shirt and smiled at Walter when he passed. Walter smiled back and Jeffrey saluted him with the same slanted gesture every night at closing. Jeffrey had taken twelve bullets in Vietnam between '62 and '69 and drove a dusty blue pickup truck with six *Semper Fi* stickers on the rear cab window. Walter hadn't done his tour until coming out of high school in '75, clean shaven and already drinking too much, but Jeffrey knew a Marine when he saw one. Walter didn't share Jeffrey's sentiment but smiled at the old man's salute. It was one of a few pleasant routines he had, beside his final cup of coffee.

At six-forty-seven, Walter rinsed his mug in the sink and shook it dry to leave next to the coffee maker. In his office, he took up his keys and jacket, shutting off his computer and lamp before locking the door behind him. The ceiling lights shuddered in and out and caused Walter to rub his eyes with a knuckle, already strained from reading over the top of his outdated bifocals all day. Down the corridor to the main archive, Walter walked through the alleys of shelves to the main staircase, and stopped.

"Nat."

Natalia hovered between two shelves in pirouette, dressed in her baggy cotton practice pants and hooded jacket. Her lashes fluttered softly, apple-red in her cheeks, apple-red in her mouth like ripe fruit, spit-shiny and full. She was a teenager again, ballet-thin and dancer-strong with arms and legs like tight cable, slim hips and small perfect breasts. The last time Walter saw her it was at the family reunion. Natalia was twenty-four, living in a clean one-bedroom apartment with her boyfriend Ben and teaching ballet to third-graders. She still couldn't look Walter in the eye then, but here, as a girl, she could. Walter stood, mouth dry and stock-stupid, watching Natalia vanish down the passage, down the rows of shelves and through the double doors into the employee corridor. He dropped his coat and keys and followed with certain steps, listening for her pointed toes on the floor. She led him to the men's room, disappearing behind the door.

He was forty-four again. She was sixteen, his big brother Ronnie's baby girl with his first wife Janice. Walter remembered Natalia as she was, the beautiful girl during the summer he had spent with Ronnie and Natalia when he was moving from Scarsdale and looking for an apartment. His wife Maggie had just filed for divorce, throwing him out after twenty years of trying and spinning her wheels, and he needed a place to stay. Everybody called her Nat then, and she was in her eighth year of ballet. She would practice in the mornings before school, in her baggy pants and hoodie. Walter remembered that. He would walk by her room on the way to the shower and catch a glimpse of her, a pillar of rigid bones, breath sucked under the jut of her diaphragm, toes and fingers pointed. He liked to watch her, the way she moved. Nat was perfect, like an angel. Walter couldn't help but think of her, alone in the guest room down the hall, the crime of her long legs giving him fever.

He was still drinking then, hitting the bottle he kept under the mattress and making bad decisions. It was the reason Maggie had finally thrown him out of the house in the first place, tired of him coming home later and later, smelling like bar men's rooms and vomit. The reason he found himself in Nat's room the night after her big recital, skin hot, breath damp with the smell of cheap bourbon. Six weeks she spent dancing for her life, stretching, practicing, awake at dawn every morning on pointed toes whenever Walter walked by her open door. She knew what he was doing was wrong but she still didn't scream, didn't try to fight as he ran a hand down her ribcage and kissed her sloppily, all tongue and teeth. She didn't cry and in the morning, after he sobered up through the hammers pounding his skull in half, he saw the blood on the sheets.

He said he was sorry. He hadn't meant to. He wouldn't do it again. Held her face and wiped the tears away. Baby girl, baby girl, just please don't tell your dad.

Walter drank for two more nights and never said a word of it to Ronnie. Natalia never looked him in the eye again, not until now, when she was still sixteen and he was fifty-six.

Walter followed after her, into the men's room, pushing the door open to find her at the bathroom sink, hands behind her on the porcelain. He couldn't help but reach for her shoulders, touching along her thin arms to her wrists to hold them, firmly and without fear. Nat looked at him like a piece of meat, eyes hard and black under false light, sighing between her teeth in television static.

She tried to kiss Walter but he turned away. Her bones made sounds akin to falling dominos when she righted herself, shoulders back, chin up, predatory and bird-like. She looked hungry, ready, sure, coming to claim the blood that was taken from her. He took a deep breath and closed his eyes.

"Natalia," he said, dropped to his knees before her, the cold tile hard on his joints. "I know, Nat, I know. I'm so sorry for what I've done to you. I'm sorry for everything."

The lonely cosmic sound that escaped Nat frightened Walter but he took one of her small hands to press a kiss to it, over the bony knuckles and to the wrist. Opening his eyes Walter could see Nat's chest open under her jacket, the nauseating splinter of bone and flesh, splitting her wide at the breastbone. She was ready to take him.

He nodded, held her hand to his forehead. It was time.

"Okay," Walter said. "Okay."

The first bite took the flesh from his face, the second his head, neck and shoulders. There was no time to scream, only to bleed and breathe out in a gasp. What was left was taken by a crush of bone and sinew, gulped in and tucked away behind the folded teeth. In the end Natalia devoured her uncle in a snap of jaws, swallowed him up without a sound and leaving only the blood behind.

Chapter Forty-Five

The house was still empty when Mariska came back with her crowbar and flashlight, retracing her steps through the yard to the kitchen. Mooreland Street was dead by the time she parked on the curb and retrieved her things from the trunk, streetlights out by one o'clock and the neighborhood black. She hadn't known what she expected to find when she left for work, lying to Billy with a tired smile and a kiss of his cheek. I'll be saying at Casey's, she lied. He's having a hard time without Joel. I'll be home in the morning. Love you. Be good without me. He smiled in that dumb way he always did and told her, Okay, no problem, do what you need to. I love you, be good, too. She said she loved him twice more. Closed the door behind her, turned over her car and drove away.

The dust hadn't yet settled in her boot prints, kicked up and fresh as she made her way through the kitchen, living room and down the hallway to the bedrooms. Specks of it shimmered in the beam of her flashlight, held close to her face with one hand, the other fisted around the crowbar at her thigh. Flight-or-flight made her strong, ready, tight like tension wire and prepared. Heavy boot prints raced circles around the kitchen island counter, Casey's size-nine Converse shuffling to the living room, disappearing in the carpet. She hadn't expected to find new footprints, but it would have made the looking easier. The trash in the living room parted like a sea to the empty fireplace, new beer cans with old gas cans and nothing seemed all that different.

A monster had been living there, if Casey was right. It hid in boxes made of their childhood, wearing other people's faces. Only Casey saw these things but she believed him, wanted to prove him right. There was no trace of it now. No claw marks on the doors or teeth left behind in the dust; no sheets of torn skin or shed hair marking its territory. She half-expected to find David Way's skeleton in the corner, creeping out from the shadows to choke her. It would have given her proof, something more to cling to than the box of flesh Casey had been carrying. It would have been more to hide from, more to hate than just David's face in old photographs. She was done hating people. David was dead. He just needed to stay dead. It was easier that way.

Mariska stopped in the hallway. She counted the steps that stretched from door to door. Ten to their parents' bedroom, five from Casey's to hers. The bedrooms were scars in the home, ugly things scored into the walls from the nights Casey hadn't slept. His eyes had burned holes into them, whispers from the cracks beneath her bedroom door etching words into the plaster and under the paper, to the studs where the nails remembered. She didn't see them now, but she remembered. The same way she didn't see the devils that had rested there once before, lying in the trash and the dirt where the box had sat in the fireplace and held court over its possessions. She didn't see the evidence of their chains in the dust, the trails where they had dragged themselves across the carpet from one room to the next. Instead she sighed and walked away.

In her car, she checked her phone for Casey's voice mail, a small quiet sound. I can't explain how, but I'm okay, he said. I saw Dad. I think it's going to be okay. I hope you're alright, don't worry about me. I'll talk to you tomorrow. I love you.

Mariska looked at the house and sighed again. The whole street was lit up again in her rearview mirror when she drove away, waking up slowly with the rise of the sun between trees and over high-pitched roofs. There were no monsters left, only memories and an empty house. She didn't know which disappointed her more.

At Billy's apartment, she hid in the bathroom while he slept crooked across the bed like a golden retriever. Toilet seat pulled down, her knees pulled up to her chest, toes wriggling over the edge of the bowl. She listened to the message once more and dialed Casey's number with a held breath.

Hey, I got your message, she said. I went to the house but I didn't find anything. Makes sense, I guess. She sighed. So, anyway, I just wanted to let you know I was okay. I'll talk to you tomorrow. Call me back. Love you.

Closed her phone, tapped her foot on the floor. She tried not to think of monsters or claws or teeth as she got into bed and wrapped herself around Billy's big chest. She wanted everything else to go away. She wanted Casey to be right. David Way was dead again and maybe he never rose, and maybe he took the box with him this time. The world held no place for monsters and closing her eyes, Mariska didn't dream.

Chapter Forty-Six

Casey had left the notebooks on the couch with his empty bag. The box had vanished in the library when his father did. At home he searched all over but didn't find the box, only his notes in his bag. It was gone. He was alone. The fear that had gripped him in the library had bled out on the long walk home, melting from his muscles to warm into a strange, empty euphoria. Like the medicated happiness of the candy-colored downers he stopped popping after college, or the fading easiness of a tequila buzz moving over him before waning into a lackluster hangover. It was something welcoming and airy and fleeting, like when he woke to Joel's lips pressed to his back, fingers at his bicep, just breathing. His father was dead again. His father was gone and he had taken his devils with him. Everything would be alright.

On the patio he smoked two cigarettes amid the flytraps. He was alone and it felt strangely, nakedly good. Beyond the balcony the city slowed to a half-sleep, the streets empty but for a few lamps and passing headlights in the distance. He opened his phone to call Joel. Instead, he called Mariska.

I can't explain how, but I'm okay. I saw Dad. I think it's going to be okay. I hope you're alright, don't worry about me. I'll talk to you tomorrow. I love you. He wanted to say that to Joel, but he told Mariska instead. She needed to hear it, too. He could tell Joel tomorrow, if Joel still wanted to hear it. He could, if Joel still answered the phone if Casey called. Still took him back, still wanted him back. Maybe they could start over then.

The burn in his muscles told him he should sleep but the urge never settled in. Casey crushed his cigarette out and walked inside, closing the patio door and padding to the bathroom. He undressed and showered, letting water run hot to cold down his face. Washing the last week from his skin, scrubbing at blood stains that he had long since rinsed off until only the redness remained behind. Burning the dust and fingerprints from his scalp, both the real and the imagined, to run down the drain in a mud of rust. He toweled off, dressed, took his pills with a cupped hand of water and a sigh. In the mirror his eyes were captured by the spider web fractures, splintering into the faces of five different Casey Ways, all with black in the hollows of their eye sockets and darkening stubble. His father was nowhere to be found. He took a deep breath.

"It'll be okay now," he said to himself. Took out the razor from the plastic tray, ran it under water, lathered his face and shaved. Felt clean, took another breath. "It's going to be okay."

In the next room something dripped. From his narrow field of vision at the sink he could make out a red puddle on the bedroom carpet. Two bloody foot prints, dribbling to the doorway and down the hall. He walked out into the living room, held a breath and followed the blood that pooled in patches across the apartment to the kitchen in cautious steps. Walter waited at the kitchen table, quiet with his mug in hand, still sipping the day's coffee. He bled from his mouth and eyes from unseen wounds, pumping hard and thick onto his clothes, his heart thudding sluggishly from inside the window cut into his chest.

The box sat on the table beside Walter's coffee mug, swallowing to itself. At the doorway Casey's stomach dropped.

"Hey, Casey." The red ran heavily down Walter's chin, catching in the corner of his mouth in a sad half-smile. "I didn't mean to scare you."

"No." Casey stepped forward, dropped boneless into the chair across from the administrator and the waiting box. "No, no, no. Christ, Walter."

"I know. I'm sorry it came down to this, I am."

"I thought I stopped it." The room spun around Casey, hot in the air at his cheek, cold beneath his feet. Sickness crawled over his skin, dizziness putting his hands on the table to steady him. "I tried to stop it, Walter. I did. This wasn't supposed to happen, not to you."

"I know you did." Walter shrugged limply. "You can't blame yourself, Casey. I had this coming, you know. It was only a matter of time."

"What should I do now?" Casey swallowed on the taste of bile at the back of his throat. "How can I stop this? Every time I try to fix this it only gets worse, and I can't – I just can't do this, not anymore."

Another sip and the box shivered, Walter's broad fingers tapping gently on the mug's wide belly. "I don't know. I don't have any answers for you, Casey. I just—"

Walter sighed. Casey pressed his lips together to wet them.

"Just what?"

"It's just that it's got to end with you, Casey. As long as you're alive, people will keep dying."

"Walter, no, please." Casey shook his head. "Please don't say that. Not you, too."

"It's the only way out of this now. I'm sorry, Casey." Walter's big basset hound eyes looked darker than ever, the whites filled in red with blood and regret. "I wish I had better news."

"I know, Walter. I know you do."

Between them the box was quiet, its stomach churning into a final satisfied calm. Casey closed his eyes, brought his hands to his mouth to cover the stutter of his breathing. Walter finished his coffee in peace but for the gentle patter of his wounds, weeping from his head and to the floor. When Casey opened his eyes again Walter was gone, his blood smeared on the table the only proof left behind that he was ever really there.

Chapter Forty-Seven

"Lucas?"

Joel poked his head outside his mother's heavy white door. It was just past six o'clock and Lucas had buzzed the ringer three times, knocking twice as Joel came from the kitchen to the door. The morning chill bit at Joel's face, skin still shower-damp above his shirt collar. Lucas looked over from his slouch against the wall outside Sarah Britton's brownstone, straightening up. He reached into his jacket pocket for a cassette. It was in a sealed plastic bag, marked with red tape and catalog tags, dates and names, police notation.

"All the files from the case were moved to another facility," Lucas said. He looked tired, cheeks pink from the cold. "The only thing left was a few copies of the police reports and the 911 tape."

"The 911 tape?" Joel asked. "Is it from the neighbor's, or--?"

"It's from inside the house," Lucas answered stiffly. "Made by the wife."

Joel nodded. "Okay, that's good. That works. Thank you so much, Lucas. I owe you for this."

He reached out an open hand. Lucas held the tape to him but didn't let go.

"I'm not sure you need to be listening to this."

"I need it."

"You already said that." Lucas squared himself, like he had practiced this. "What you didn't say was why."

Joel sighed, brought his collar up to cover his cheek.

"I read through the reports, you know. Woman waits for her husband to come home from work, and then guts him like a pig with the kid in the room. Cuts his face off; his dick, too. Then she sits outside for the police to show, screaming that the kid has no face."

"I need to know what's on the tape. I wouldn't have asked you to help me if I didn't."

"Yeah, but that call." Lucas shook his head. "It's bad, okay? Really bad. I'm just warning you."

"That kid grew up, Lucas. He needs to know what's on the tape. I owe it to him."

"That friend of yours, right?"

"I love him." Joel put his hand on the cassette, ready to take it. "He's in trouble right now. If I can do something to help him, I have to try."

Lucas sighed. "If anybody finds out about this, I can kiss my career goodbye, Joel. You know that."

He let go of the cassette. Joel swallowed.

"I'll give it back to you before that happens, Lucas. I promise."

"Yeah, well." Lucas stuffed his hands in his pockets. "You better."

Chapter Forty-Eight

I was wrong about Dad. It's not him, it's something else. I can see it now. I think...I think I just about got it nailed down, though. I'm following a lead, okay, and I know it doesn't make any sense, but. But, look, we'll talk later. Call me when you get this.

Casey didn't get Mariska's message. He didn't sleep. The box had slept in the middle of the bed, making quiet satisfied sounds under the lid, throat flapping, swallowing like a full stomach. He didn't clean up the blood pooling in the kitchen, living room, or hallway. It felt like cleaning up a crime scene, toweling Walter's blood from his skin, scrubbing it off his hands. Walter deserved better than that. Instead, he watched the sun rise, called Mariska's number, hung up. Drank two cups of coffee and called her back to leave a message. He forgot to say I love you. He almost wanted to call back and tell her.

By noon, Casey dressed, gathered his things into his bag, notebooks and the box. Swaying through traffic on the crosstown bus, he tried not to look anyone else in the eye. Not the pretty college students with notebooks under their arms, old ladies with green fabric grocery bags, or the skeevy-looking Harold clones listening to expensive iPods with holes in their lips and designer pants around their asses. He got off a block from Paul's office and walked it, unable to look back without shivering under his clothes. Up the monolithic elevator-cave to Paul's office, seated on dollhouse furniture. Paul looked tired and impassive in his operatic armchair, notepad in his lap, pen in hand. He didn't smile this time.

On the couch, Casey avoided his eyes, too, looking at the floor instead.

"Well, I have to be honest: I'm surprised you came, Casey.

After our last session, I thought you wouldn't be back."

"I need to go under again," Casey said.

After a moment, Paul sighed. "We already discussed this, Casey."

"No." Casey looked up. Blinked twice, eyes wide and ringed by sleeplessness. "I give up, okay? I'm done. I just need to do this. There's...there's something locked up inside me, okay? I get it now. The only way to get past this is to find out what it is I'm not remembering."

Paul leaned forward. "What brought this on?"

"I'm tired." Casey shrugged. "I'm tired of fighting. I don't want to hurt anybody else anymore."

Paul tapped his pen to his chin. "So you admit that you were wrong?"

Casey made a fist of his hands. "Yes."

"That Joel is better off without you?"

He let the fists go. "Yes."

At that, Paul smiled. "Alright then, Casey. Let's get started."

Casey lay down on the couch, closed his eyes. Paul counted backward from ten, slower and slower, deeper and deeper in the dark. The leather melted away under his palms, the floorboards and the concrete foundations. A wooden skeleton grew in place of Paul's office, rounded out by plaster and paint, carpet and fixtures, capped by roof shingles. Somewhere else, Paul breathed evenly like a metronome.

"You're at your childhood home, Casey. Can you see it?"

Casey opened his eyes to the gentle flicker of a shaded orange wall sconce. He stood, looking up and down the stretch of the white hallway that connected his bedroom to Mariska's, his father's to the linen closet and bathroom.

"Yeah, I can."

"Where are you?"

"In a hallway."

"Travel down the hallway, Casey."

Out of the corner of his eye, something moved. A glimmer of motion made of arms and wisps of hair. Casey turned to see a door at the end of the hall open and then slam shut. He followed after, finding himself outside his bedroom door. It came to him slowly, remembering the wobbling knob with the keyhole stuck tight with the green plastic army man he shoved into it when he was four. Jiggling the handle, the door opened. His bedroom used to be blue with white trim, a wooden bunk bed, dresser and white curtains on the windows. Walking inside, it was now a cavern, a dim windowless room with a big bed in the middle. It stood on tall legs with a broad headboard, dressed in lush white blankets and pillows, Christmas lights with white bulbs wound around it like wreathes to make a fake halo. A church altar made of neon light.

Joel lay in the middle of the bed, naked, clean and perfect. A Renaissance painting or a Christ statue, smooth and unspoiled, made of light. Hail Mary, full of grace, Casey recounted in the back of his mind from Sunday school lessons of decades past, Our Lord is with thee. Snow fell backwards from beneath the bed like the glow of television static. It caught in Joel's eyelashes and the hollows of his chest, making him look thinner, more delicate, carved out of ivory and bone. Casey swallowed.

"I miss you," Joel said.

"Where are you now, Casey?"

"I need you," Joel said.

"I'm in my bedroom," he lied.

"Come home," Joel said.

He tried not to look into the glassy lull of Joel's weighted eyes. Joel crawled to the edge of the bed on hands and knees, reaching out to stroke a thumb over the edge of Casey's jaw.

"What do you see?"

"Pray for us sinners," Joel said, "now and at the hour of our death."

"Nothing," Casey also lied. It wasn't for Paul to see. "It's nothing."

He took Joel's hand from his face, smoothed the fingers open to kiss the center of his palm.

"I'm sorry."

Behind the bed was a door. Casey closed his eyes and took it to a hallway where Mariska stood in a green sundress and sandals with flowers on them. The air was warm and Casey immediately recognized his father's foyer, the front door, coat rack and umbrella stand. Mariska was eight-years-old with her hair pulled up in a high ponytail that bounced when she moved, hula hooping in a swing of her waist. Alyona used to dress Mariska then. She stuffed her daughter into dresses with flowers and birds printed on them, making her straighten her hair, wear patent leather shoes with little heels like grownups did. Mariska smiled at Casey anyway.

"Hey," she said. "Are you looking for David?"

"I-I don't know," Casey stammered. His mouth felt dry. "I'm looking for something. He might know where it is."

"He's in the kitchen," Mariska said as though she hadn't heard. "It's through the living room. I think he's in there, anyway. Ask Mom."

She pointed through a wide doorway to their old living room. A canary cage grew from the floor where the fire place had been, made of metal wire and bone flint, Alyona Kovol inside. She stood in the center on the tips of her pointed toes, twirling slowly with a stuttering motorized rhythm, arms and head hanging like the limbs of a defunct robot or broken marionette. From the cage she smiled broadly with black-blank eyes, teeth white like the pearls around her neck and the bone-shine of the buttons on her red dress. When Casey came near to the cage Alyona's neck made popping sounds, head swiveling to orient itself. Crunch, crunch, snap like broken clockwork, the gears and bolts rattling together until it curled down to her toes and in a jerk of her arms. Up close he saw the blood on her fingers, making pink stains of her skin, the soak of it on the front of her dress and underneath, coloring her neck and kneecaps in smears.

"Where are you now, Casey?" Paul asked.

"My living room."

"Go to the kitchen."

Casey wanted to shake the cage, kick it over, break Alyona's wilted neck. Instead, he took a breath and moved away, through the room to the doorway where the kitchen would have been. It was sealed over now. He put his hands to it, looking for a seam, a keyhole, or lock. A twitch in his peripheral stole Casey's attention. In the corner of the room by the bookshelf and his father's writing desk there was a boy. Small and skinny under a mess of dark hair, sitting with his back out and head between his knees. Casey swallowed and approached the boy, reaching out a cautious hand.

"Hey," he said. "Hey, are you okay?"

As he drew close Alyona began to scream, a primal, ugly sound. When he turned the boy got up to run, speeding past Casey and through the door appeared in the wall, black and made of iron and slamming it shut behind him. Casey didn't reach it in time, pulling and shaking at the locks and chains.

"No, no, no, no—"

Behind the door someone began to moan, a twisted animal noise, tinny and distorted through the metal.

"Casey, I'm going to begin counting back from ten," he heard Paul say.

"No, I'm almost there," Casey said, beating on the door. "I can get in."

"Ten, nine, eight—"

The moans rose into fever-pitch, a nearly orgasmic shudder that melted into Alyona's screaming.

"Dad," Casey screamed. "Dad, open the door."

"Seven, six, five, four—"

"Dad, I know it isn't you. Just let me in – fuck, Dad, please. Open the door."

"Three, two, one."

Casey sat up to find Paul's office spinning. He grabbed his head as the last tremors of seizure rolled over him, blood dripping from his nostrils, tasting iron in the back of his throat. Paul held out the waste bin but Casey pushed it away with a shake of his head.

"There's something in the house," he said. "It was a boy. It was in there with my father."

"It's the memories you've repressed, Casey," said Paul gently. "You're nearly there."

"No, it's something else." Casey swiped his hand across his nose, licked the blood from his lips. "I thought it was my Dad but it's using him. It's using my parents' faces to try to get to me. That's how it does it. It's a trap. The whole thing is a trap."

Paul sat back. "I thought we were past this."

"I just needed to get a look at it, that kid or whatever. It's trying to pull me back in."

"So you lied."

Casey's laughter was short and rough. "I told you what you wanted to hear."

"You're delusional, Casey."

"Yeah, well. I've been called worse."

"If you don't want to accept treatment, fine, but I can't let you use me to justify your paranoid fantasies."

Casey stood and walked to the door. Paul got to his feet.

"You walk out now, Casey—"

"Yeah, I know." Casey turned as he pulled open the door. "Don't come back."

"You can't beat this, no matter how smart you think you are," Paul said. "You will end up hurting somebody, I guarantee it. Do you really think you can live with yourself?"

"No, I can't." Casey shrugged. "But I'm going to make sure it doesn't happen again."

Chapter Forty-Nine

Mariska was on her second cup of coffee by the time Casey found her in his corner booth, working off of five hours sleep and a full pack of cigarettes. She looked up as he sat down, shrugging off his bag and dropping into the seat across from her. She looked bad, restless and worn-through. He looked worse, black under his eyes, blood dried to his knuckles and his shirt collar. Before she could speak, he waved her off.

"Relax, just a nosebleed. I'll make it." He looked her up and down. "Are you alright?"

"I got your message this morning," she said. "What happened?"

"I was wrong." There was still blood in Casey's sinuses. He snorted and wiped at his nose. "It killed someone else last night."

"Christ." Her stomach dropped. "Do you know who it was?"

"My boss."

"Fuck."

"Yeah." He lit a cigarette. "It's not Dad."

"How do you know?"

"I saw him last night at the library, just like Mom. But it was just using him to lure me in, back to the house."

"So you think it's the house." She ran a hand through her hair, licked her lips, tried to think. "Okay. What do we do now?"

"Not the house, something in the house. It was there, and it followed me out inside that box," he said, breathed out smoke. "It's something I saw there, something I locked in my head. I saw it, or saw part of it. I don't know. I thought it was hunting people, but it's waiting for them. It's been waiting for me, since Dad died. It's just been feeding on whatever's close, now it's loose and going after people near me."

Casey took two notebooks out of the bag, opened dog-eared pages to fresh notations and slid them across the table.

"Why you?" Mariska looked at the notes, the names and faces. "I mean, all this – what does any of it have to do with you?"

"It wants me to remember, to go back. I just don't know why, or what for."

She looked up, swallowed. "Mom said something happened that night. Like something changed in the house, or changed in you, or something."

Casey leaned forward. "What did she say?"

"I don't know. It created a hole there, like." Mariska shrugged. "Like what she cut out of your dad left a hole in the world, you know? Or in you, I guess. It just changed things. I don't even know, okay? She just says it."

"I'm so fucking stupid." He sagged back, shook his head. "Your mom's the only one left who was there. I need to talk to her."

She straightened, closed the books, pushed them back across the table to him. "Why?"

"She's the only one who remembers what happened."

"Casey, you know what happened."

"Maybe? Whatever it was, it's locked up in my head. She was there. She'll know."

"Case, no."

"Mar."

"No, okay?" She sighed, turned her palms face-up on the table. "Look, I wanted to help you, I did. But this shit, Casey? I don't know what it is, but I know it's not on you. It's not your fault. You can't fix it."

He shook his head. "I'm close to something. It's right

there, I can feel it."

"Close to what? You're killing yourself like this. You need to let it go."

"I can't."

"You can," she said. "Just walk away, Case. Throw the box off a bridge, bury it in the dessert, I don't know. But doing this? It's going to kill you."

"If that's what it takes."

Casey's phone rang in his back pocket. He reached for it, saw Joel's number, and stood to answer.

"Joel?"

"Casey." Joel sounded small, flat. "I wasn't sure you'd pick up."

Casey pushed past the front door, far out of Mariska's ear-shot, and slumped against the brick-face under the dirty yellow sign. "Are you okay?"

"Yeah, I'm fine. I just." In his mother's apartment Joel examined the cassette tape at the kitchen table. Alone, looking at it like it could snap at his fingers at any moment. The notebook sat closed beside it, untouched where he had left it nights ago. His voice died on the line.

"I've been meaning to call you." Casey heaved out a breath. "It's been bad."

"Yeah, I know." Silence. After a moment, Joel spoke up. "I read it, you know. The notebook you gave me, I mean."

Casey closed his eyes. "Yeah?"

"Yeah. Or at least I tried to. I'm not going to pretend I understand this, Casey, I'm not."

"Look, I know it's bad. I know and I'm sorry."

Joel swallowed. "But that's not why I called. I have to tell you something."

"No, Joel, just. Look, I know I didn't always do right by you, but I want you to know I never wanted to hurt you." The words stuck in Casey's throat, dry to the roof of his mouth. "You deserved a lot better than I could give. I get that now."

"Casey? Casey, no, I'm not. It's not that. I don't want you to think—"

"I just want you to know that no matter how bad it gets from here, I'm going to fix it, okay? I'm going to fix all of it. So no matter what happens – no matter what you hear – I loved you. I always did."

Casey hung up, closed a hand over his mouth to cover the hoarse sound that climbed out of his chest. On the other end Joel stared at the tape. Ten minutes later Casey came back inside. Mariska watched him fish through his wallet for a ten dollar bill and leave it on the table, gathering up his things into his bag.

"Where are you going?" she asked.

"Go get ready for work. See Billy. I'm going home to look through my notes, see if I missed anything."

She stood. "Go to sleep."

"Mar."

"Go get some sleep. I'll stop by after I get off to check in on you."

"Mariska, don't."

"Shut up the fuck up, Casey," she said softly. "Okay?"

After a moment, he nodded. "Okay."

Chapter Fifty

Joel had waited until after work to listen to the tape. He had finished getting dressed that morning with it on the dresser after Lucas left, eating breakfast with it on the table beside his coffee and paper. It came with him in his bag to the office, on the desk while he took lunch between calls and appointments. The weight of it made his fingertips itch whenever Joel looked at it. It wasn't his, not like the notebook that had been given to him and that he chose to read and then keep closed. It belonged to Casey, some piece of memory or pound of flesh he hadn't been privy to. Maybe, he thought, it had been that way for a reason.

He didn't listen to it until he was at his mother's stereo, a fat silver box-system with broad speakers on the third shelf of the entertainment center. He popped it into the cassette player, wiped his hands on his trouser legs, and sat down. Took a deep breath and held it.

911, please state your emergency.
I killed him.

Alyona Koval's voice was softer than Joel imagined it would be. He always heard Mariska's voice in his head whenever Alyona's name was dropped in conversation, mentioned in passing. Mariska's voice was darker than her mother's was, even through the choking sobs that rattled over the surface of the tape.

Who did you kill, ma'am? What happened?
He destroyed us. I tried so hard and he ruined everything. That fucking bastard.
Ma'am, slow down. I need you to tell me where you are and what's happened.
My husband is dead. I cut him. His face is gone. I killed him.

Joel's stomach did a sick flip, a gnarled summersault.

I killed him. Oh, god, I killed him. Now he's here. He's going to kill me.

The tape growled in the cassette player. It stuttered and spat, jerking like a rip had split in the reel.

Who's trying to kill you?

His face, it's like a hole. Just like his father. I cut it out of them. I cut it out.

Jumping. Burning. Tearing. Harsh animal noises, grubby old pornography blown out on speakers or dying carbine engines, sputtering into nothing.

You have to stop him. Oh, god, oh, god.

Alyona sniveled. Someone screamed. Joel frantically pressed the stop button, pulled the tape out, and slammed the cassette player shut. He caught a shaking breath and put the tape back into his bag. I have to take this back to Casey, he told himself. I have to show him. I have to make this right.

That night he crawled into his mother's guest bed and dreamt of boys without faces between fitful spells of sleep. Behind his eyes he saw David Way's corpse in a white kitchen and some blurred facsimile of Alyona Kovol screaming in the corner, blood on her dress and in her hair, hiding from a child with a void in his skull. Somewhere far away Casey stood in a burning house, pages from his notebook falling from the rafters in the stop-motion sway of snowflakes. Casey with dirt on his knuckles and in his clothes, the flames lapping at his legs until Joel finally woke before sunrise. Staring at the shadows for faceless children, he regretted sleeping at all.

Chapter Fifty-One

Casey hadn't slept in a day. He didn't tell his sister that. Mariska had already worried enough, stayed up late enough, lost enough sleep. He left the box on the bed and smoked two cigarettes on the patio before the sun died out between the buildings across the street. The flytraps smiled at him. His chest felt tight. The apartment whispered on the other side of the glass door but Casey hadn't heard. If he had, he would have told himself it didn't matter. Not a whole lot mattered anymore, under the weight of things.

Crawling into bed, his head had cleared enough to appreciate how the burning under his eyelids had spread to his neck and down his arms, into his fingers and toes. It hummed with his pulse in a dull, stinging throb, making fire under his skin as he stretched out beside the box. Cheek pressed to the pillow, limbs loose and made of gelatin. He hadn't even realized he had fallen asleep until Joel woke him with cool skimming fingers, tracing the shell of his ear and carding into his hair.

"Casey," Joel breathed out. He was warm to the touch as Casey came around, a hand holding his face, knees bracketing his waist. The way Joel did when Casey woke up from nightmares, keeping Casey close to himself, holding him there until Casey settled again. "It's okay, I've got you now. It's okay."

The box was gone. Casey didn't care to where.

"Joel?" Casey tried to sit up but the warmth of Joel's was too soothing, his heaviness in the mattress too familiar. The burn in Casey's muscles made him weak and he gave in. "How did you get here? I told you before."

"I just wanted to be here." Joel kissed him, wet lips and gentle tongue, soft and well-intentioned. "I'm sorry."

"No." Casey put his hands on Joel's elbow and knee, keeping him to himself. "No, it's me. I was wrong. I was always wrong. It wasn't my father. It was something else, something that wants me and I can't let you stay, okay? I can't protect you here."

"Hey," Joel said. "Hey. It doesn't matter now, alright? I'm not going anywhere."

They kissed and Casey couldn't say no to Joel's hands, working under his t-shirt to slip it over his head. Joel undressed him and then himself, all greedy fingers and teeth, putting Casey on his back under whispers and bites. Casey couldn't say no to that either, not even to the quickness of it, the urgency, the lack of the care that they always took, even when it was fast and hard between them. Perched in Casey's lap Joel took him in, eyes closing and mouth opening in the slow connection of their hips. The urge to question thinned as a sigh and Casey shut his eyes and turned his head, lulled by the clutch of Joel's body. All sucked in breaths and spread ribs, spine arched, perfect under Casey's hands. Up and down in his lap, slow-sex and slow-burn, like nothing had ever changed.

Love you, Casey wanted to say. Miss you, need you. I'm sorry, I'm sorry.

From the floor the box opened in a creak of hinges and metal parts. Casey heard it but didn't have to, already aware of the lid moving, opening its throat. Out of the throat crawled five fingers, one arm and then another, two hands reaching out for leverage. A boy with no face lifted himself from the box's guts, lean under his clothes and mop of dark hair. There was a hole where his face should have been, an empty space that made a void of his skull that the light coming from the bedside lamp couldn't reach. Casey knew this before he saw it, the boy dragging himself to his feet in a pop-snap-pop of ligaments and bones, unfolding himself into flesh. Bare toes wriggling, solid weight on the floor, breathing like Casey breathed, shallow like a rabbit.

The boy picked up the box, closed the lid and held it, skinny fingers tap-tap-tapping behind Casey's eyes. He opened them. Above him Joel smiled in a way he had never seen before, rabid, starved. He reached for Casey's chest, fingers splayed over his heart, first to stroke then to dig, scratch, claw. Peeling flesh from bone, stripping it bare, and working blunt fingernails down to breastplate layer by layer. Casey meant to scream but the sound dried up and died as Joel pulled the skin away, through the muscle and deeper. Broke through the bones, unfolded the ribs from around Casey's heart and reached between them. Blood on the sheets, on Casey's skin and on Joel's hands, up to his elbows in smears. The boy, tap-tap-tapping.

"Let me inside you," Joel whispered, sex making his skin red and his breath a wreck. Back flexed, riding Casey harder, faster. Casey pushed against Joel's hands, his wrists, his chest, mouth open in silent scream. "Let's just go home together."

The faceless boy opened the box. Joel threaded bloodied hands into Casey's hair, panting into his mouth to kiss him. He smiled in orgasm, taut like cable, a filthy sensation that started in Casey's hips and radiated out until Joel shivered. Casey screamed. Until his throat was raw and his jaw muscles burned, and he could only the see the blood on Joel's mouth, the blood that connected them. Casey's heart to Joel's hands, spit and semen and sweat between them. Then there was nothing.

Mariska came by after work as promised. Casey was under the bed when she found him, half-fetal and still shivering. Joel was gone, the impostor, the puppet, like he had never existed. The box sat in the middle of the bed and blood had dried dark to Casey's skin, sticky in his clothes and hair. He said nothing as she pulled him out by the wrists, hauled him to the bathroom. Threw the box under the bed, parked her brother at the sink, and she wet a rag to wipe him clean.

"You have to destroy it," Mariska said over and over, shaking her head each time she found another fleck of skin in Casey's hair. "You have to, okay? Tomorrow, okay? We'll burn it. We'll hide it. Tomorrow, we have to do this tomorrow."

Casey said nothing then, either. Mariska closed the bedroom door, propped a chair under the knob, and told him to sleep. She said she would hold down the fort until morning, keep watch, standing guard with the steel flashlight dug out from the top kitchen cupboard. Lying on the couch to sleep under his sister's vigil, Casey stared at the corners for shadows and faceless boys, and waited.

Chapter Fifty-Two

Mariska slept in a fetal curl in the corner armchair. She had fallen asleep sometime after four in the morning, when Casey faked sleep long enough to put her at ease. The box was waiting under the bed where she had left it. She would destroy it. That was what she told Casey. Burn it or bury it or throw it off a bridge. It would die because she promised it would, but Casey knew better than that. It would live as long as he lived, hunting as long as he still breathed, wearing faces and hiding in plain sight.

It was barely dawn when Casey rose from the sofa with limbs numbed by half-sleep. He held a breath making sure Mariska wouldn't wake as he moved through the apartment to gather his things, shoes at the door, keys and bag on the table. In the bedroom he knelt to look under the bed. There was blood there, staining the carpet where he had laid his head and tried to forget. The box was there now. He held a breath and reached for it. It moaned under the lid, the wet static of bad television signals, the tinny cadence of porn on old film, bubbling and crackling. He stroked the lid with the blade of his thumb, jumping and scratching in his hands.

It made Casey think of Joel. Not the impostor Joel, the trap that had worn Joel's face and tried to ruin him, make him some ugly, filthy thing. It made Casey think of the Joel that held his face and kissed him and promised everything would be okay. It made him think of home, or something like home, some place warm and safe. He thought of his mother, her garden, and the flytraps. Then he thought of his father.

The primal stutter of it lulled him for a moment, until the taste of blood in the back of his throat brought him back to reality, hot like a slap. For a moment Casey thought to stuff it back under the bed with a fearful shiver, but with Mariska in the next room he put it in his messenger bag instead. He would just try to ignore the smell of his blood in his sinuses and the weight of the box over his shoulder. He would just have to deal with it later.

Casey took the car keys from Mariska's bag on the coffee table. She didn't move. In their place he left a message, a bright yellow sticky-note stuck to the strap.

M

I have to go. I'll be back soon. Don't try to follow me.
Love you.

C

Mariska still didn't wake. Casey felt guilty, but it wasn't enough to stop him. A last look over his shoulder from the front door and he promised himself he would make it up to her. He would make it up to Joel and to everyone. If he couldn't, he would kill himself. Either way it would be over. He closed the door and locked it, and didn't notice the changing weight at his shoulder. Down the stairs and out to the parking garage, driving to Rosedale Glade Mental Facility in Mariska's car. Behind the front door the box waited for the faceless boy, stooping down to pick it up. Tap-tap-tap.

From the armchair Mariska stirred with a sigh, pushing the sleep from her eyes with a twist of her knuckle. The boy walked out across the living room on softly padding feet, stroking the box's lid. She saw the bony slip of him, the empty crevice of his skull staring back, gentle familiarity in the fall of his clothing, the shag of his hair. Shoulders she recognized from Christmas photos, skinny legs that used to stick out of oversized swim trunks in the summer, little hands that used to fit in hers in a time when she had no one but her baby brother. Her breath caught in her chest, bringing her up straight in the chair.

"Casey?"

The box moaned inside of itself. Mariska recognized David's voice in the static. She told herself she wouldn't scream. Wouldn't cry, wouldn't give an inch to the terror in her stomach as the boy and his trap filled Casey's apartment with devils.

Chapter Fifty-Three

The hospital walls of Rosedale Glade were grayer than Casey had remembered them being. He had never been here specifically, but a hospital was a hospital. Cages were cages. He had only been committed once before, when he was twelve. A week observational stay arranged by Aunt Cheryl and the pediatric therapist on-call when he was taken to the hospital, after being found in the puddle of his father's blood. Dazed, half-awake, nearly catatonic on the examination table as a nurse in blue scrubs cut off his clothes, rushing to discern whether or not Alyona had cut her seven pounds from her step-son as well as his father.

It was a week in patterned green pajamas made of papery cotton, locked up in a white cell of a bedroom with a television in the corner. There were other children down the hall in the same green pajamas, dosed on little blue pills like hard candy to keep them quiet. Nurses gave Casey pills, books to read and coloring pages with used crayons, hoping to goad him into speaking. A therapist in a beige pantsuit said her name was Dr. Stevens but he could call her Nancy if he wanted. She was his first therapist. She said everything would be okay. Every time Casey closed his eyes he saw blood in the snow between his toes. Static poured from the ceiling and the television to settle on his hair and eyelashes. Somewhere in the dark, facedown in white, his father smiled with the meat left on his face. Nancy still said everything would be okay. From then on, Casey hated therapists.

Now he was thirty-two, walking down the cold static hallway to the day room. Patients shuffled around in blue pajamas, some playing cards and watching television, others muttering, pulling gently at their clothes or hair. They didn't look at Casey. He didn't look at them, either. Alyona sat in a chair at a wide window, back to him, a closed book of poetry in her lap. Casey recognized it from the care package Mariska had sent to her two years earlier. She had asked if any good books had gone through the acquisitions department at the library lately. He remembered feeling the childish urge to lie, but then as now, he swallowed and did nothing.

"Alyona?"

The word stuck in his throat. She had aged twenty years. Hair thinning, face thinning, her body shrinking into a smaller, skeletal version of his father's second bride. Alyona turned to look at him, up and then down to his feet. Her face fell into something he didn't recognize. Casey took a chair from a nearby card table and parked it a safe distance from her beside the window. In the dull light, her fingers trembled.

"Do you know who I am?" he asked.

"I know who you are. My husband's bastard."

His jaw ticked. "You still hate me, don't you?"

"We both know what you've done. You deserve to be here, in this prison, just as much as I do."

"You think I don't know that?" He leaned forward. She leaned away. "I don't care what you think of me anymore, Alyona. I really don't."

"Then why come?" she half-whispered, half-spat. "You want to see me here, see what you made of me?"

"We need to talk."

"We have nothing to talk about. Mariska came by before, asking about your father. I told her then that I have nothing to say about it."

"Maybe this routine works on my sister, but I don't give a shit about you or your guilt-trip. You and I were the only people there the night my father died. I need to know what happened."

"You know what happened. You know."

"I don't remember anymore."

"You want me to tell you?" Her shoulders shook with fine tremors that creaked in the chair beneath her. "You think that I would help you?"

"I need to know."

"I will tell you nothing."

"What do you remember?"

"I know what you are. You're the same as your father." She shook her head, looked to the floor. "Same cloth. Same lies."

"What am I?" Casey craned his neck, meeting her gaze, bringing it back up. "What do you think I am?"

"You watched." Alyona threw the book down. No one noticed the hard thud it made on the floor. Casey leaned away. "You sat on your hands and did nothing while that pig raped my daughter. You sat there and watched it. You might as well have done it yourself."

"I was a child," he said. "I didn't know what to do."

"You lie."

"You think I wanted him to hurt her? I hated him."

"Pig," she spat. "Whore-son."

"I wanted him dead."

"Then you should've killed him yourself."

"I was a child, I didn't know."

"You always knew!" she stood and screamed. Body twisted in her rage, teeth bared, hands gnarled like tree roots. "I saw you there that night. I saw you. You watched me murder him, you watched me cut him, you liar. You demon."

Three bulky orderlies in white smocks flooded into the room, two from the north door and another from the south. Patients moved away while others shouted back, incoherent rage or spastic anxiety bleeding together under Alyona's screams. She lunged forward and Casey fell back, chair dumping him onto the floor. Two meaty men grabbed for Alyona. It only made her scream louder.

"You let all of this happen. You let him rape her so I would kill him. Look at what you've done. You're going to destroy all of us."

"What did you see?" Casey shouted, scrambling to his feet. The third orderly came from behind to hold him back. "Tell me, what did you see?"

"You used me! You're just like him!"

"You fucking bitch, what did you see?"

"It's you. It's always been you." The orderlies dragged Alyona to the nearby sofa, holding her by the elbows and arms. One stuck a needle into her neck and pushed the plunger down. "You see it, don't you? You see the hole? It's inside him – oh, god, it's inside him."

Her words softened and slurred, body going doll-slack. Alyona slipped into chemical sleep pressed into couch cushions by bulls in scrubs. The two men carried her back to her room and the third let Casey go, sliding to his knees, left there. He was helpless, hapless, just as he was as a child.

"What did you see?"

Discarded on the floor there were no answers. Nothing but cold gray tile under Casey's hands and knees, the ceiling spinning overhead, his stomach making a knot of itself. Down the hallway outside, Alyona disappeared and took her secrets with her.

Chapter Fifty-Four

Mariska bled from between her teeth, coppery and hot to dribble across her knuckles. It was still warm when it puddled on her shirt sleeves, getting on the carpet as she pulled herself across the living room floor by hands and knees. She had meant to fight but the signal got lost in translation somewhere between her brain and fists, the urge to run dying in her feet. The boy hadn't let her go. He kept her pinned to the chair by weight at her throat, making her lungs ache, the force pushing out against her front teeth to make a bruise of her lips. Tap-tap-tap against the lid of the box, a cracking sound in her ribcage, eye socket swelling black, her nose dripping red down her chin.

Tap-tap-tap on the box. She hadn't heard it, only the television static. Rearranging her bones, setting fire under her skin, and all she could think of was the phone in her bag on the coffee table. Her hand reaching for it, dialing 911, running out of the apartment, down the hall and far away as fast as her feet could carry her. The box-cutter left in her kitchen, the box's bloodied guts under the blade, survival. She thought of freedom and safety. She thought of the box dead and buried in the desert and this boy wearing her baby brother buried with it.

It was the knock at the door that had stolen the boy's attention from her. He turned his empty skull to look over his shoulder. Mariska let out a damp animal sound and melted to the floor, clawing at the carpet between the chair and the kitchen doorway. On the other side of the door, Joel knew he should have called Casey before he came. Should have called and asked for permission, maybe forgiveness. The cassette tape felt heavy in his coat pocket, the borrowed notebook tucked under his arm. He knocked again. No answer. Sighing, he entered with his house key even though it felt like cheating, pushed the door open to the cold apartment.

"Casey?"

The blood on the floor met him first, brown smears that led him to the kitchen. A rustle in the hall made him flinch, aware of the unnatural hum of signal interference, the shallow breathing underneath it. Joel followed it, finding Mariska on the floor where she had dragged herself. He dropped to his knees, holding her head and smoothing blood-wet hair from her face.

"Oh, god," he said. "What happened?"

"S'Casey," she slurred, "but he doesn't have a face."

"It's who? Who did this?"

"She – she cut it out of him—"

The front door slammed shut. Joel took a deep breath. He tried not to panic. Panic never helped anyone.

"Okay." He pulled her arm over his shoulder, helped Mariska to stand. "We need to find a place to hide."

They moved quietly down the hallway to the bedroom, listening for the shuffling of feet. Joel helped Mariska slide under the bed, following behind her. Bellies pressed to the floor and a hand over her mouth to cover her quick, wet breathing. Footsteps followed after them, small bare feet in the doorway that circled their way around the bed. Mariska shivered in Joel's arms and he held a breath, tried to think. Shuffle-step, shuffle-step, stopping briefly in a cautious wriggling of toes before turning to walk away. Out the door again, down the hallway and gone, leaving only the sound of static behind.

Joel waited ten minutes and listened for signs of life. After ten minutes he crawled out on hands and knees. Blood trickled down his cheek, cold on his chin when he wiped it away. He hadn't realized that he had been bleeding, leaking from his ears and nose in the static noise that filled the apartment. Joel didn't hear Mariska scream, only felt her hands grabbing at his ankles from under the bed. He looked up and saw the faceless boy, the void, gently tapping the box. Mariska's fingers dug through his clothes down into the bone, the boy's fingers stroking the lid like a pet, or a child. Movements unfolding, repeating, like broken clockwork or stop-motion animation.

"Wait," Joel said, or thought he did, voice lost in the hum and the blood in his ears. "Wait. You don't have to do this. Just let us go."

He didn't take his eyes from the vacuum of the child's skull. Instead he reached for Mariska's hands to hold them. Pulled her out from under the bed, and repeated the words over and over.

"It's okay. It's going to be okay. She's hurt, she needs a doctor. Just let me help her. Just let us go."

The boy didn't move. The tapping stopped. Joel swallowed.

"I know Casey and I know he's hurt and I know you don't want to hurt us too, okay? So why don't you just let us go?"

If Joel could hear, he might have heard crying. Up to their feet, he helped Mariska to the doorway, down the hall and into the living room. The boy just watched them.

"It's okay. I promise."

Joel didn't see the boy throw the box, or hear the clatter of metal pieces on the floor. Twenty men and women moved through the apartment behind them, holes in their chests just as Casey had said. Drawn in by the box and the faceless boy, faces flayed of skin or torsos chewed by teeth, leg bones shattered and splintered. They clawed at the walls or screamed at nothing or beat their heads on the floor, wild like animals locked in cages. Around each of their waists a chain connected them to the box, a tether that kept them in place, kept them close, like dolls or toy soldiers. Joel didn't see that, either. He pulled Mariska out of the apartment and closed the door behind them. He still couldn't hear through the blood, but if he had, he would have heard her screaming.

She cut a hole in him.

She cut a hole.

Casey.

Chapter Fifty-Five

When Casey saw Paul at Rosedale Glade Mental Facility, he already knew that he had failed.

"So how does it feel?"

Paul was smiling at Casey from the passenger seat of Mariska's borrowed car. Buckled in tight inside his brassy-buttoned cardigan, blood dripping from under his eyelids and the box cut into his sweater. Even his heart sounded smug--*tha-thump, tha-thump*. Casey didn't flinch when he got into the car and saw Paul. He didn't even feel sorry for it, just cold and numb.

"I don't know what you're talking about." He didn't want to argue but did it, anyway; a kneejerk reaction to Paul's face. "And you're not dead."

"Oh, no, not yet." Paul smiled. "But you'll make sure of that, won't you? Daddy's favorite little weapon."

Casey took a deep breath and concentrated on keeping his arms from shaking. "What do you want?"

"I want you to admit that I was right."

"About what?"

"About you," Paul said. "About everything."

"I didn't do this."

"Maybe you didn't pull the trigger, Casey, but you loaded the gun."

"I started this, okay? I get that. I let Alyona kill my father." Casey shook his head. "The box's hurting people to get to me, but it's over now. I'm going to stop it."

Paul laughed. "You really think it's that easy?"

Casey swallowed. He wanted to beat the smile from Paul's face, stomp that pleasant condescension into the curb. Instead he gripped the steering wheel. "It doesn't matter now. It can have me. Joel and Mariska, they'll go on. It'll be over."

Paul's face fell, rearranged into something slick and pitiful. "You're so close to it, and you still don't see it for what it is."

Paul leaned forward. Casey leaned away, trapped against the driver's side window.

"Your father was a destroyer, Casey. It's in your blood."

"No."

"You're built to tear things down. It's hard-wired into you, just like your father. You're a predator."

"No." Casey's voice cracked. He reached for the box, for his bag in the backseat. It was empty.

"You have to accept this in yourself."

"I'll kill myself. I'll stop it. All of it."

"You couldn't even kill your own father, Casey. How can you possibly kill yourself?"

Casey's phone rang. Lips pressed to the shell of Casey's ear, Paul grinned.

"Daddy's little weapon."

Casey reached for his cell, flipped it open. He tried to clean up the mess made of his voice. "Joel?"

"Casey?" Joel sounded soft and broken on the other end of the line. "Are you there?"

"It's me, I'm here. Are you alright? What's happened?"

"You have to come to the hospital. It's Mariska. Something's happened. It – I think it, I don't know. Just come here, okay? I need you here."

Paul disappeared. Casey listened to the wreck of Joel's breathing before telling him, "Okay. Okay, okay. Don't move." He closed the phone, started Mariska's car and stood on the gas all the way back into the city.

Chapter Fifty-Six

"She cut a hole in you."

That was what Joel said when Casey got to the hospital. He found Joel in the waiting area outside the emergency room, pacing the floor. There was blood on Joel's clothes from where he had wiped his nose and ears. It was under both of their fingernails as Casey checked him over for bruises or scrapes, signs of violence. Joel grabbed Casey or maybe it was the other way around, standing between two rows of white metal chairs, arms around one another, bodies wracked, breathing hoarse.

"That's what she kept screaming," Joel muttered against Casey's neck, eyes closed. "That someone cut a hole in you. But that's not possible. That boy, he isn't. He wasn't."

Casey said nothing. He moved them to a wide metal bench with cracked blue upholstery to sit together. They stayed like that for an hour. Later, Joel would have to tell the emergency room doctor that came around, clipboard in hand and routine questions to ask, that someone had broken into their apartment. He could deal with these things better than Casey ever could, and Casey's mouth was too parched, his throat too tight to lie. A man had found him and Mariska asleep, Joel said, and had attacked them in a panic. He tap-danced his way through the story, remembering the minutiae of rape trials he had sat through, home invasions turned violent. The doctor didn't ask any more questions.

Casey eventually left Joel to sit next to Mariska in her oversized bed in the Intensive Care ward, hooked up to a halo of machines. She slept in a hard chemical sleep, bandages on her arms and neck, her head and sides. The clothes cut from her body had been replaced by a paper gown that swallowed her up. Thirty-seven stitches, two broken ribs. Her face was made purple by invisible fists, swelling her eye sockets shut and ringing her throat. She was lucky not to have internal bleeding. That was the official diagnosis: She was lucky.

The box was missing. Casey tried not to think about that, and instead parked himself beside her and held her hand. It seemed too small now, too bony, her fingers too cold. The box was gone and she was lucky. Alone with Mariska and her halo of machines, Casey sobbed into her open palm and wished he had swapped places with Alyona. He wished that he was lying there instead of Mariska. He wished that he had died, instead. By six o'clock that night, a doctor with a receding gray hairline and red plastic glasses looked over Mariska's chart, checked her bandages and made an encouraging gesture with his hands. He said that they would keep her there for another two days for observational purposes. Then they should prepare to take her home. Keep her on bed-rest, keep her hydrated, and she would be okay.

She was lucky, after all.

Casey and Joel had already spent the better part of the afternoon and into the night sleeping in an uncomfortable coil on the sofa in Mariska's room. Elbows in ribs, knees bumping armpits and resting heads on stomachs and collarbones. Lulled by the whirling of machines and woken periodically by the nurses who came in with fresh bandages and water pitchers. They took turns walking to the fast-food joint around the corner for coffee or limp French fries. They never really slept and Mariska never really woke. Casey called Billy before dawn, had to tell him what happened with a knife in his chest. Billy, who took it like a champ, didn't even scream or curse or ask why no one had bothered to call him before. He just rushed downtown, into the room, at Mariska's side to stay.

Once Billy took up watch at Mariska's bed, Casey felt safe enough to go outside and smoke a cigarette. Joel followed.

"It's the tape," Joel said.

"What're you talking about?"

Casey and Joel stood in the parking lot next to Joel's hatchback, leaning against the hood. It was almost seven in the morning. Casey smoked the last cigarette in his pack. Joel shoved his hands into his trouser pockets, his shoulders bunched, and tried to get his story crystal-clear in his mind.

"That's why I came by. I'd called a guy I know in police evidence. He got a hold of the 911 tape from the night your dad died."

Casey sucked the smoke in, let it out in a gray stream between his teeth. "Joel."

"There's something on that tape. Something that Alyona said, that Mariska said at the apartment."

"Joel."

"What?"

"I know, okay? I already saw Alyona about it, she's not talking."

Joel had been trying to explain it since the doctor left them the day earlier. Casey didn't care about that anymore. It made Joel sigh, kicking at the dirty concrete beneath them with the toes of his white hi-tops. It made him mad but he didn't show it, too tired in this light, too grateful to have Casey next to him.

"What I don't understand is why it didn't kill us." Joel ran a hand through his hair. It laid flat to his forehead, barely sticky with the previous morning's hair product. "It had us, then it just let us walk out."

"I don't think it can hurt you." Casey shrugged limply. "You saw its face, right? You recognize it the way I do. You're close to me, so you're close to it. And it just...I don't know. It's angry. It just lashed out."

After a moment, Joel shook his head. "It's not your fault."

"Of course it's my fault. I didn't listen. I left it behind."

"Casey." Joel turned to face him, invading his space. "I know what it did to her. But I saw that boy, and I saw that box. It's – it's something else, okay? But it's not you."

"You saw what it can do, Joel. It's killing people. There's no stopping it."

"Don't say that."

Casey looked down. Joel pressed him against the car hood, waited for a response.

"It wore your face."

"What?"

"The night before last. It hid in the apartment and it was wearing your face, your body, and I just. It looked like you, okay? I couldn't stop myself. Felt like you, smelled like you, but I knew that wasn't you. Because you could never do that to me. You would never hurt me, not like that. And I knew I'd made it angry, but I kept it anyway, even though – even though Mariska begged me to get rid of it."

Joel swallowed the knot in his throat. "Casey, please."

"I let this happen."

Joel held Casey's shoulder, squeezed it. "We can figure this out, okay?"

"We can't, Joel. This is on me."

"Tough. We'll go to Paul. We already know it's in your head, whatever this is. The answer's there, okay? We just have to go get it."

Casey stiffened. "Not Paul."

"We don't have a choice."

"Don't you know somebody else?"

"No, Casey, I don't."

"He hates me. He wants you to himself. You think I'm crazy, whatever, but I'm not going back to him."

"Casey."

Casey stared at Joel for a hard moment, and then shook his head. "Fine."

Chapter Fifty-Seven

Joel navigated his hatchback down wide streets Casey didn't recognize to a tall condo on the other side of town. In the passenger seat, Casey said nothing. Joel kept promising it would be okay, it would be okay, Paul owed him this much. Paul owed both of them. Up the elevator and knocking at Paul's heavy black door, Joel just squeezed Casey's arm and waited. Paul opened the door. He didn't bother smiling this time.

"Joel, you're out of your right mind to bring him here."

"Paul, please," Joel said softly. "I don't have time to explain, but we're in trouble. I need to ask you a favor."

"I've had it with doing you favors," Paul said. "I'll have to ask you to leave now."

He moved to close the door. Joel stuck his foot in the jamb. Paul's eyes flickered with a look of danger.

"You must be joking, Joel."

"You know I wouldn't do this if I wasn't desperate."

Joel pushed his way past Paul and through the door. He tugged Casey inside by his wrist and Casey followed, closed the door behind them.

"I'm done with him," Paul said. "I'm done with his little games. I want him out of my house now or I'm calling the police."

"Please, wait. Just listen to me." Joel held a hand up, separating Paul and Casey, his body between them like a shield. "We need this, okay? I wouldn't have come here if we weren't desperate."

Paul looked unimpressed. "Why do you waste time with this?"

"Because we're close to something here, Paul. We just need a favor."

"Like?"

"I need to go under again," Casey answered.

Paul laughed bitterly. "Spare me, alright? If you think I'm going to do anything for you, Casey, you're sicker than I thought."

"Then do it for me, Paul," Joel said. His brow was stern, mouth shiny from licking his lips, eyes a little wet.

Something in Paul softened. Casey held a breath and felt sick.

"Please, Paul."

Paul sighed.

"For me?"

Casey looked down, his face hot.

"Fine." Paul pointed to his study. "After this I want the two of you out of my house."

Casey wanted to ask why, why, why, but instead he stretched out on the black chaise lounge with Joel settled on the end at his feet. He held Casey's hand like a vice. Paul noticed this as he sank in the armchair across from them, eyes flicking to their hands from Casey's face in a tight look. It took everything Casey had left not to feel justified and closed his free hand over Joel's wrist.

"Close your eyes, Casey," Paul said.

"I'm right here," Joel said.

Paul went through the guiding mantra, counting forward to ten. Casey closed his eyes and listened to Joel breathe, the calming metronome of his body. He awoke on his back in his father's living room. His mother stood frozen in a glass case where Alyona's cage had been in his last vision, the fireplace before that, an upright casket adorned with flytraps and rose stems. Alyona laid before it in a heap of defective parts, bleeding from wide slits in her wrists and throat. Cuts like the wide smiles of his mother's flytraps, running red down her arms and into the carpet in human sacrifice.

Casey stood. Mariska was eight-years-old, skipping rope in the foyer at his back. Laughing, skipping. One, two, three, four, five, six, seven, all good girls go to Heaven. He turned, she smiled. There was blood on her yellow party dress, a crown of red dripping into her eyes and onto the floor.

"It's time to go home, Little Brother."

The door to the kitchen rattled its chains. The locks shook, jumping to the tinny melodic hum of static and fuzzed-out pornography. Blood pumping, hips bucking, the wet slap of flesh on flesh in death and as in orgasm, the sex and violence of a single act. Casey pulled at the chains, tearing through the locks. Fucking and dying, his heart hammering, deaf in the static that settled around him in invisible banks of snow. He held his breath and pushed the door open.

His father's kitchen in 1990, clean white wall tiles, clean white floor, new countertops in the white granite that his stepmother had picked out the summer prior. His father was face down on the floor. Blood soaked through the twenty-seven wounds in his back, making his white button-down red. The distinguishable features of his face were gone, carved away and melting into a growing puddle on the floor. Beautiful Alyona sat in the corner on her haunches, the knife between her bare feet. Her arms braced the cabinet doors, blood cooling on her face and the front of her dress. Beautiful and screaming in static electricity, makeup running down her face, pictures of Mariska's naked body strewn all over the floor from the mouth of the open lockbox.

Casey was twelve-years-old when he saw himself sitting next to his father's corpse, hands and knees stained in blood. Another boy stood beside him, a hand on his little shoulder, looking down at his father's body. Holding him, protecting him, heads together like conjoined twins. One shaking, fearful, empty, the other keeping him close.

"It's okay," Casey could hear Joel say from somewhere else. "I'm not going anywhere."

The boy looked over his shoulder at Casey. He had no face. Alyona kept screaming. Casey stared back at himself as a twelve-year-old boy, a hole where his humanity used to be.

"Just squeeze my hand. I'm here."

"I'll protect you," the faceless boy whispered, gently like a secret. "I'll take you away from this. You won't have to remember. I'll take it from you. It won't hurt anymore, I promise."

Somewhere far away, Paul counted backwards.

"And then one day we'll be together again."

Joel's fingers tightened. Casey woke up choking.

"I've got you," Joel said, helping Casey up, stroking his back. "It's alright, I've got you."

Casey retched into the waste basket Paul held out for him until there was nothing left. Blood smelled tangy in his sinuses, dribbling down his nose and onto his chin. The whole room spun.

"What did you see?" Joel held his head, wiped the blood away on his sleeves and with his thumbs. "Come on, I'm right here, you can tell me."

"It was me," Casey breathed out. His chest was sore, his stomach tight from vomiting. "I killed them. It was me."

From the armchair, Paul scoffed. "Don't tell me you actually buy this crap."

"Paul," Joel said, "shut up, please."

"He's delusional and you're playing right into it."

"Paul, shut up. Just shut the fuck up."

"We need to go," Casey said, getting to his feet, still shaking.

Joel stood, steadied Casey to keep him upright. Paul followed.

"You want to feed into his psychosis, Joel? Fine. You deserve one another."

Joel led Casey to the front door, Paul at their heels like a yapping dog.

"Spineless, absolutely spineless. I can't believe you. I hope you're happy, Joel, wasting your life on this train wreck. He's a mess and you're insane if you think you can fix him."

Stopping in the foyer, Casey turned to put his fist into Paul's nose. Paul didn't see it coming. He grabbed his face with a sharp cry, blood tricking out between his fingers.

"Shut up, Paul."

None of them noticed the lockbox sitting on the coffee table in the living room. Joel helped Casey out, closing the door behind them. Looking at the blood in his palm, Paul just laughed. In an hour he would be dead. Casey knew this. Paul would draw a bath as he tended to his bleeding nose in the vanity mirror. The running water would mask the sound of footsteps in the bedroom, radio interference in the air. A boy named Jacob Haas would sit down in his bed as Paul emerged from the bathroom for fresh clothes from the bureau. He would wait for Paul, with his pouting mouth and dead-doll eyes.

Jacob looked just like Joel in a long line of Joels, both before and after. Fine bone structure, blonde hair, light eyes, fatherless and raised by sickeningly-supportive mothers. There was Jacob and Andrew, Devon and Michael, Caleb, Aaron and Shaun. Not Joel, though. Not quite. They came to Paul with sad eyes and sad stories. Paul liked to watch them undress in his office. He liked to urge them on, gently aroused by their shame, the creep of guilt climbing their thighs, up their lean chests to their faces. They didn't have a daddy to love them but Paul did. Drawing the blade of a finger to the end of their long skinny dicks, he liked for them to earn it first.

Paul would have liked Joel to earn it, but Joel never did. Never asked, never begged, and never quite got close enough. There was always Casey. Casey who picked Joel up after class, and waited outside Paul's office when they were discussing Joel's thesis to walk him to lunch. Casey who had Joel checking his phone every five minutes, and said that maybe they should move in together. Casey who had Joel in his bed each night, smelling like his cheap aftershave and sheets, smiling every time Joel stopped them in the hall to kiss Casey. Licking his lips and pressing them together, to savor the memory and the taste in ways Joel never would do for Paul.

Jacob would wait on the bed. When Paul saw Jacob, he would blanch. Jacob would only smile, something ugly opening up inside his chest. In an hour, Paul would be dead, but that was his and Casey's secret.

Chapter Fifty-Eight

Casey went to the hospital to say goodbye.

Joel dozed off on the sofa in the makeshift visitor's lounge where Casey had left him, in front of the fuzzy television and two cans of Pepsi from the machine outside. He needed the sleep, and Casey hadn't told him about Paul yet. Chances were he would never have to, and he didn't know how much Joel would even miss Paul if he did. By the time Casey made it to Mariska's room, Billy slept squeezed into the armchair beside her bed, folded like a paper crane under the film of artificial light around her machines. Two nurses on duty at the desk at the end of the hallway, a janitor pushing a mop bucket from one end of the floor to the other, but the Intermediate Care Ward slept.

Mariska had slept all night, so Casey was told. Billy said she was up before Joel drove them back from Paul's apartment, eating food and responding to questions from the nurse who checked her eye movements and heart rate. The doctors said it was a good sign. Then Mariska fell asleep, and Billy fell asleep, and Joel fell asleep and Casey was alone. Seated next to his sister in a chair stolen from beside the next bed, Casey counted the bruises hollowing her face as she slept. It didn't feel like a good sign. He reached for her hand, skimmed across the back of her knuckles the way she used to comb her fingers through his hair when he was little, hoped for some sign of life. When she didn't wake, he sighed.

"Doctor said you were going to be okay within a few days, take you home. Take it easy, plenty of rest, lots of fluids and you'll be fine. Like you just fell off a bike or something. I think he's a fucking idiot, but whatever." Brushed the hair from her face, felt the warmth of it, the dried sweat between strands. "You were wrong, by the way. It was me. It was always me. I couldn't deal with what I was, what I felt, so I just…I cut that part out. But it didn't die. It just waited, so it just fed on anybody that got too close, feeding on what was inside of them, I think. Something that it could dig into and use against them."

Wetness stung at the corners of his eyes. He dug it out with a knuckle, took a deep breath.

"So, yeah, I fucked up. I got Sherrie hurt. I got you and Joel hurt. People died, and I don't know why, but I know I did it to them. So I'm sorry. I'm sorry for everything. I'm sorry I never stopped Dad and I'm sorry I let this shit happen to your mom and I'm sorry I didn't listen to you."

Under the chemical fog of sleep she murmured, rolled her eyes under her lids. A machine at her side beeped. "You're full of shit," she said, her voice cigarette-and-whiskey rough.

He laughed softly. "Shut up. You're supposed to be sleeping."

"Yeah, well." She licked dry lips, turned her head to her pillow. "You're talking too much. Go home. Go to bed."

"I know. I will. I just wanted to see you first."

"Take Joel. S'tired." The words started to slur, running together into syrup.

"I know."

"And don't do anything stupid."

He sighed again.

"Love you, Sister."

Another murmur and Mariska was gone. Casey took her hand and kissed two bruised knuckles. Smoothed the blankets and let it rest there.

"Hey."

He sat up, turned to see Billy blinking at him from the armchair. Billy pulled himself upright, wiped his mouth with the back of his hand. Casey pushed the wetness from under his eyes and stood. Put on a good face, tried to lie.

"Sorry. I'm just going."

"Hey."

Billy followed Casey out into the hallway, closed the door behind them. It was the most serious Casey had ever seen him, a hand planted on a denim hip, reaching out to grab Casey at the shoulder to face him. He looked tired. He looked hollowed out like Mariska did. Maybe they belonged together after all.

"It wasn't a break-in, was it?"

"No, it wasn't."

"I knew the three of you had been sneaking around lately, like you were hiding something. I knew it." Billy shook his head. "What happened?"

"I can't tell you."

"Bullshit." Billy urged Casey back a step toward the wall. "You didn't even call me when she gets to the hospital. I have to find out that she's been here for hours before anybody bothers to tell me. I put up with that, fine, whatever, but tell me what happened to her now. You have to."

"I can't."

"Can't or won't?"

Casey squared himself up. "I can't tell you because I can't prove any of it."

"I don't give a shit."

Footsteps came down the hall from the nurse's desk. Casey waited for them to pass. "She was pulled into something because of me. But I'm going to fix it."

"How?"

"You don't want to know."

"Tough shit."

"You don't." Casey's voice was cold, certain.

Billy huffed out a breath. "Fine."

"Look, just, make sure Mar gets this, okay?" Casey took out a folded notebook page from his pocket, handed it to Billy. He couldn't tell Billy it was a suicide note. Mariska wouldn't take it if she knew what it was. She would come for him, pull the plugs out of the walls and threaten his life for even thinking about it. "It's for her, and nobody else."

"Yeah," Billy nodded. "Okay."

Casey turned to walk to the lounge to get Joel. Go back to the apartment, do the same thing all over again. Billy called out after him.

"Hey. You're not the only one who cares about her, you know. I love her, too. It's my job to take care of her."

Casey stopped and after a moment, shrugged. "I know that. I wouldn't leave her here with you if I didn't."

Chapter Fifty-Nine

Their apartment was less of an apartment and more like a crime scene when Casey and Joel got back, quiet and stiff-legged from waiting room chairs and car rides. They hadn't talked about Mariska or the suicide note. There was nothing to discuss. The apartment was cold. Gray morning sliced between the curtains that Joel pulled partly open, the blood that had dried brown in the carpet impossible to ignore. It made the apartment itself a trap. They said nothing of that either, and kept their hands to themselves on opposite corners of the living room.

Joel's shirtsleeves were still dark from Casey's nosebleed. He crossed his arms to hide them with a held breath behind his teeth and said "That's better."

Casey had pulled the curtains shut before, locked himself in with the box. It seemed stupid in retrospect as he watched Joel at the window from the sofa, still tasting blood in his sinuses. Mariska's blood on the floor, Casey's on Joel's sleeves. It made his teeth feel gritty and his stomach turn, dirty from the inside out.

"Hey." Joel had turned away from the window. His eyes looked darker in the light, the lines around them heavier. "You need to sleep."

Casey shook his head. "Not yet. We need to talk."

"No, you need rest. We can talk later."

"Joel." Casey wrung his empty hands between his knees. "There's only one way out that I can see."

"Don't." Joel sighed, shoulders sinking. "I know what you're going to say, so don't."

"So?" Casey looked at the floor rather than at Joel. It was easier that way. "Look, what I've done – what I've let happen...it's bad, okay? It's fucking awful and I can't do anything to make that right."

"Casey, I don't care about that."

"I do. And it hurts because I can't fix it. Not ever."

"Enough."

The sharpness in his voice made Casey look up. Joel sighed again, ran a hand through his hair. "I'm not leaving you."

"You should."

"I won't."

"I would."

"No." Joel crossed the space between them, crouched to his knees to meet Casey's eyes. "You wouldn't. Because I know you."

"You know what I have to do. You don't deserve to be put through this, anymore."

The totality of it made Joel feel sick. He took a breath and reached out for Casey's fingers, still as cold as they had ever been. "It's not a matter of deserving it, Casey. This happened to us." Joel peeled Casey's hands open to lace their fingers together. "It just happened."

"It's in me. It's a part of me. This whole time, it's wanted me back. I can't walk away from that, not now."

"You were a child."

"It doesn't matter." Casey took a shaking breath. He sat forward to push a hand into Joel's hair, gripping it. "I'm damaged, okay? I'm fucked up and I'm twisted inside and I can't – I won't bring you down with me. It has to stop."

"You can't save me from this. I don't want it, Casey, I don't. I just want you to stay, okay?"

"Joel."

"No."

"If I kill myself, I take the trap with me. This will all be over."

"Don't you dare. You're staying right here."

"I don't have a choice."

"Maybe when this is over, and when Mariska's out of the hospital, we can – I don't know, we can just go. Just us, Casey, we can get away from this." Joel grabbed Casey's shirt to drag him closer, made a fist of it until their foreheads touched. "We can get a house somewhere where it's warm, with a patio where you can keep the plants. I can go into teaching or something, and you can go back on your meds and it'll be okay. We can start over again."

"Joel." Casey held tighter. "Stop."

"We have a choice here," Joel breathed. "You don't have to do this."

The kiss they shared was a fierce wet thing, all lips and tongues and teeth. Casey started it and Joel finished it, trying to quiet and be quieted, pushing and pulling. They held each other tightly by the hair and shirt until Casey finally pushed back, closed his eyes, and swallowed.

"Joel, I know. I know, I know, I know. But can we just – can we just go to sleep? Please? Just give me a day and I'll find a way to make this right again, I promise, Joel. I swear."

After a moment, Joel nodded. "Okay," he said, "okay. But you'll have to be here when I wake up. You have to."

"Yes," Casey promised and kissed Joel again. It was the worst lie he had ever told, and it would be the last. "I'm not going anywhere."

Taking Casey's hand, Joel led them to bed, kissing, touching, blind, fingers caught in shirt hems and hair. They undressed each other without looking, shirts peeled away, belts undone, jeans shoved down. Joel lay out on his back on the mattress, arms wrapped around Casey's neck, ankles crossed behind him, chest-to-chest and mouth-to-mouth. Lotion in the nightstand drawer, hurried and convenient, opened onto fingers and spread out across skin into moans and sighs. Casey's hands on Joel's knees and asking him, please. Just us, just this, just what I can give you.

"Stay here," Joel said against Casey's top lip. "With me, okay? You're with me."

Casey closed his eyes and nodded. That, too, was a lie. Joel sucked in the sounds Casey made when he pushed forward, their hips meeting in a shiver that started in Joel's chest and radiated out. Joel's fingers tugging at Casey's hair, arching them forward on the back of every thrust, pulling them back down into the mattress. Pushing and pulling, shudder, murmur, and sigh. Fleeting sex, slow-fucking, measured out in haggard breathing and the stretch of Casey's spine, like notches in a sun dial, rises to mark the passage of time. Joel held on and didn't let go, the way he always did and always would. There were no secrets between them now, no clean nice sheets for Casey to sully. No clean white anything, just their breathing, their bones and skin, and the shapes they made together.

Alone in their apartment, in their bed, and for everything else that waited outside, for one day, it was enough.

Chapter Sixty

Casey was half-asleep in the soft catch of Joel's arms when he saw his father for the last time. David sat on the foot of the bed. His face was whole again, like Casey's face but older and stronger, his fingers tented to his mouth like silent prayer. That wasn't possible as far as Casey knew; the dead and the devil didn't pray. The sunshine coming from between the shut curtains painted his father's back in a clean white stripe, defining the mountain ranges of his shoulders, the wrought-iron of his sturdy hands in midday light. Casey moved carefully across the bed as not to wake Joel, finding a safe distance on the other edge. His father on one side and him the other, the way it always had to be.

His father smiled. "Hey there, kiddo."

"Don't," Casey breathed out. "Don't do this now."

"So this is him, huh?" He looked at Joel. Sleeping, guiltless, unspoiled. "He's yours?"

"Leave Joel out of this."

"He's not what I had expected from you. I always thought you'd go off, find a nice girl, and have kids by now. Live the American dream."

"And do what, Dad? Marry women I couldn't stand just to look good in front of the neighbors? Just like you?" There was a certain pleasure in saying it, like rubbing salt in a wound just to feel the burn. "Guess neither of us got what we wanted."

"I didn't come here to fight you." His father rubbed his hands together, dropped them into his lap. "You think this stunt is going to solve anything?"

"I don't have a choice, Dad. As long as I'm alive, people will die."

"I don't think Joel would agree."

"I'm doing this for him. But you wouldn't know anything about that, would you?"

"You might be surprised, kid."

Silence in the bedroom, Joel breathing between them. Casey finally spoke, "I wanted to kill you myself."

"I know."

"I should've done it. I wanted to. For so long, Dad, you don't know how badly. It would've saved everyone from this. Mariska would still have her mother. Joel could've gone on to something better. Everybody would be safe."

"Well, maybe that's true. But, one way or another, I think you'd still be here, talking to me. We're the same, you know, the two of us. Sitting here, you try to hide that but you know it's true, Casey. We've both got demons. They just come with different faces."

Casey felt cold all over. "Don't say that. I'm nothing like you."

"You're everything like me, Casey. We were both built up to do great things, but we both failed." David shrugged, like a giant would shrug, all heaviness and musculature. "I failed you. I failed everyone because of what I was. Now you're here and you can't get over it because you can't get over me."

"You did this to us, Dad. You destroyed all of us."

"Yeah, I did. And now you have to put it back together."

"I don't think I can."

Just like that, Casey was twelve-years-old again, looking up at his father. He was too small, too weak, and too helpless to stop him. Save him, kill him. David just shrugged again.

"Then I guess you'll just have to die."

Casey swallowed. "You never told me why."

"Why what?"

"You know why what."

His father looked away, to the corner where the sunlight didn't reach. "I never had a reason. I hurt her because I wanted to, because it felt good. It was easy to do and I liked it." He sighed. "I don't expect you to understand. But it wasn't your fault. You need to know that."

The room suddenly felt too small, the air too hot. "How many others, Dad?"

"Casey."

"How many?"

"Eight, maybe nine, I think. They were just girls. I found them at church when I was in middle school or from the neighborhood in high school, because I was taller than all of them and they liked the attention at first. There was one or two when I was at college, when I saw a young girl in a mall or at a movie theater and I couldn't help myself. But I promised myself I'd never do it again. I straightened up, married your mother, tried to do the right thing. I never did it again, not until Mariska. She was my last mistake."

Joel slept on between them, murmured into the pillow, fingers splayed to the mattress where Casey had been. Casey wanted to be there with him, to sleep and dream and know nothing of devils. Instead he made a fist in the sheets. "And you were my first."

At that, his father smiled. "Yeah, kid. I guess you're right about that."

When Joel woke at five o'clock, Casey was gone. The bed was cold. His jacket, keys and shoes were missing with him, the front door locked. Tented on the living room coffee table was a note, carefully folded, written in Casey's chicken-scratch.

J

I meant what I said before. You do make me want to be a better person. The person that you think I am, the way I feel when you look at me. This is the only way I can be that person now, and keep you safe from all of this.

You made my life worth living. I just want you to know that.

I love you.

C

Joel read the letter three times, folded it over twice and put it back. He left it there. He should have thrown it in the trash. Suicide notes were stupid cries for help. They didn't count for anything. Joel didn't let it count, not after four years and all the blood on them now, on their clothes and in the carpet. It was something shared, under fingernails and in the threads of the sheets where they slept, not to be forgotten or washed away. With the television on in the dark, sitting on the sofa, Joel watched the door and waited for Casey to come home again. Home to him, as it should have been.

Chapter Sixty-One

Casey took a can of gasoline and put it in Joel's hatchback, driving to his father's house on Mooreland Street. The sky had gone from pink to purple when he pulled to the curb, almost black. He took the gas from the backseat and made his way around to the back door. Up and down the street porch lights were flicked off, cars tucked inside garages. No one across the street was out to see him. Even if someone had they wouldn't have time to call 911. The house would be gone by the time the fire department arrived. He would be dead before anyone could pull him out. Back in the city, Joel slept, warm in their bed. Mariska slept with Billy at her side. At least that was what Casey hoped: they would sleep through this, waking when it was over, when it was safe.

Through the dark kitchen, the stale mold smell of the turned-over fridge made him cough. Around the island counter to the doorway to the living room, where his father's den was, was a three-ring circus of shame and despair. A crowd of men and women with holes in them, the strange and familiar alike tethered to a single chair in the corner. Carroll Robinson, Harold, Walter and Paul, other faces from missing persons fliers and waking dreams, strung together and gathered around the faceless boy in the middle. The victims filled the house, dragging their chains down the hallway to the bedrooms, huddled in the corners and under the counters in the kitchen. Some scratched into the walls while others clawed at their leashes until their fingernails splintered and bled.

An old man moaned into the arms hugging his knees; another banged his head against the cabinet door. Harold was there with his shattered ankle and Walter his bloodied face. Carroll Robinson bled into the dirty carpet and moaned about Claire, precious Claire, beautiful Claire, the whore Claire. Paul with the sopping mess Jacob had made of his face tore at the peeling wallpaper and scraped at the plaster, tugging at the tether shackled at his feet. A woman with a bruised eye cried red tears to herself, and another with slender bones sticking out from flaccid arms shivered on the floor, dirt in her hair and on both of their clothes. The trap sat in the armchair, holding the lockbox in his lap, holding his audience.

It was his collection of souls, people that hurt people, or tried to hurt people, or thought about hurting people. That was what they had in common, in urges that ran bone-deep. The trap didn't do anything to trick them. It didn't hunt or stalk, or wear down the tired and the sick like frightened deer. It only opened doors to people who couldn't say no. People like Paul, or Harold, or David Way, people who had the potential to destroy. If Casey had killed his father in the first place, none of this would have happened. And so his trap waited in its house of flies. The crowned boy-king with his court of devils, the child that was born the night Alyona carved her hate from David's hide to waste in the fireplace in a box made of flesh.

Tap-tap-tap.

"I know what you are," Casey said, if only to bolster his own nerve. "I created you. I know that now. I'm not afraid anymore."

The trap said nothing.

Casey took the can of gas and poured it out in a circle, splashing the walls and soaking the carpets. The whole house had been eaten by moths and termites, plaster falling from the studs. It would only be a few moments before the support gave way and the roof tumbled down on their heads.

"I'm here, alright? You have what you want." Casey dug the matchbook from his jacket pocket. "Let everyone else go."

The trap said nothing.

"You have me. This is mine; let me fix it."

Tap-tap-tap.

Casey screamed, *"Let them go!"*

Nothing. The cold of it ran down Casey's spine.

"Fine."

He lit the match.

The trap stood. All the bodies dropped, toppled over from where they huddled in on themselves, severed from their lines. They shriveled up and died, like the faces of his traps when Casey wasn't keeping up with his garden. They disappeared, into the carpet, the foundation and the earth.

Casey told his child self, "It's just you and me now."

He dropped the match. The carpets ignited in a flash, spread to the walls and crackling and sparking to the ceiling. Haggard window dressings smoked into nothing, heat jumping in the foyer, the kitchen, filling Casey's lungs with black smoke. The trap stepped forward. Twelve-years-old and skeletal under his clothes, made up of all the awful things that had broken Casey's heart years ago, sleeping down the hall from a rapist. He was a framework of everything Casey feared he would become, splintered off and left behind. The empty space was filled with fights in high school and college, all that anger Casey carried in him; all that hate, the sadness and denial, the what-ifs and maybe-sos of his father's legacy made flesh.

Casey swallowed. "What do you want?"

Let's go home, the trap didn't say. Let's be together.

Instead, he held out the box, the battered shell of memories and flesh, old skin shed. All that was left was the empty lockbox with its broken lock and dented lid. Casey took it. It didn't mean anything now, hollow of the seven pounds of flesh that had birthed it somewhere in the dark. The ceiling creaked and moaned overhead. The room turned black. His stomach tightened.

"It wasn't your fault. He did this to me, to all of us. You couldn't have stopped it."

Nothing. Casey felt the tremors under his skin, working down his arms into his fingers. The urge to run, to fight, to survive, wrestled back by the void, tamped down by fire. He didn't want to die. He didn't want to live in a world with devils, where Joel couldn't be safe and Mariska had to live with scars. He didn't have a choice, anymore.

"I'm sorry."

Silently, the boy-trap sagged to the floor at Casey's feet and trembled all over, sobbing to himself on knobby knees, bent under the weight of the dead. Still a child, still Casey, still angry and alone, for all the horror he had swallowed down in fearing he would become his father. After a moment, Casey let out the breath he had been holding. He sat down on the ground beside the boy, set the box aside and pulled the boy to himself, head to his chest, ear to his heart. He closed his eyes and breathed in the smoke until the boy stopped shaking, their bodies making shapes in the firelight. They would die, and it would be right. To die for all the times Casey could have killed his father, and couldn't, and let others die instead. They would be together in the end, just as the boy had always asked.

Chapter Sixty-Two

"Hey."

By the time the old woman at 6627 Mooreland Street thought to call the fire department, the house had already burnt down to the foundation. The boy-trap had died in the firelight, his flies dust under booted feet, bodies scorched away and scattered in the earth. Not even the box remained, a skeleton of metal pieces or milk-teeth left behind to prove it had existed at all.

"Hey. This guy's alive."

Casey opened his eyes. He saw the mouths of overgrown flytraps amid the gnarled weeds of his father's Technicolor yard. Beneath him the grass was green and warm. Above him he thought he saw his mother. She smiled through the sunlight he imagined there, like a clean white crown, white like her dress. White like Heaven must have looked like, if Casey believed in Heaven. If his father's backyard was Heaven and his mother was God, and he would be allowed to rest in her fields of traps.

"Hey, baby," she said. "Time to wake up."

He must have been three-years-old again.

"Help me get his feet."

He must have been dead.

Two firemen with sweat on their brows and ash on their suits moved Casey, out of the backyard to the ambulance parked sideways in the street. They promised him he would be okay, they had him now. They promised he would live. Everything would be fine. A woman in a blue jumpsuit and a tight black ponytail asked Casey his name. It was hard to answer under the oxygen mask. He blacked out twice before the paramedic dug his wallet from his back pocket and read aloud from his expired driver's license. When he was coherent enough to respond, he figured he probably wasn't as dead as he first thought. There was a ridge on his breastbone when the paramedic pushed down his collar to listen to his heartbeat. It was raised like knuckles under the skin, two hands pushes together, or the meeting of two jaw bones. Pulled open, stuffed tight and stitched together again. The skin looked old and healed over. Casey touched it, felt the ridges move gently out then back into place, fitting there. It was made of flesh and bone, muscle and sinew. She didn't ask about it. He took a deep breath, said nothing.

The cops wanted a statement. Casey blinked through the black circles in his peripheral as the paramedic poked and prodded at him, asking if he remembered his address and if he could follow the flashlight with his eyes. He lied and said he saw somebody in the window when the house caught fire. Rushed in to help, then crawled out into the lawn and passed out. The old lady across the street waved a small wrinkled hand and said yes, yes. There were always kids over there, having parties and loitering around. They must've accidently started the fire and run off. A fireman said it was a gasoline fire, probably just kids messing around, and the cops taking his statement said Casey was free to go. He said that there was a twelve-year-old boy inside, that he had seen a child when he was inside. The same fireman shook his head and shrugged.

Casey didn't say anything else, let the paramedic close the ambulance door and take him far away, speeding past green trees and highway cinderblock to the hospital. Nurses in blue scrubs poked and prodded him. They asked him questions, checked his lungs for smoke inhalation, and rechecked his reflexes for carbon dioxide poisoning. They said he was lucky to be in such good shape, no burns, no irritation, no damage or complication. There was just dirt in his clothes and ash in his hair, blood still ringing his fingernails in rust stains, too dark to rinse away. The scar on his chest looked like a face when his eyes refocused in the sterile fluorescent light, shaped like the mouth of a flytrap with its fanning teeth. No one said a word of it, made him sign some insurance forms, agree to payment terms, blah, blah, blah. They let him go on the condition he drink plenty of fluids and get some rest. Casey nodded his head and said nothing.

Outside it was dawn, purple on the horizon and turning pink and blue. The street was quiet, abandoned at the hour, air clean and cool on his face. A ride across town in an empty bus brought Casey home, up the stairs like a ghost tracing its steps. Joel was awake and waiting for him when Casey scratched his key up in the lock, still wearing the previous day's clothes, blood still on his shirtsleeves. Joel hadn't moved from the couch until Casey appeared at the door. Blood under his fingernails, ash in his clothes, smelling like burnt wood and dirt, the way a fireplace smelled when it needed cleaning. Joel stood. Casey dropped his keys and jacket and felt numb, his brain cottoned, mouth dry. The stupid suicide note still sat on the table and Joel looked like his was going to cry but didn't. He just crossed the ten steps between them and held Casey's hands. Spread his thumbs over the knuckles, scratched and dirty.

It was on the morning news, an aside between mayoral races and weekend weather forecasts. A bored-looking anchor in a blue blouse and black blazer, feigning interest over a wide shot of firemen and police cars. House fire on Mooreland Street, no deaths, neighbors fault unsupervised teenagers with baggy pants. Casey made no mention of it. Joel knew better than to ask.

"I'm sorry," Casey tried to say. I'm sorry I lied. I'm sorry I left.

"Okay," Joel said like it was nothing at all.

From the bathroom, they listened to the television down the hall. Casey propped himself against the counter, reflection half-dead in the mirror, sleeplessness still black in the hollows of his face. Joel wet a wash cloth in the sink. They didn't have to look at each other. Casey wouldn't say anything. Joel wouldn't ask about the ash on Casey's elbows and on his knees, the way it got under his shirt to stick in the sweat. Took Casey's hands to scrub his knuckles first, cleaning the dirt away. He turned Casey's hands over palm-up, smoothing his fingers open, kissing the center of his right hand. Casey made a low sound behind his teeth, swallowing it with weighted eyes and dry lips, the bottom cracked in the middle, the top chapped.

"Joel," he started to say, stopped short when a sigh claimed the sound. "Joel, I."

Joel didn't answer. He closed Casey's fingers and wiped the cloth across his neck, under his jaw and up his cheek. At his temple, he kissed Casey's broken lip, at his ear the peak of his cheekbone, under his shirt collar the corner of his mouth. He tasted grit and licked his lips. Casey cupped Joel's arm at the elbow, the other at his wrist, pushing against him weakly, watching Joel's mouth. Urgent in the ridges of his spine and the faint veins in his arms when he tried to hold Joel close and let Joel go, anyway. He closed his eyes and Casey found himself on his knees in a dry sob, Joel following, arms wrapped around him, holding him up. Sitting there, not speaking, and just breathing, hands fisted in shirts fisted in hair, close together for all the nights kept apart.

And for the first time in twenty years, Casey Way felt whole.

Epilogue

The house on Elizabeth Street was tiny and blue with green window shutters and flowerboxes to match, the walls inside various shades of cream and the floor laid in new wood. It was built up on a brick foundation with wrought-iron fencing around the little covered front and back porches, skinny trees fanning across the backyard and over the shed by the garden, empty of flowers and ready for planting. Quaint like a watercolor painting or a picture in a brochure, fifteen minutes outside of downtown, near two schools and three shopping centers. Joel circled the listing three times in red pen and held it up to Casey. Casey said Okay, we'll go to the bank tomorrow. It was, after all, perfect.

When Sarah Britton saw it, she got out her checkbook. Joel said no. She said it was a birthday present. Joel said still said no. Then she said it was a down payment, because she expected it to be filled with grandchildren and they needed a head-start on college funds. Casey shrugged. Joel just sighed. By the end of the month, they had packed up the apartment on Davis Street and never looked back. There was no staying there, in the face of things. It was filled with too many ghosts, witness to such scars and ugliness that couldn't be vacuumed or scrubbed away, no matter how hard they tried. Because Joel had tried, armed with rubber gloves and steel wool pads, carpet cleaners and bleach, and it never felt any less haunted.

So when Joel said he wanted to move out, Casey packed their things up in boxes and bags, and didn't say a word about it. Joel wanted a house. Joel deserved a house. Letting him have that was the least Casey could do, something he felt compelled to make happen even without Sarah and her checkbook.

On Elizabeth Street there were no ghosts, no memories or faces in cracked bathroom mirrors. Joel just seemed to breathe a little easier there, standing in the foyer or looking out the bedroom window. Casey liked that most of all. In the kitchen he changed out burned-out bulbs and put up cupboard shelves, moving to the backyard to replace a loose hinge on the shed door and dig holes in the waiting garden for his traps. Joel unpacked boxes of books and blankets inside, his footsteps soft through the open screen patio door. Billy came with Mariska, to put new blades on the ceiling fan and look into the grinding sound the dishwasher sometimes made, sleeves rolled up to the elbows, his box of favorite tools scattered all over the kitchen floor. Outside with Casey, Mariska arranged the newly acquired lawn plastic furniture like pieces from some oversized doll house.

It had been three weeks since she had gotten out of the hospital. The bruises on her ribs still gave her trouble when she slept on her side or lifted anything, but when Casey told her that he didn't need her help moving in, she heard nothing of it. My baby brother's moving so I'm going to be there, she said, even if you have to wheel my broke-ass around to do it. Casey knew better than to argue with that. Instead, he handed her the light boxes from the moving truck and let her carry the lawn furniture. He said if he caught her moving the sofa she would be dead before she hit the ground. She just made a face and went back to arranging plastic chairs.

They hadn't talked about the faceless boy since the hospital, or the box or the old house Casey had burned to the ground. It never felt like the right time or place to try. There was nothing else to say about it, no apologies to make or condolences to share. Even if Casey had felt the burden to speak Mariska wouldn't have let him, just as Joel didn't let him when he came home after the fire. It was over. They were all even now. It felt right to just let it die.

Digging holes in his new garden, Casey stopped to lick the taste of dirt from his bottom lip. He sighed and drove the shovel into the ground.

"Hey."

"Hey what?" Mariska asked over her shoulder.

"I was thinking."

"Sounds painful."

"Ha, ha." He sighed again, dusted off his hands. "I was thinking, maybe this is a good thing."

She turned around. The look on his face was earnest, hopeful. For it, she shrugged and dropped into a nearby chair. "I mean, yeah. This is a good thing. You guys got the house, you're settling down. It's cool, you know?"

"Yeah, but, I mean for you and me. To get some space between us, if only for a little while." It was Casey's turn to shrug, sitting down beside his sister to look over the yard. "We're good together, and we're good for each other, I think. Until somewhere along the way it stopped being a good thing. And it hasn't been good in a long time, Mariska."

"So what're you saying?"

"I'm saying that, you and me? We're each other's blind-spots, and we always have been. I love you, I do, but…I have no idea who the hell I am without you. I don't think either of us really knows for sure. You have your own life, and your job, and Billy."

"Yeah?"

"And I want to see you go be happy and stop worrying about me. I'm going to try to do the same."

"I guess we never really learned to live without each other, ever since we were kids. Did we?" Mariska sat on her hands, unsure of what else to do with them. "So maybe it's time for us to try, right?"

He nodded. "Maybe it's time."

She shrugged again. "I get it. I do. And I mean, it's fine. Billy's kind of talking me into moving in with him, getting a bigger place together. We both decided it'd be good to get me out of my old place. It's just got a lot of bad memories attached to it. Time for a clean start."

"Yeah? That's good."

She looked through the open blinds. Billy was still in the kitchen on a step-ladder, fussing with the uprooted ceiling fan. She smiled. "Yeah, I thought so, too. "

"You love him?" he asked. "Makes you happy?"

"Yeah, I love him." Her smile broadened, bunching her shoulders with a sigh. "It's lame, but I really do. We're thinking about making a proper go at this whole boyfriend-girlfriend thing. You guys seem to make it work, you know? Maybe we can, too."

Casey made a face. "Joel is not my girlfriend, thank you."

"No, but he does own you."

"He does not."

"He makes more money than you, Casey. And he picked out your house."

"Shut up."

"And his mom paid for it. I mean, c'mon. You're basically married."

"I'm not letting you come over, anymore."

"I'm just saying." Mariska smirked, leaned back in her chair. "Better put a ring on that thing before he starts asking questions."

"Before who does?"

Casey and Mariska turned to find Joel at the patio door. Casey's jaw clicked shut. Mariska sat up.

"Nobody," she said.

"Should I ask?" Joel ventured.

"I'd rather you didn't," Casey answered.

"Alright. So is anybody else hungry? I was thinking of ordering something in, since the kitchen's still a mess."

"Nah, I'm good. Actually I'm supposed to go get some food with Billy after he finishes up. We're gonna go over apartment brochures, or whatever it is normal people do." Mariska stood, swiped at the lingering cardboard shavings stuck to her shirt. "I figured we'd take off, let you guys settle in."

Joel and Mariska shared goodbyes and a hug before she bent to kiss Casey's cheek. When she left to retrieve her boyfriend and his tools, Joel took up her seat beside Casey. He noticed Casey's incredulous look.

"What?"

"I didn't realize you two were on hugging terms," Casey answered. "It's kind of like seeing Reagan and Gorbachev holding hands."

"Rude." Joel swatted at Casey's arm. "Is that where your plants are going?"

Casey looked over to the flowerbed. "Yeah, as soon as I add some peat moss and sand to the soil so their roots don't burn up." After a moment he leaned back. Let his eyes fall on Joel's hands where they sat in his lap and reached over for a skinny wrist. "So, is this good?"

"The house?" Joel asked, watching Casey's fingers skim over the fine bones.

"The house, us. All of it."

"Yeah, it's good."

"And you're happy?" Casey shrugged. "Here, with me?"

"Yes, you idiot," Joel smiled. "Of course I am."

Casey looked to the empty garden, the shed, and the fence beyond it. To the tops of swaying trees and the soft blue sky stretched overhead. No clouds or sun, just an endless sky. He eventually nodded, and never let go of Joel's wrist.

"Good."

"What about you?" Joel watched Casey's face, the faraway look of his eyes. He closed a hand over Casey's, held it tightly. "Are you happy?"

Casey swallowed. "No. Yes. I mean, I don't know yet. But I think I can be. I think I can try."

Joel squeezed Casey's hand. "And that's all I ask."

Made in the USA
Charleston, SC
05 April 2014